CAPE
RAGE

BERKLEY TITLES BY RON CORBETT

The Sweet Goodbye

Cape Rage

CAPE RAGE

RON CORBETT

BERKLEY
NEW YORK

BERKLEY
An imprint of Penguin Random House LLC
penguinrandomhouse.com

BERKLEY and the BERKLEY & B colophon are registered trademarks of
Penguin Random House LLC.

Library of Congress Cataloging-in-Publication Data

Names: Corbett, Ron, 1959– author.
Title: Cape Rage / Ron Corbett.
Description: New York: Berkley, [2024] | Series: A Danny Barrett novel; 2
Identifiers: LCCN 2023025950 (print) | LCCN 2023025951 (ebook) |
ISBN 9780593440384 (hardcover) | ISBN 9780593440391 (ebook)
Subjects: LCSH: Undercover operations—Fiction. |
Organized crime—Fiction. | Revenge—Fiction. | Wilderness areas—Fiction. |
LCGFT: Detective and mystery fiction. | Thrillers (Fiction) | Novels.
Classification: LCC PR9199.4.C6677 C36 2024 (print) |
LCC PR9199.4.C6677 (ebook) | DDC 813/.6—dc23/eng/20230530
LC record available at https://lccn.loc.gov/2023025950
LC ebook record available at https://lccn.loc.gov/2023025951

Printed in the United States of America
1st Printing

Book design by Alison Cnockaert

For Kai and Leo,
Glimmer Twins who like a good adventure

We must go on, because we can't go back.

—*Treasure Island*,
Robert Louis Stevenson

CAPE
RAGE

PROLOGUE

PEOPLE HAVE STARTED asking me questions about Henry Carter. "How did it feel to be sitting that close to him?" "Was he as good looking as his picture?" I tell people I only met him once but that doesn't stop them from asking. Most people have only heard stories about Henry Carter, so I understand the interest.

And I can talk about my work. I'm not like some undercover cops who think talking about what we do is bad luck. I'm not superstitious, don't keep talismans, don't believe karma is much more than people getting what they deserve from time to time.

So, I can talk about Henry Carter. That's not a problem. But the question everyone ends up asking—"Was he as bad as people say?"—is one I can't answer. People are disappointed. I see it on their faces. Sometimes they press—"But you were there, right? When it all went down, you were at Cape Rage? You talked to him for, what was it, an hour?"

True. And in an hour-long conversation with someone when you're not talking nonsense, when you're only talking about things that matter a great deal, you can learn a lot about that person. I probably know Henry Carter better than most of the people he grew up with in Snow Corners.

But what happened that night, and why Carter did what he did, I can't tell you. I'm already wishing people would ask me different questions, because there are some things I can say with certainty about that night, some things beyond dispute. I wish people would ask me questions about revenge and betrayal and family because I can answer those questions; revenge was how this story started, betrayal was how it played out, and family—it was everything to this story. Everything that mattered.

Because it's that sort of story—a family story of revenge and betrayal—it's difficult to know where to begin. Such stories go back centuries. That's another thing I've been thinking about lately—beginnings and endings and why we get to thinking we ever decide things like that; wondering if it's hubris, to even open your mouth and say something has ended, or something has begun.

Everyone got it wrong with Henry Carter, that's for sure, off by miles, or as many miles as it would be from Seattle to that logging road in California where he was shot in the back. Maybe we're always kidding ourselves about beginnings and endings, pretending we have a seat at that table, that we're one of the players. Although you need to start somewhere. It's human nature. And for me, this story began the morning I met Gardner and Hart.

1

THE TWO MEN sitting across the table from me hated each other. That was easy to tell. One wanted me there and one didn't. That was just as plain.

Frank Gardner was old-school FBI and dressed the part: cheap blue suit that didn't fit well, shoulders too tight, cut too long. Gray hair in a brush cut probably as short as the settings on a home-barber shear could go. What looked like permanent, indigo-colored chin stubble.

I would have guessed him to be midfifties, but fit as hell, with a chest and arms you only get from going to a gym a few times a week. When I walked into the FBI office in Seattle, Gardner stared at me the way you'd stare at an ex-spouse entering a courtroom.

Jason Hart, sitting the other side of a desk from both of us, was everything Frank Gardner wasn't. He had blond hair running past his collar, feathered and layered the way no home-barber shear could do it. No chin stubble. Wore a dark-gray suit with a checked pattern so subtle you almost had to be standing on top of the guy to see it. He looked to be in his early forties and smelled of cologne, talc, success and a thousand other things Frank Gardner would never have or be.

Jason Hart was Frank Gardner's boss.

That would have been enough right there for a lot of men to hate each other, but it always seemed like there was something else to it. Should have thought more about it at the time. Easy to say today. Doubt if you'll find anyone to argue with you.

But there was a lot to consider that morning, and career-related hatred between FBI agents wasn't on my list. The request for me to be seconded to Hart's task force had come in two days earlier, and it was my first trip in Seattle. I was thinking about that. The window of Hart's office looked out on Elliott Bay and the sky was the electric-blue color you get sometimes after a good hard rain, a sky that should have had rainbows and water droplets falling from trees beneath it; but it hadn't rained in Seattle for eight days and that sky looked restless and mean, a sky that probably wasn't doing anyone any good.

The FBI agent who'd picked me up at the airport had talked about little else. Look at the sky. No rain for eight days. Talked about it in a breathless, childish way. He was a short man who wore a salt-stained trench coat, even though it wasn't that cold, and besides the weather he only talked about one other thing. As he was putting my bag in the trunk of his sedan, he asked, "What are you here for, Pete Flarety or the Danbys?"

When I answered "Danbys," he groaned and said, "Good luck, pal. That family is a piece of work." Then he started talking about the weather.

What I was thinking about most that morning though was the CCTV tape I'd just watched. The tape had shown a bank robbery three days earlier at a Wells Fargo in San Francisco; the last two and a half minutes of it, anyway, when the robbery went south after a robber accidentally set off a tear gas cannister inside the bank.

We were silent a long time after that tape finished: Gardner looking at me with a sneer on his face; Hart fidgeting with one of the brightly colored file folders on his desk; me staring out at that hopped-up, neon sky.

It was Hart who spoke first.

"Want to see it again?"

"No."

"Really? Most people want to see it again. You don't get camera angles like that very often."

"What happened to that second guard was an execution. Don't know why anyone would want to see it again."

"Squeamish?" asked Gardner.

"No. Just don't like snuff films."

"Squeamish. That's what this job needs. Glad we sent for you."

"Frank, ease up," said Hart, and he leaned across his desk to open a file. "The guy's right. We've gotten too used to seeing that damn tape. I don't want to see it again either." He leaned back in his chair. "So . . . what do you think?"

He crossed his fingers and cupped his hands under his chin. Like an attentive student waiting for the answer to a clever question. Maybe he *had* seen that tape too many times.

"Professional crew. They didn't hesitate with the second guard. One or two makes no difference in Washington?"

"None."

"Woman is different. That's how you were able to ID the crew?"

"Tess Danby. She doesn't fade into the woodwork, does she? Did you get the material we sent to Detroit, about the family?"

"Got it last night."

"All three—Ambrose, Finn and Tess?"

"Yes."

"Any questions?"

"It's quite the family. How long has your investigation been running?"

"Eighteen months."

"How close are you?"

"Until the bank robbery, not that close. We have paperwork that might get Ambrose and Finn, financial irregularities, some dirty money. The Danbys make most of their money running contraband out of Cape Rage. They've been doing it since Prohibition, from on an island in the Strait that the family bought back in the thirties. But those aren't the crimes we want them for. We have eight unsolved homicides and scores of armed robberies in the Pacific Northwest linked to the Danbys. This task force was set up to clear those cases."

"The background material you sent on the robbery has it as four robbers, but you only sent three jackets. You can't identify the fourth robber?" I asked.

"Close, hotshot," laughed Gardner. "Real fuckin' close."

"Frank, please," said Hart, flashing Gardner an angry look. "All of the robbers have been identified. The reason we only sent three files is because the fourth is dead."

"How?"

"The Danbys shot him after the robbery; on their way back to Cape Rage."

"How do you know that?"

"Confirmed in a wiretap. Not our case. Danby associate. We also have witnesses to an argument between Finn Danby and his sister where he's referred to in the past tense. And he never came back to Danby Island after the robbery, which rather proves it."

"He lived on the island?"

"He did. Tess Danby's husband—guy's name was Henry Carter."

"Why did they kill him?"

"Working theory is this was a once-in-a-lifetime score, and Ambrose didn't want to split it with a son-in-law. Or maybe it was Tess's idea. She gets bored easily, as you would have seen in her file, Mr. Barrett."

Gardner laughed when Hart said "Mr. Barrett" and his boss gave him another nasty look—but it was still as nasty as a man with feathered hair and a gray-checked suit could muster. Gardner laughed a few more times before saying, "This is a joke. Are we really supposed to call this guy Barrett?"

"That's his operational name, Frank."

"Not his *real* name. This guy can't even play straight with us, the people he fuckin' works for?"

I turned to Gardner with what I hoped was a look of great weariness upon my face. People in my line of work don't have a lot of fans. I get called in when cases have stalled or are about to go bust. The agents already working those cases don't usually like the help. I've almost come to expect a bit of hostility, and I'm not above responding in kind.

"I don't work for you," I said to Gardner. "It was your *boss* who put in a request with the Detroit police. That's who I work for. And you're calling me Barrett because I know men in the ground today who are there because some local suit got the names mixed up. I will never be anything *but* Danny Barrett to *you*."

He wasn't ruffled. "Professional spook. Your family must be proud," he sneered.

"Frank, we've gone over this a thousand times," Hart almost yelled. Then he looked embarrassed at almost yelling, looked at me and said, "There's been some disagreement . . . internally . . . about your vocation and its . . . necessity."

"Debate away. I don't need to be here."

"I'm glad you are. I'll make sure Frank plays nice, don't worry about that. I'm the boss, just like you said. *Frank, explain it to him.*"

I was startled. Hart couldn't pull off the look, but his voice dropped about an octave when he said *Frank, explain it to him* and there was some sand and grit to it suddenly, something menacing and surprisingly competent. Gardner still gave his head a slow shake—the recalcitrant puppy being brought to heel—but eventually he got around to telling me why Hart put in the request, and why I was in Seattle.

"We need corroborating evidence that the Danbys were the ones who robbed that bank," he began. "Our lawyers don't think the security tape will be enough. They think that *without* corroborating evidence the tape would be ruled inadmissible at trial. Because of the ongoing investigation into the Danbys that is being conducted by this office, the robbery case has been transferred from San Francisco to Seattle and is the reason we have requested your services, *Mr. Barrett.*"

It took him ten more minutes to explain the FBI's plan. He must have used six or seven sneers in the telling, saving the biggest for his close, which he probably had rehearsed in his mind and went like this, said without pause or hesitation: "So that's pretty much it—we need you to go to Cape Rage and get hired by the Danbys; we need you to get over to Danby Island and find evidence that will link the Danbys to the bank robbery in San Francisco; if you get on that island, by the way, you'll be the first cop to ever see it, and congratulations to you; once you're on the island and have secured the corroborating evidence we need you to get that intel to the operation commander—that will be me—then we need you to be ready and prepared to assist the operational commander in any way he deems necessary when we come over to that island and shut the motherfuckers down."

The last words came out in a rush, the syllables smashing into each other like boxcars in a train wreck, and when he was done, Gardner laughed, and sneered, and asked, "What do you say, *Barrett?* Want the job?"

Maybe it was the laugh. Maybe it was not wanting to give a sneer-freak the last sneer. I've thought about it a thousand times and I'm not sure why I didn't take more time with my answer that morning; why I didn't take another look at that mean, restless sky outside Hart's window and ask myself what sort of story comes with a sky like that.

Instead, I looked at Gardner, shrugged my shoulders and asked, "Is that all?"

———————

THAT IS ONE beginning for this story. There is another: three days earlier, when Henry Carter awakes on a patch of fern moss and finds himself staring at high cirrus clouds. He hears the one-note trilling of a cardinal. The spinning of car wheels. Feels the moss beneath him turn warm and wet, as he bleeds out.

In time, the cardinal flies away, the car wheels fade, and after that comes a great silence, a muteness broad and deep enough for him to tumble into. He spins in the silence a long time, what seems like days, until a foul smell comes over him and he reawakens.

He rolled when he was shot, and he is grateful he isn't face down. He lifts his head and sees blood pooling around his waist. It is starting to discolor. The reason for the smell. He lays his head down and goes back to watching clouds.

He doesn't spend time thinking about the betrayal. Not right away. It happened. He should have seen it coming. He doesn't allow more than that, not until the last minutes before he loses consciousness a second time, when he remembers her face.

The way she looked when he saw her last. Surprised. But not as surprised as she should have been. Questioning. But not in a good way. Wondering whether she should run. Whether that was the smart play and whether she had the time for it.

He knew the look.

When he reawakens, the air has chilled and there are black dots in front of the clouds, as though they have mottled. He wonders what would cause a thing like that, but no answer comes to him.

His father had an expression for her. He remembers that. "Tess Danby ain't no hand-upper, son." When he asked his father what that meant, he'd answered, "Means that gal is a great many things, Henry, but one thing she'll never be is any help to a man when he's down."

Funny. Is that funny now?

He ponders the question for the rest of the day, until the wind gathers strength and the late-afternoon gnats come and then are blown away; until the shadows climb down from the upper branches of the trees and begin to lie for the night; until the last of the day's light fades, glimmer by glimmer, from the forest floor. Just before the world goes dark, Henry Carter decides the question doesn't matter much—Tess Danby isn't there now—and it would be right and proper, an action befitting the facts, to kill his wife if he ever has the chance.

2

THE NEXT MORNING, I was on a Greyhound to Cape Rage. It was the milk run, stopping eight times before I got off, another eight after that before the bus reached its destination of Vancouver. We stopped at Everett and Mount Vernon, at Bellingham and Ferndale; stopped at a railway switching yard in the foothills of the Cascade Range where two young line workers jumped off and the bus stayed parked just long enough for the driver to have a cigarette.

We stopped at the Lummi Indian Reservation, where half the bus got up and walked off, each person carrying shopping bags, or children's toys, one old man carrying a wooden kayak paddle. It was at Lummi that I first saw Cape Rage. It looked like a distant white hill at the southern tip of the Strait of Georgia, the San Juan Islands in the foreground, each island with second-growth Douglas fir, the tree line of each looking roughly the same, almost too uniform to be natural, and in the shadows cast by Cape Rage those islands looked like boats making their way out to sea.

When the bus left the reservation, I put my duffel behind my head and resumed thinking about the work ahead. I had the three back seats, the ones that don't recline and nobody ever wants, but I can stretch out on those seats if I'm traveling solo and the bus isn't full. Which they never are anymore. Lot of days, I worry about Greyhound.

Artemis Danby came to Washington State, from Buffalo, New York, in the 1890s, one stagecoach ride ahead of an arrest warrant for a string of holdups and assaults along the Erie Canal towpath. He came west with money and soon built a sawmill near Cape Rage, at the mouth of the Drayton River. It was said by some that the reefs around Cape Rage sank more ships in the nineteenth century than the Columbia Bar, but Danby didn't care. Keeping visitors away seemed a good thing. And it made the land for his sawmill that much cheaper.

After the sawmill, Danby bought tugs to start moving booms up and down the Strait, then some seiners to go crabbing, and then—in a stroke of entrepreneurial brilliance that secured the Danby family fortune—some three-mast schooners to run Canadian whiskey through the San Juan Islands during Prohibition.

By the time the United States entered the Second World War, Artemis Danby—King Arthur, as he was known by then—owned salmon canneries in Blaine and Tacoma, a fleet of dry-haul steamers, five more sawmills, two pulp-and-paper mills and the entire town of Cape Rage, the settlement that had grown up around his first sawmill.

The Danby family business was now run by his grandson, Ambrose Danby, who lived on an island in the Georgia Strait with his son and daughter, the island bought in the '30s by Artemis from a bankrupt railway company, a grand hotel on the cliffs of the island that had once been the jewel in the company's portfolio. The Danbys turned a decent profit on their legitimate businesses but earned ten times more smuggling contraband up and down the West Coast. The family also—carrying on a tradition started by King Arthur—stole, almost for sport.

Why would the Danbys bother with armed robberies when they owned a town, and had more illicit money coming in than they could spend in ten lifetimes? For the same reason Gambinos robbed planes sitting on the tarmac of JFK and Mafia dons in Palermo have Renaissance masters hanging in their bedrooms. Because they're criminals. Because they can.

The robbery of the Wells Fargo in San Francisco was a rather dramatic case in point. The CCTV tape had begun full frame on a half-blind robber pushing open the heavy, plate-glass doors at the front of the bank. Tear gas wafted out. The robber stood on the top of the steps and pulled off a black balaclava. When the balaclava was removed, long, auburn hair tumbled out. The robber was a woman. The tear gas swirled and billowed around her and for a moment the scene looked like an '80s music video. Just needed an Aerosmith song.

Then it didn't look like that at all. A security guard had been walking up the steps of the bank. An armored truck was parked in front and, until the front doors opened, the guard had been unaware of the robbery taking place inside.

The guard stopped walking. He was an old man with gray, patchy hair. His uniform hung loose on his body. He stopped walking. Looked at the woman. Then he took a step back, keeping his eyes on her, never moving a hand toward the gun holstered at his hip.

The woman hurriedly put her balaclava back on and, just then, another man appeared on the screen. He was running toward the steps, dressed in the same black camouflage as the woman. The guard must have heard the footsteps because he suddenly turned his head, and when he did that, when he saw the man approaching, his knees buckled.

I've seen this happen so often I've begun to wonder if it's universal, a reflex action that happens to people when they see doom coming from ten feet away. The avalanche snow. The cresting wave. The stone-cold killer with the Glock 9 mm. I haven't decided yet, but on that security tape, the knees of that guard buckled, he was *already falling* when the bullet hit him in the head. A clean shot from twenty feet away, after the shooter ran across a street and assumed a stationary position for no more than a second. On the tape, it looked like continuous motion.

Then came the hard part. The part that was difficult to watch because you knew a bad thing was coming, but you could never stop it. The woman ran off the steps and out of camera range. The killer didn't follow her. Instead, he looked around, rotating his body, completing a full 360-degree turn without taking a step. He didn't seem in a hurry. He looked around while he was moving, holding his head back and taking deep breaths through his nose.

No way he could have sniffed out that second guard. I tell myself that, and each time I tell myself that, I remember the security tape and how it looked to be *exactly* that. No evidence to the contrary. That guy stood and sniffed and then he dropped to all fours, like he was about to do a push-up. Then he looked under the armored truck and saw the second guard.

I hadn't seen him until then. A young guard, his eyes wide with fear, his body trembling. I could see him clearly once I noticed him. He stared at the killer, and the killer must have stared back; I couldn't see his face because of the camera angle, but it seemed to take longer than what was needed, neither man moving for a few seconds, until the man holding the Glock moved his hand slightly and the guard's head snapped back and out of the frame. Then the killer got up, ran away, and that was the end of the tape.

Henry Carter killed those guards. Gardner had said the identification was beyond dispute. Said I'd caught a break when the Danbys decided to kill Tess's husband on their way back to Cape Rage. I stared out the window of the Greyhound, at the gray-green islands of the Georgia Strait, and the distant white cliffs. It was comforting to know that although he didn't like me much, I was going to be able to agree with Frank Gardner about some things.

⸻

THE GREYHOUND PULLED into Cape Rage just as dusk was falling, the last of the day's light casting long, distorted shadows on the narrow streets leading to the bus station. Gulls shrieked overhead, flying off to wherever gulls spend the night. The station was in the back of a hardware store, the Greyhound ticket booth closed, same for the store. I stood on the street waiting for the driver to unlock the undercarriage cargo bins, watched the mountains to the east turn rose, then purple, then lose distinction and turn to black contour lines carved into the horizon.

When the bus pulled away, I couldn't see anyone on the street. Couldn't see any cars moving either. With a population of 1,200, Cape Rage was big enough that there should have been people downtown at eight p.m. But the streets were empty. I picked up my duffel and started walking.

Judging by the redbrick buildings and the wooden garages, the narrow streets and the corner stores with the old-fashioned bay windows, downtown Cape Rage had been built during the bootlegging years. Maybe a few years after. It looked the way a lot of mill towns and port towns look today, the ones that had seen their best years in the golden decades of the Industrial Age. Everything around me looked a little tired, a little underused, in need of some sort of repair.

I walked three blocks before seeing signs of human life—a corner store that was still open, yellow light coming through the window, a weak color that didn't light up more than a few feet of the sidewalk. There was an old man sitting on a stool behind the sort of metal cash register no company has made in half a century. He was thin and his hair was slicked back straighter and wetter than a beaver pelt. He didn't even turn his head as I walked by.

A block past the corner store, I heard the surf. Another street past that, I heard voices, the sound carrying over the water, men's voices that sounded closer than what they were, the voices growing, the surf getting louder, until I rounded a corner, and the ocean was there in front of me. Fifty feet down the shoreline sat my destination, the Spyglass tavern, every window lit, voices now so loud it was like men were standing next to me at a bar. After walking the deserted streets of Cape Rage, finding the tavern was like finding a cruise ship that had run aground, although the bar had somehow managed to stay open.

3

THE MORNING AFTER he is shot, Henry Carter awakes to a wayward light, one that had snuck onto the forest floor as no more than a glimmer, then grew and strengthened, turned to predawn glow, then, finally, to this light. Carter looks at it in wonder. He has hoarfrost on his cheeks, his lips, his hair. He already looks like a body in a morgue.

The Danbys had chosen well, he thinks: a gully one hundred yards off a rarely used logging road, one left in shadows most of the day. It is possible his body will never be found.

This saddens him and Carter is surprised when the emotion comes. He never thought he would care. Dead was dead, and you need not pity a dead man. His problems were behind him. This is what he has always believed. Until this morning.

He lies with this strange new emotion and listens to the songbirds awaken. Feels a weak wind begin to melt the frost upon his face. In time he grows tired, closes his eyes and goes back to sleep.

=====

MIDMORNING OF THAT day, a teenage girl comes through the gully picking fiddleheads. She works on her hands and knees, searching for the dark-green buds hidden beneath the pine-needle undergrowth of this forest. She snips the fiddleheads carefully at ground level when she finds them, so the roots will be left for next year, moves on in search of more, so focused on her work she is five feet from Carter when she sees him.

Not him—his blood she sees first. The girl has crawled onto the fern moss, is enjoying the momentary softness of the moss upon her knees, is looking for the hidden fiddleheads when she raises one hand in surprise, blood dripping down her fingers. When she finally sees Carter, she screams, then scrambles backward, dropping both the canvas bag holding the fiddleheads and her Buck knife.

She puts both hands over her mouth, so she doesn't scream again, doesn't make a sound. Looks at Carter. He lies on his back, his face pale and wet. It looks like he's been swimming, the girl thinks, although he is dressed in a black suit and white shirt, with what looks like an expensive watch on his right-hand wrist. His shoes are black as well, thick soled and polished, the toes pointing straight up, like garden spikes. His jacket is thrown open and she sees a leather shoulder strap with no gun.

The girl pulls herself to a crouch. She has long, straight blond hair, wears a man's parka with soot stains on the fur collar. She stares at Carter, then at the forest. Hears gray jays nattering and something moving in the woods nearby—nothing large, probably a racoon or porcupine. She looks back at Carter.

She guesses him to be in his early thirties, maybe a little older, tall enough, and built right, broad shouldered, lean in the hips. He'd been shot in the back and the blood around his body has darkened and hardened and is now the color of wet terra cotta. He looks like he belongs in this forest about as much as a beach blanket belongs.

The girl listens one more time to the sounds of the forest, then stands and walks toward him. She kneels and puts two fingers against his neck, recoils when she feels a tremor.

You're not dead?

The girl is surprised, then annoyed with herself. Guilt is a rare emotion for her, and it is several seconds before she puts her fingers back on the man's neck, telling herself this man is trouble—anyone can see that—and surely there is no shame in wishing she'd never crawled onto this patch of fern moss, never seen this man. That's what she meant to think. Not that other thought.

She keeps telling herself this, and in a minute, she takes her fingers away, finally convinced it is no trick. As dead as this man looks, he is not dead.

The girl stays in her crouch, and just then a squirrel runs past her, no more than two feet away. It runs up a tree, perches on a low branch and breaks into the quarrelsome chatter squirrels use sometimes. The girl stares at the animal awhile before saying, "Don't know what you're complaining about. He ain't your problem."

After that she walks into the woods and begins to look for young hemlock trees.

4

THE SPYGLASS TAVERN had been built in 1910 by Artemis Danby and it still had the original cedar-shake siding, weathered and beaten down now to a kindling-smoke gray. It had been built right on the town's main wharf and there were large windows on the two sides facing the Georgia Strait, and what looked like portholes on the two sides facing the town of Cape Rage. The back half of the tavern sat on stilts over the water.

There were several tin chimneys, a few gables and a wooden carving of a spyglass hanging from a metal rod above the front door. The spyglass swung and the metal bar creaked when I opened the door. I was stepping inside the tavern before I remembered Spyglass was the name of John Silver's bar in *Treasure Island*. Artemis Danby had a sense of humor.

The bar was to the right as I walked in, a solid piece of white oak running almost the length of the room. There was a mirror behind the bar and liquor bottles stacked on shelves in front of the mirror. There were round tavern tables spread across the room with short, spindle-backed chairs around them. A pool table and shuffleboard table were opposite the bar.

Men were sitting at about half the tables. They wore jeans and flannel work shirts, a few wore the rubber waders they would have worn that day on a boat. There were no waiters, just a bartender, who stood behind the bar wearing a denim shirt with the sleeves rolled up past his elbows, full-sleeve tats on both forearms. There were no women.

I got some stares when I walked in, and the next shot in the pool game seemed to take longer than necessary, but that was it. The Spyglass didn't turn quiet as the door closed behind me. No one stared at me like the next thing I did was going to be important to them.

The bartender took his time about coming to see me though. Like he was deciding if he wanted to serve me, or deciding how friendly he wanted to be, neither decision apparently being an easy one. When he finally walked over, he was wrapping a towel around his knuckles, like a boxer getting taped.

"Coors. Jack on the side," I said. He turned and walked away. When the drinks came, I gave him a ten and told him to keep the change. It worked out to a three-dollar tip. That got me a nod of the head.

"Busy night?" I asked.

"Look busy to you?"

"Don't know what a Tuesday night looks like in Cape Rage. This could be a rush."

"It ain't a rush."

I drank the shot of Jack Daniels, throwing my head back just a little and putting the glass down gently on the bar, not making a show of it, letting him know I could be civilized if the situation required. "I'll have another," I said, and he walked away.

I gave him another ten and again told him to keep the change. This bought me a half smile.

"Whatta ya looking for, pal?" he said.

"Cold beer and Jack. Looks like I've come to the right place."

"Don't think so. Man tips like this wants something. You don't seem the lonely type. Or the chatty type. Just so you know, drug dealers in this bar . . . I stomp on their fuckin' heads."

He smiled and wrapped the towel tighter around his knuckles.

"I don't see a problem," I said.

"I don't see a problem either."

"Good."

"Good."

We stared at each other, me wondering if it was my turn. Eventually, he unwrapped the towel and went back to where he'd been standing before I walked in; opposite end of the bar, near the back doors, next to an ashtray with smoke trailing from a nearly burned-away cigarette. He butted the ashen stalk of his last cigarette and lit another.

I looked around. The men sitting at the bar were solo drinkers, like me, and they all looked like men who worked outside to make a living. Hard physical labor, their bodies crooked and angular, knobby elbows and knees, hands more burnished than the wooden bar in front of them. No one was at the shuffleboard, but the pool table had four players and coins stacked for players waiting to get up. The game looked serious, with little talking and most players walking around the table a few times before taking their shot.

There was a microwave behind the bar, and this was the kitchen for the Spyglass. Chuckwagon sandwiches in plastic bags cooked on high for forty-five seconds. Clam chowder sitting in cooking-oil jars atop an icebox, ladled into chipped bowls and cooked for thirty. The tavern had the aroma of melted cheese and cooked ham, draft beer and rye whiskey. It smelled the way a good tavern should smell.

I had been sitting there about thirty minutes when I heard the creak of the metal rod and three men came walking through the door.

One of the men was huge, a giant, really, six-foot-eight or somewhere around there. One looked like a kid not old enough to be there. The third, the man who walked in last, had long black hair and a half-grown beard that didn't hide bad scarring on both cheeks. He was wearing a three-quarter-length black leather coat that he unbuttoned when he came through the door but didn't take off.

I watched the men in the mirror behind the bar. They walked toward an empty table near the pool table. Halfway there, the man in the leather coat stopped to talk to someone. He bent over to say something in the man's ear, and that's when I saw it. The bulge was right where I expected it to be—back of the leather coat, waistband height. Finn Danby was always armed. I'd read that in his police file.

———

WHEN YOU'RE WORKING undercover, it's easy to get too clever, start overthinking every situation. But when you get too many moving parts, you're asking for trouble. A simple plan, like a simple life, is what you want in this world.

It was Bert Fleming who taught me that, the FBI agent who saved my career when I was about to be kicked off the Detroit Police Department. Fleming would have loved Jason Hart's plan. Overthinking was not going to be a problem.

A Danby associate named Jimmy Metcalfe was sitting in the Terre Haute Penitentiary doing an eight-to-ten stretch. Metcalfe had been born and raised in Cape Rage and was the same age as Finn Danby. He was considered a close associate.

With very little orchestration on the part of the FBI, Metcalfe got himself a three-month solitary sentence when he punched a guard. He started his ninety-day stretch the day I arrived in Seattle. It was impossible for anyone outside Terre Haute to contact him. I was a friend of Metcalfe's, looking for work.

That was the plan. *I'm looking for work. Jimmy said I should see you if I was ever out this way.* It was flimsy enough to be embarrassing. Not the way you ever want to start a case. Perfect world, it's the people you're chasing who take the first step. Perfect world, I would have hung around the Spyglass a few weeks and got myself noticed. Then a situation would get set up where I'd be needed. I'm a driver and the gang's regular driver just got arrested. Or I brought home the mobster's sixteen-year-old daughter after finding her stumbling outside a rave club, the ecstasy pills an FBI informant sold her earlier in the day still in her purse. Never touched her.

All sorts of ways to arrange an invitation, but this case didn't have the time for it. There was an urgency to the Danby case right from the start, and in the beginning, I thought I understood it. The San Francisco FBI office wanted the Danbys for that bank robbery. But the Seattle office—because of the ongoing investigation—had first dibs on them and had told San Francisco to back down, they'd handle it.

But two security guards executed half a block from where tourists buy cable-car tickets—they weren't going to back down forever. Hart had to wrap up his investigation or the much-larger San Francisco office was going to take the Danbys away from him. I figured he had a few weeks, at best.

Which meant I was going in by dropping the name Jimmy Metcalfe and not doing much more than that. It was the undercover equivalent of a smash-and-grab jewelry heist. The same level of finesse and forethought.

I finished my beer, got up from the barstool and made my way to Finn Danby's table.

5

HE LET ME stand there awhile, pretending not to notice. Up close, Finn Danby didn't look as big as he did when he walked in. His skin was slack and there were jowls beneath the scruffy beard. I could see now that the beard didn't hide knife marks, but the residual scarring of bad teenage acne. I stood beside his table drinking my beer until he stopped talking to the man next to him and finally turned.

"Can I help you, pal?"

"You're Finn Danby, aren't you?"

The other men at the table tensed when I said that, but Danby didn't blink. His eyes were lidded, and his movements seemed slow. "Who the fuck are you?"

"Danny Barrett. I'm a friend of Jimmy Metcalfe."

"I don't recognize you. . . . How you know Jimmy?"

"Back east. I worked for him in Duluth. One of his ships."

"You were dry goods hauling, were you, pal? Never understood why a sailor would want to shovel rocks for a living."

"Iron ore wasn't all we were hauling."

"No, suppose not. Jimmy's inside, ain't he? Thought I heard that."

"You heard right. He got jammed up with a boat. Took it from a guy who owed him money. Guy reported it stolen."

"Right, right, it's coming back to me. . . . Piracy?"

"Yeah. Jimmy took the boat from the guy in the middle of Lake Superior. Grand theft if that boat is moored, piracy if you take it from him in open water and tell him to take the lifeboat home."

Danby started laughing. Then the giant laughed. Then the kid decided what I'd said was the funniest thing he'd ever heard.

"Fuckin' Jimmy," said Danby, still laughing, "sounds like something he'd do. He should have stayed home; I would have rigged him out with a boat. Didn't need to go halfway 'cross the country and start fuckin' 'round with tramp steamers."

"Jimmy had big plans," I said. "He wanted to build a steamship line. Said that's where the serious money was. Like fuckin' Onassis."

"Yeah, like fuckin' Onassis—he used to say that all the time." And Danby roared again.

"Still does. 'Danny, we're going to make out like fuckin' Onassis. Sit back, count the money, fuck babes that used to fuck a president.' I thought he was going to make it too. Shame about that boat."

Finn Danby stopped laughing and began nodding his head sadly. Yeah, shame about that boat. I made a mental note to thank the desk agent who'd compiled the dossier on Jimmy Metcalfe, including the appendix of frequently used expressions and words culled from his police wiretaps and court transcripts.

"What are you drinking, pal?" Danby asked.

"Jack. Coors for the chaser."

"Thatta boy. I'll buy your next round." Danby raised his hand and the bartender looked in his direction. He pointed at me, then at himself, then he turned and went back talking to the man next to him.

I stood there like a waiter left hoping for a tip. "I was actually hoping to speak to you a minute, Mr. Danby."

He was slow to turn. Being a friend of Jimmy Metcalfe had bought me a beer, a shot and not one ounce of goodwill.

"'Bout what?"

"I'm looking for work."

"Ain't got any, pal. Sorry."

"You sure? I'm probably better than any guy you got right now."

"A steam tramper from Duluth? Shit, pal, you probably ain't better than my sister."

The giant that came in with Danby slapped the table so hard the bottles jumped and clinked. The kid had spittle running down his chin. I waited until they were done laughing and said, "I don't know your sister, Mr. Danby, so I can't comment on that. When I said I was probably better than any man you got, I was looking at who you got sitting here with you tonight."

Danby had a beer bottle going to his mouth and it stopped midway. The giant sucked in his breath so fast it sounded like a wind tunnel. The kid looked like he'd just been slapped.

"What did you just say?"

"You heard me. I'll tell you more—I came two thousand miles to see you, Mr. Danby, because Jimmy Metcalfe's a pal of mine and he said if I ever needed a place to go and start over, Cape Rage was the place to go, and Finn Danby was the man to see. Stand-up guy, our kind of people, Danny. That's what Jimmy always told me.

"But here I am, standing right in front of you, telling you I'm a friend of Jimmy's, telling you I need work, and you try to blow me off with a beer and a shot. I'm getting pissed off at the unfairness in this world, Mr. Danby, I truly am."

Danby kept the beer bottle where it was before slowly taking it the rest of the way. He took a big, long gulp, and put the bottle back on the table.

"Know what, pal? Don't think I'm buying you that drink anymore. Say hi to Jimmy for me."

It had always been a long shot. The Danbys had run Cape Rage for more than a century and the last time someone worked for them who wasn't from Cape Rage was probably around the time they started. I was going to need to improvise and had always suspected as much. Although I didn't even have a backup plan this time, and I normally won't leave home, cross a busy street or climb a high flight of stairs without one of those.

It would come to me. That was the new plan.

I stood and waited. Eventually the giant stood, walked around the table and put his hand on my shoulder. "You wanna take this outside, pal? Finn just told you to blow."

The giant smiled. It was the sort of smile someone has right before they accept an award or take a large sum of money from an out-stretched hand—a smile of sweet, entitled superiority.

I smiled back. He couldn't have looked more like a backup plan if he'd had the words tattooed to his forehead.

"TAKE YOUR HAND off my shoulder," I said quietly.

"I'll put my hands wherever I fuckin' wanna put 'em, asshole, including upside your fuckin' head if you don't get your ass out of here."

Finn Danby laughed. The giant gripping my shoulder laughed. The kid laughed. Men sitting at nearby tables started laughing too and I wondered—Why is there always laughter? Most acts of violence have someone laughing just beforehand, and half the time, the person laughing is the last person who should have been. Fifty percent. From what I've seen of the world, those are the odds of ever knowing where you're truly standing in this world.

"I'll leave when I finish my beer," I said. "Already paid for it."

The giant looked at Finn, who shrugged his shoulders and started talking again to the man sitting at the next table. I raised the bottle, taking my time about it, took a good, long sip—it was nearly full, which seemed a waste—and then I threw the bottle over my shoulder.

It missed the giant, but he yelled in surprise and lessened his grip on my shoulder enough for me to slip free. Without turning around, I drove my elbow into his gut. It bounced off like I'd hit a guardrail. The giant never flinched, let alone buckled or lost his balance. I was diving to the ground when his punch came, a right-handed undercut that would have ended the fight right there if it had connected.

But it swung over my head harmlessly, and when it did, I kicked out with my right leg, hitting the giant above the ankle. This time he screamed. When he bent down to grab his ankle, I hit him in the face with my other foot.

It was a beautiful kick. So square in his face I never saw it land; only saw my boot pasted above his crouched-over body, like my boot had become his face, then he flew backward. When he started to get up, I rolled in his direction and gave him a second kick to the face, almost as beautiful as the first. This time he fell backward and when his head hit the wooden floor it sounded like a high-noon cannon shot. He stayed down and an awkward silence filled the tavern.

It didn't last. I'm not sure how many men tried to jump me right then, but it would have looked like a football scrimmage for a while: men pawing each other trying to reach me on the floor; the kid trying to bite my arm; the man who had been talking to Finn now scream-ing, "Pin the bastard's arms an'll give'm a kick he won't forget."

I stayed on the ground and brought them down one by one. I like fighting on the ground, Brazilian jiu-jitsu some people call it, and it *was* a Brazilian—an old cut-and-corner guy in Detroit—who taught me how to do it. He told me not only the techniques but the history, stories about the Gracies and other fighting families from the jungles of Brazil, showed me grainy black-and-white videos of matches in outdoor rings, thatched buildings in the background, thousands of people watching a way of fighting I had never seen.

"People think being on the ground is a bad thing," the cut-and-corner guy told me. "In Brazil, we made it a weapon."

The man who wanted to give me an unforgettable kick went first. I waited until he had raised his foot and then I kicked him in his right shin. He dropped like dead weight. When he started screaming, I knew I had ripped the tendon.

I pulled the kid off me and got my knees around his head, squeezing until his eyes rolled back and his hands stopped clawing my legs. People stopped to look at that, and then I threw the kid aside, arched my body while still on my back—as though I were doing a reverse plank—and crabbed my way to the nearest man.

He looked at me like I was a circus act. Was still looking at me like that when I grabbed his leg with one of mine and brought him down. I jumped onto his chest and gave him a flurry of short jabs to the head. He was helpless from the first blow, unconscious from probably the second or third.

But I kept punching him. I broke his nose and blood squirted out in a fine, high arc, like a pipe bursting. I kept punching. I knew I had probably done enough to get Finn Danby's attention, but there was a way to ensure it. Violence was considered a good thing by men like Danby. Gratuitous, over-the-top violence—that was considered a better thing.

I feigned the last couple punches, but it wouldn't have made much difference by then. I'd been careful to avoid his eyes, and his teeth, but he was never going to thank me for what I'd done. Both cheekbones looked broken. His nose was a mess.

I finally stopped, took some deep breaths and stood. The tavern was quiet now. Except for the cries of one man, writhing on the ground and clutching his shin. Three other men lay around him, unconscious. One was a giant; one was a kid; one was the man I had just beaten to a bloody mess. I looked at all three, to see if there was an *urgent* need for an ambulance, then I went and stood in front of Finn Danby.

"They'll live," I said, and didn't say anything else as that seemed to be all that needed to be said right then. Danby flipped his hair back, took a last sip from his beer bottle, put it carefully on the table, smacked his lips and asked, "What did you say your name was, pal?"

6

THE GIRL'S CABIN is on a bluff overlooking a pine valley and a distant river, although on most days the fog and the mist swirling on the knoll are so thick the river cannot be seen, and it seems as though the girl lives among the clouds. She pulls Carter inside, tethered to a sled she has made from the trunks of young hemlock, props the sled up straight, cuts the sumac strands, and he falls onto a bed.

She walks to an airtight stove and starts a fire. Her cabin has two rooms, divided by a curtain she has hung from a length of plastic clothesline. One room is larger than the other, about twice the size, and in this room are the stove and a wood box, a kitchen table made from rough-hewn planks of wood, two foldout metal chairs tucked beneath the table. A door sitting on sawhorses is her kitchen counter. Underneath are two large plastic containers of water. A couch has cushions stuffed with cedar boughs. The coffee table is the cut burr of a large maple. There are two small windows in the room and a closet by the front door that holds winter clothes and rain gear, a .22-caliber hunting rifle and some fishing rods.

The smaller room has a four-poster metal bed and a wooden dresser with an oval mirror. Another closet, a thin one this time, the way they used to make them, has a blue summer dress and a pair of overalls hanging from wooden pegs.

The girl puts two pots of water on top of the airtight, dips a washcloth in one pot and returns to her bedroom. Carter lies on his stomach, and she can see his wound clearly now. It was a shotgun that struck him down, the metal fragments pockmarking his flesh. There is one large ugly hole in the middle of his back, where the brunt of the charge hit. There is singeing on the torn flesh around the hole. Whoever shot him was standing close.

The girl returns to the airtight and looks at the tools she had placed in one of the pots: a Buck hunting knife, two sewing needles, a pair of needle-nose pliers. She isn't sure how long you need to boil metal before it is sterile, but five minutes at a roiling boil seems a good number to her. She has no watch so she counts off the time.

When she is done, she pushes one pot to the back of the airtight and takes the other into the bedroom. She kneels beside the bed and waits for the water to cool. Looks again at the burned flesh and ugly scarring. Eventually she uses a washcloth to take the hot tools from the pot. She tosses the Buck knife from hand to hand, blowing on it, then begins popping out the metal from his back. She uses the pliers to pry free the shards that have meshed with flesh and muscle. When she has been working a few minutes, she realizes she isn't going to need the needles.

After removing the metal, she goes outside. It is nighttime now and the stars are splashed against an onyx sky. The contrast is striking, more vivid than normal, like looking at diamonds pinned to black velvet boards. It hasn't rained in more than a week, and she thinks that has something to do with it. She walks to a stand of red cedar and uses her Buck knife to cut strips of bark. When she has two dozen strips, she returns to the cabin.

She puts the bark in the pot she left on the airtight. Counts off two minutes, watching the bark curl and the water turn yellow. She stokes the embers in the airtight and puts on two more logs, then takes the pot into the bedroom. She puts half the strips on Carter's back and then wraps a towel around his torso, lifting him gently and pulling the towel beneath him two times before pinning it. She takes a fresh washcloth and dips it in the pot. The bark has now shriveled so the edges are touching. She wrings out the cloth and pushes it against Carter's lips. Keeps it there. In a few seconds, Carter opens his mouth, and she squeezes.

For the rest of that night, the girl stays beside her bed doing nothing more than that. She isn't sure if cedar tea is what you should give to a man who's been shot in the back. She has no experience with such things. But cedar tea is good for many things, was what the Huron gave French explorers back east, the ones who'd traveled too far inland and were found half dead on their pinnaces. She knows those stories. Half dead would be half dead, right?

Night passes into day without the girl noticing. The trance of repetitive motion: dipping the washcloth in the water, squeezing the liquid into Carter's mouth, wiping his cheeks, laying the back of her hand on his forehead to check for fever. Dipping the washcloth in the water.

Day becomes a second night. The weak sunlight in the room disappears without the girl noticing it has come. A sleepy light that never chases away the shadows. She hears geese flying overhead, and wind rustling through the cedars. Halfway through the night, she looks at Carter and thinks he doesn't look frozen anymore. His skin has a reddish hue, and his breathing is no longer shallow and ragged. She puts down her washcloth and goes to the other room.

DESPITE THE GIRL'S exhaustion, when she lies upon her couch that night her sleep is troubled, filled with dreams that run one into another without pause. She is a young girl, traveling with her father, backseat of a Buick Regal. Boat of a car. Everything they own in the backseat and trunk. Highway in the Midwest. Cornfields unfurling to the horizon, late in the season, so the tassels are golden and full. Then she is on another highway, up north, skiffs of snow in a plowed field, pine in the high country. Her father is driving, a pint of bourbon tucked between his legs.

They are looking for a way out of the pines, but the forest stretches further than the cornfields. So long since they've seen the sun it seems like a town they passed five hundred miles back. Driving and driving until suddenly she sees a light. But not a good light. Not a welcoming light. A muzzle flash of light seen inside a cabin, the girl standing outside looking through the windows. Then another flash of light, this one inside a car, parked far down a gravel road. Then a flash inside a corner store, an old man with slicked-back hair clutching his chest and falling over a metal cash register no one has made for fifty years.

She runs and runs and suddenly she's back in the Buick, craning her neck to see in the back seat. Cardboard boxes. A vinyl case of CDs. A girl's pink suitcase. "Are we there yet?" she asks.

Her father laughs. Takes another sip of whiskey.

The dreams keep running until she awakes with a start. She's out of breath, confused for a moment where she is. Looking up she sees a gray mist showing in the south-facing window above the airtight. It comes back to her. It's morning, she realizes, and she stares out the window awhile.

When she turns her head, the girl is surprised, yet somehow not as surprised as she should have been, to see Henry Carter in the room. He sits on the cut burr of maple. Wears a buffalo robe several sizes too big for him. In his lap is her hunting rifle.

———

THE GIRL DOESN'T say anything right away. Carter is sitting straight on the maple burr, his right hand on the stock of her rifle, forefinger on the trigger, not so much as a tremor.

"You're feeling better," she says.

Carter doesn't answer.

"I thought your pulse was too strong last time I checked it," the girl continues. "Not making that up. Really did. Too strong for how you was lookin', anyway. How long was you fakin' it?"

Carter looks around the room. At the airtight stove, the old-door kitchen counter, the pails of water under the door. Eventually, he says, "Whose robe is this?"

The girl is surprised to hear his voice. She still thinks of him as a man about to die.

"My dad's."

"Where is he?"

"He don't live here anymore. I kept it 'cause of how warm it is. He was a big man, it's a good coat in the winter. . . . Why you got my rifle?"

"I thought it'd be best if I had it."

"You thought it'd be best . . . ? I saved your life, mister. I found you nearly dead in the woods. You know that, right?"

"Where are my clothes?"

"What?"

"The clothes I was wearing. Where are they?"

"Corner over there," and the girl points toward her bedroom. "I had to cut 'em off you. They ain't going to be any good to you."

Carter stands. He does it slow and easy, without taking his hand off the rifle, without needing to steady himself. He walks to where the girl has pointed, picks up his pants and shakes them.

"Your stuff's in a bowl on the dresser," the girl says. Carter drops his pants and walks to the dresser. He peers inside a cereal bowl sitting atop the dresser, then he picks it up and shakes it. There is a clinking-metal sound. He empties the contents of the bowl into his hand and then puts his hand in a pocket of the buffalo robe, comes back to the living room and sits on the cut burr of maple.

"Has anyone been here?" he asks.

"Since you been here, you mean? No."

"No one has come looking for me?"

"No."

"Have any neighbors come?"

"What neighbors? Go outside and have a look."

Carter stares at the window above the airtight. "That's a good thought," he says. "Stay where you are."

Carter walks outside and looks at the mist moving through the trees in the valley below, and a fog hanging over the ocean, so thick only small patches of light-blue sea are showing, like tears in a fabric. He sees no ships, no rooftops in the forest below, only a narrow, crooked road running beside a small river. He goes back inside.

"Where is your nearest neighbor?"

"'Bout ten miles downriver, at the forks."

"And your father?"

"He don't live here anymore. Already told you that."

"He's dead?"

". . . Why you want to know something like that?"

"So I can understand you."

The girl tilts her head when Carter says that. She is curious. Surprised. "He left one day and never came back."

"When was this?"

"Be a year next month."

"How have you survived?"

"Same way I was surviving before he left. . . . The work didn't change any."

"You have no other family?"

"Just my dad. Far as I know."

Carter turns away from the girl, takes another look around the cabin. "This is true . . . what you're telling me?"

"Don't know why I'd make up a story like that. Don't make me sound all that special."

Carter nods and says, "Where you found me—can you find your way back?"

"Sure I can."

"Take me there."

***

HER DAD HAD been a bigger man than Henry Carter, but the girl finds a pair of jeans that can be cinched to fit, and a flannel shirt that fits better than the jeans. She cuts new strips of cedar and changes his dressing before they leave. He sits in the cinched jeans, naked to the waist, the Winchester in his lap. The cedar has a sweet resin smell that fills the cabin.

They follow a path down the bluff, then down the logging road Carter saw through the mist. There is a river running somewhere, but he doesn't see it. The girl walks five paces ahead of him, the hunting rifle aimed at her back.

When the logging road forks, they turn left, away from the river. The road begins to narrow. They are walking an old-growth forest now, the trees so tall and plentiful that only glints of sunshine show on the forest floor. A gull shrieks overhead, a mournful, distant sound that echoes off the trees and seems more pitiful with each fading cry.

They reach a small rise in the road and the girl stops walking. "Over there," she says, and points to a gully a hundred yards away, "that's where I found you."

Carter looks to where she is pointing. It is a gully the other side of a clearing, one of the few clearings in this forest, a small patch of land where a building must have stood once. He crouches on his ankles and examines the road. Picks up a cedar branch and sweeps away some gravel. Walks fifty paces down the road, crouches and sweeps again.

He comes back to the girl. "Take me to the exact place you found me."

". . . Are you sure?"

Carter motions with the rifle and they walk off the road and into the gully. The dew on the stunt cedar makes their jeans wet from the knees down by the time they reach the fern moss. Carter's blood can still be seen, a ragged, chocolate-brown stain that resembles a continent. Africa, perhaps, if it were tilted on a different axis. Europe, if it had been blown up and put back together wrong.

Carter walks into the gully, then onto a wide swatch of moss. He closes his eyes. Starts taking deep breaths. The girl watches him. His breathing is steady as a metronome. Six seconds in. Eight seconds out. When he opens his eyes, he says, "What day is it?"

"I'm . . . I'm not sure."

"How many days have I been in your cabin?"

". . . Brought you home three days ago. . . . You been there two nights."

"What time of day did you find me?"

"Morning . . . not that late. I'd been out picking about two hours."

Carter looks around. A few seconds later he says, "We'll wait over there."

The girl looks to where he is pointing: a large red fir on the edge of the logging road.

"We're staying? Why?"

"Someone will be coming."

7

I SPENT THE night on the bench outside the hardware store, moving inside when the Greyhound ticket booth opened. I used the washroom in the store to wash up, stripping to my waist and getting a nasty look from an old man who came in with a broom shortly after six.

"There ain't a bus till noon," he said, his voice sounding more authoritative than you would expect from a man holding a broom.

"I'm not waiting for the noon bus," I said. "I got in yesterday."

This got me another nasty look, along with some tsk-tsks as the old man worked his way around the room with his broom. I couldn't see there being much of a homeless problem in Cape Rage, but when it came, this man would be ready.

When I finished at the sink, I put my shirt back on, took my duffel and headed outside. The old man had left by then and was talking to another man in an aisle of the hardware store. The two men watched me leave, then watched me through the glass windows of the store while I made my way down the street, watched right to the end of the block, as though it were important to them to know which direction I was heading.

I turned left and found a diner two blocks down. I had what the menu called the Fisherman's Special, which was eggs with fried haddock instead of bacon. The fish tasted fresh enough to have been caught that morning. The eggs were runny, the coffee bitter. When I had walked in, half the tables had dirty dishes on them, like the breakfast rush had come and gone. I wondered what time you needed to be sitting at the Twisted Reach diner to get fresh coffee.

I walked around Cape Rage for a couple hours after that. There were people on the streets now, but not that many, and the ones who were out didn't seem to be going anywhere in a hurry. Most of the working men must have been out in boats. The buildings I walked past were wooden cottages and two-story Cape Codders; not many were brick. I didn't see a school, but I saw children's toys in the yards of some houses, so there must have been one somewhere.

The spit of land stretching far into the strait cast shadows upon the town as I walked. I'd read in the Danby files that the cape first appeared on a 1792 map drawn by Jose Maria Narvaez, although the Spanish explorer mistakenly identified the cape as an island—Isla del Rey. Narvaez can be forgiven. At high tide, that's how it would have appeared to him—a wooded island with soaring white-granite cliffs so tall they cast shadows over the strait.

Low tide would have been a different story. Then the half-mile reef that ringed the "island" would have become visible, a reef so large it connected the granite cliffs to the mainland. Maps of the nineteenth century corrected the name to Cape del Rey, and when the English took control of the area the name was changed once again, this time to Cape Rey, the anglicized name it had had for nearly two hundred years. Although no one ever called it by that name.

For Narvaez had made one last mistake when he named the cape in honor of the king of Spain: the hapless explorer honored his patron not with a place of beauty and grandeur, as he thought, but with a cape and reef so deadly Cook called the place "foul" and Vancouver said it was "cursed." Cape Rey marked one of the most dangerous stretches of water in the Pacific Northwest, a place where scores of ships had floundered and sunk, and because of this no one ever called the cape by the anglicized name a Spanish explorer had mistakenly given it. It had always been called what it was—Cape Rage.

I went back to the Twisted Reach to see if the late-morning coffee was any better. It wasn't, and by noon I was back on the wharf, standing in front of the Spyglass and watching a Mercedes cigar boat come into the harbor. The boat was Day-Glo red, the driver a stocky man with a full beard and black watchman's cap. He slipped the boat into neutral and let it drift into the wharf, the two Mercury engines sounding like a prop plane about to take off.

"Barrett?" he yelled when he was close enough to yell. When I nodded, he slipped the boat into reverse, bringing it to a dead stop as neatly as if he'd put on brakes. I threw my duffel in behind him and got aboard. He'd slipped the boat back into drive before I was seated, turning it around in the basin. He hadn't cleared the break wall before he took off again, throwing a wake behind us that was taller than some of the fishing boats anchored in the outer harbor.

Danby Island was twenty miles out in the Georgia Strait on a dead northwest bearing, although you couldn't see the island because of the cape. The peak of Cape Rage was too high to be seen from the boat as we traveled past, and I wondered how these cliffs might compare to the ones in Dover. I suspected Cape Rage would be grander, made as it was from one of the toughest rocks God ever invented, then imbedded with red and pink quartz that must glint in the midday sun. In comparison, the cliffs of Southern England were made from rock little different than schoolyard chalk.

We traveled in the shadows of Cape Rage for several minutes before we reached open sea and finally saw Danby Island. It was one of the larger islands in the strait, with cliffs almost as tall as Cape Rage. When the cigar boat banked right to go down the channel running between the island and the shore, the sky disappeared. It seemed as though we had entered a fjord.

It was a long time before the sun came back. I stared at the cliffs, and the shoreline of Danby Island; so many rocks and shoals there didn't seem to be clear beach anywhere. The sun still hadn't come back when I started to see buildings atop the cliff. Small cottages, then a massive white house with gables and widow's walks and so many windows it would have been hard to count them all, even if we'd been going slow enough to do that.

There was a shipping channel on the west side of Danby Island, and the wharf was off that channel, leeward side, in a bay so well protected it probably didn't need a break wall. The driver finally slowed his speed as we approached the harbor, where I saw three longline trawlers moored at the wharf, each with a Danby Fisheries logo. There was also a logging tug and two more cigar boats.

A man sitting on an ATV was waiting for us at the end of the wharf. He looked like a smaller version of the boat driver. Smaller beard on a smaller face. Smaller watchman's cap on a smaller head. Again, the boat driver didn't bother mooring, just cut the engines and drifted into the wharf. I stepped off as though I were walking down the street.

Soon as I was off, the boat turned around, the bow sticking out of the water as straight as a navigation buoy. When the boat was pointed in the right direction, the driver applied some gas and the bow started to drop. When the boat cleared the harbor, he applied more gas and the bow kept dropping. Five seconds later, the boat looked like a whitecap far out in the channel. "Barrett?" was the only thing he'd said to me.

His smaller clone was chattier.

"That's all you have in the way of bags?" he asked.

"That's it."

He picked up my duffel, shook it and put it in the back of the ATV.

"Turn around, hands on the hood."

I put my hands on the hood of the ATV and he patted me down. It was good and thorough, and if I was carrying anything, he would have found it. As he was searching, he took out my wallet and my phone.

"Give me your watch," he said. I unbuckled my watch and gave it to him. "You won't be getting the phone back. You can have the watch after we've checked it."

"My wallet?"

"Up to Ambrose. Come on, jump in."

The switchback road that brought us to the top was about a mile long. It was steep in a couple places, like scaling a rock face, nothing growing around us except heather and stunt pine, some small shrubs I'd never seen before, desperately clinging to the escarpment. When we reached the top, the land leveled off to a bluff with views of the ocean in every direction.

The old hotel was directly in front of us, a two-story, three-winged wooden building with too many windows and gables to count. There were widow's walks with cast-iron fencing and what looked like leaded windows on the dormer windows below the roof line. A garden was off to the right, surrounded by a white-picket fence.

Further along the cliff was a line of six cottages, what looked like a three-bay garage large enough to also be a warehouse and, beside the garage, a bunkhouse. It looked like every bunkhouse I'd ever seen, a long, rectangular one-story building with dirty windows running down both sides, an industrial steel door propped open at each end. Standing in front of the bunkhouse was Finn Danby.

"Good trip over?" he asked when the ATV was parked in front of him.

"It's beautiful country," I said, stepping out of the vehicle.

"Ain't country—it's salt and fuckin' fir," he said and wiped the back of his hand over his lips. He was unsteady on his feet when he turned and said to the ATV driver, "You have his bags?"

The man pointed to my duffel.

"You've searched him?"

"Got his phone, his watch and his wallet. Didn't have anything else."

"No gun?"

"No gun."

Finn nodded and turned back to me.

"Welcome," he said. Then he laughed and started walking up the stairs to the bunkhouse. I followed him.

The walls in the hallway were tobacco-stained drywall. Fluorescent lights hummed above us. There were twelve rooms, six to a side, and we walked to one of the last rooms. Inside was a metal-frame bed, a wooden dresser with cracked oblong mirror, a nightstand and a closet with a man's winter parka, some gray suits and rain pants. On top of the nightstand sat a framed photo of a young boy standing in front of a Christmas tree. The lights on the tree were bright. The eyes of the boy were dark and menacing. The boy looked to be about seven or eight.

"We'll put you in Billy's room till he comes back," said Danby.

"You don't have any empty rooms?"

"Don't know if you're staying, pal. This one's already made up. We'll bring your bag back to you later today. You can't have a phone. . . . Washroom is down the hall. . . ."

Danby paused and started tapping his lips with a forefinger. Trying to remember what else he needed to tell me. After telling me the bathroom we had just walked past, the one that had the door open, was halfway down the hall. More useful information like that.

Finally, he snapped his fingers and said, "Dad wants to see you at eight in the dining room. He'll send someone to get you."

I STAYED IN my room and waited. I'd be waiting nearly seven hours, but I thought it best to stay where I'd been put. I walked to the window and looked out. I could see the Pacific, but only a slice of it. Mostly I saw the back of the old hotel. I walked back to the bed and opened the drawer of the nightstand. Inside was an ashtray, an empty box of .45-caliber shells and a badly curled *Penthouse* magazine. The date on the magazine was August 1988.

I tried to conjure up a mental image of the man who lived in the room. He smoked. He had a son who was going to be trouble. He was a man who didn't mind spending money on a good suit and good parka.

Not much to go on. I looked around the room for more clues. Mail, some more photos, a shoebox of mementos, a souvenir of some sort. I found nothing. For the most part, it was an anonymous room.

I wasn't surprised. Personal belongings, in rooms like these, were never much more than what you could shove into a duffel, what you could have bought at a Stedman's department store the week before. Rooms like these, for the men who lived in them, might as well be truck stops.

There was never much difference in these rooms. I'd seen them in off-the-grid lumber camps, biker clubhouses, in the back of mansions on Miami Beach. People who go into a life of crime thinking it's going to be high-rise condos and hotel rooms in Vegas are always surprised when they finally see the long-term staff accommodations.

If you're serious about being a crook, that is. If you're in it for the long haul, lived through the highs and lows that come with any career—the scams and the rip-offs, the bench warrants and shakedowns, the pen time and hole time—if you've lived through that, you know these rooms.

I walked back to the window. Ten days now without rain and the sky over the ocean was still the electric-blue color it had been the first day I saw it. A shiny, almost unnatural-looking sky. I heard seals barking. A lighthouse bell going off somewhere. Why do these rooms always make me feel like if I took one wrong step I'd fall off the edge of the planet?

I sat on the bed and went back to my what-do-we-know-about-the-last-hood-to-live-in-this-room game. Didn't get any further. Lay down on the bed. There was a pine-plank ceiling. The same planking was on the floor. The walls were drywall. Why didn't they continue with the wood?

Ten minutes before eight, the ATV driver came to get me. "They're waiting for you in the dining room," he said.

"Do I just walk over?"

"I'll show you where you're going."

He looked around the room. "So you're the one from the Spyglass who knocked out Jean. When I picked you up at the wharf . . . I was expecting someone bigger. You're big enough, but . . ."

"Sorry to disappoint."

"I ain't disappointed. I think it's funny as fuck. 'Bout time someone gave it to that fat prick."

"Where is he, by the way? He'd be staying in this bunkhouse, wouldn't he?"

"Three doors down, opposite side of the hall. Room next to the bathroom. He's been in Cape Rage most of the day. You probably passed him in the channel, on your way in. . . . What's your name?"

"Danny."

He nodded. Didn't bother giving me his name. "You good to go?"

"Yeah."

"Come on."

I followed him outside. We walked toward the house and when we were twenty feet away, he said, "You go through the front entrance.

That's the lobby. The dining room is behind the lobby. They're waiting for you there."

"You're not going in?"

"Fuck no. You don't go in that way unless you're a Danby. Or you're someone Ambrose wants to talk to, like you. Our kitchen's round back."

He pointed at some shadows behind the house. Then he looked at me, up and down, not trying to hide it, before saying, "I really did think you'd be bigger. Don't know what you want from Ambrose, but if I were you, I'd want a way off this island before Jean knows you're here."

8

THERE WAS A front porch on the Danby home the size of a baseball diamond. The wooden boards creaked and moaned as I strode across them and moths—attracted by the glow of gas lanterns burning at every post along the porch—dived my head. The porch was big enough to make the moths more annoying than they should have been.

I walked through the French doors and then through a lobby, which still looked like a hotel lobby, with a reception desk along one wall and wingback chairs scattered around the room. I walked through another set of French doors and into a dining room. The room looked the way it probably did when the house was still a hotel: A dozen tables were spread across the room, most with white linen tablecloths, a few with full place settings. A service bar was in the corner, next to a swinging door leading to a kitchen. In every corner were floor lamps with green globe-shaped shades, and there was a large crystal chandelier hung from beams in the middle of the room. Floor-to-ceiling windows lined two sides of the room, both looking out on the Pacific. Dead animals mounted on wooden plaques stared down from the other two walls: Black bear. Buck moose. Chinook salmon.

The light cast from the floor lamps and the chandelier was weak and much of the room was lit only by the night sky. There was more shadow than light, and the shadows fell across the room in strange geometric shapes and lines. Several of the tables by the windows had shadows on them that looked like pencil lines. At one of these marked-up tables sat the Danbys.

Tess Danby was sitting as far from her father and brother as the place settings on the table would allow. She was beautiful. Even the CCT tape, with tear gas billowing around her so that she looked like she was stepping out of an old Aerosmith video, didn't do her justice. Her long red hair seemed to capture the weak light in the room, entangle it and transform it into different hues of amber and cobalt. Her eyes were light blue, her mouth full, with tiny laugh lines around the corners. Even though she was seated, I could tell that if she stood, she'd have a swimmer's body: tall and lithe, proportioned the way doll makers used to proportion dolls until they were shamed and guilted into doing it different.

She stared at me as I entered the room, but before I got to the table she had turned away and was gazing out the window. I wasn't sure how to feel about that, being dismissed by Tess Danby in the time it took to walk across a room. Part of me thought that was a good thing. Part of me wondered what I'd done wrong.

Finn Danby looked the same as he had earlier in the day. Same clothes. Maybe a little drunker. He sat next to his father, who had not taken his eyes off me since I entered the dining room. If not for Tess Danby, I wouldn't have taken my eyes off him either.

Ambrose Danby was a massive man. I would have guessed him at 260 pounds, maybe 270. If you told me he was 300 and knew that for a fact, I wouldn't have argued with you. He had long black hair and a full black beard, wore a brocade purple vest over a butter-yellow shirt, dark-brown canvas pants, had a gold loop earring in his right ear. His chair was pushed back from the table, and his hands were clasped and resting on his stomach, which moved up and down every once in a while like lava bubbles. If he'd had a peg leg and a parrot, I would have started looking around the room for little Jimmy Hawkins.

Danby looked me over for a few seconds before saying, "You don't look like you're from Brazil. Don't look Brazilian to me at all, and I've met quite a few of those people. Where'd you learn to fight like that?"

"Detroit. Guy who taught me was Brazilian."

"Well, that would explain it. I knew Hélio Gracie. Heard of him? Met him a few times in Mexico City. He knew people I knew. Saw him fight once at that stadium they have down there, must have been a hundred thousand people, maybe more. It was a big event. I had good seats. I had *great fuckin'* seats, and you know what—that fight still looked like two men flopping around like fish in the back of a boat."

He laughed and patted his stomach. It seemed to pat back. "Although I hear you did well down at the Spyglass. Took out Jean, and a few others. Know how you beat a ground fighter, son?"

Before I had a chance to think of an answer, Danby said, "There's two ways you can do it. Both work pretty good. You can sit on 'em. Ground fighters are never that big, so if you apply a lot of weight, they're fucked. The other thing you can do, and this is the one I recommend, the other thing you can do is make a sincere and committed effort to break their fuckin' legs."

Finn Danby laughed so quickly he spit out some rye whiskey. Tess Danby turned from the window, gave her father a disgusted look, then went back to staring at the moon. Neither she, nor her brother, had spoken since Ambrose started talking. I guessed that would be a rule around Ambrose Danby.

"I'll keep that in mind," I said.

"You do that. You're only the second man, that I know about, to take down Jean. He was none too fuckin' happy about it this morning.

Don't know if anyone's told you that." He took a sip of his whiskey. Smacked his lips a few times. "Know who the first man was?"

"If there's a point to the story, I'm guessing it's you."

"Very good, my friend. A smart boy you are." Danby looked at his children. "Know how I did it?"

"How could I?"

"I shot him."

His smile disappeared. His children both tensed at the same time. You could see it. Their spines getting rigid, the muscles in their arms going taut, bracing themselves it looked like, like what you'd do if you were on a rolling ship, or an airplane that just hit turbulence.

"I forgot about that one," said Danby, giving his stomach another friendly pat and finally gesturing for me to sit down. I took a seat next to him, across the table from his son.

"Finn says you're a friend of Jimmy Metcalfe. How you know that pirate?"

"Worked for him in Duluth."

"Dry goods hauling."

"That's what he called it."

Danby smiled. "I'm sure Jimmy was into all sorts of things over there. Always a bit of an entrepreneur, that guy. Isn't that right, Finn?"

"Yeah, he is. I told him it was stupid going to Duluth. We could have set him up with a boat. Isn't that right, Dad?"

"We would have done that for him, sure. He just needed to ask."

Danby spread his hands like a waiter who had just put down a plate of food he thought particularly deserving of a sizeable tip. Just then a real waiter did appear, a man who came through the swinging door from the kitchen. He was thin as pencil lead, with the same skin complexion. An ashen-faced man wearing gray slacks and a white busboy's jacket who came toward the table as slowly and silently as a nervous cat.

When he finally reached the table Ambrose pointed toward me. "What'll you have?"

"A beer," I said.

"Is there a particular kind, sir?" the waiter asked.

"Coors."

"Very good. And you, Mr. Danby?"

"You're asking, Enrique? Thought you worked here."

"My apologies. No reason to ask Master Danby then either?"

Finn Danby laughed and held up an empty rocks glass. *Master Danby*. Like he was twelve years old.

"And Miss Danby?" the waiter said, turning to look at Tess. She smiled at him, a sympathetic smile it seemed, the kind you'd give someone if you had a shared burden. What that could possibly be, I had no idea. I suspected the waiter would also have trouble coming up with an answer.

"I'm good, Enrique," she said, holding up a nearly full rocks glass.

"Very good, miss," he replied, and with that he turned and padded his way over to the service bar.

"I ran your name," said Danby, when the waiter was out of earshot. "You haven't been in Duluth in a while. Looks like you left right after Jimmy got popped."

"I did. His business shut down. Boats went into dockage. I think they're still sitting there."

"The FBI in Maine are looking for you. You know about that?"

"Doubt if there's any warrants. If you're worried about me being a heat score, you don't have to. *Are* there any warrants?"

"No. Person of interest in what sounds like a right holy rat-fuck. Three unsolved murders. Beau Lafontaine was one of them. That guy was a Malee. How did you get mixed up with those crazy motherfuckers? You French or something?"

"It's a long story. Don't see how it matters much. I'm not in Maine anymore."

"No, you sure ain't. You go from one end of the country to the other. In a big fuckin' hurry. Anything I should know about you that isn't in the police file?"

"I haven't seen my police file, so I wouldn't know. I'm here for the reason I told Finn. Jimmy always said you ran a quality operation— 'Serious people doing serious work, that's the Danbys.' And I've looked into you—your family has been around a long time. You got your own town. I like the sounds of that. I'm tired of amateur hour."

"The Malee ain't fuckin' amateurs."

"No, but they're fucked up in ways that are almost as bad. I don't want any more psycho shit either. I want the real deal."

Appeal to a man's vanity. I get embarrassed sometimes by how obvious the ploy is, how simple and crude. If it didn't work eight or nine times out of ten, I'd stop using it.

"It's serious work we do, Jimmy was straight up with you about that," said Danby gravely. "What did you do for him?"

"Transportation. Customer relations. Jimmy allowed freelance work too, had some that he lined up for us. I did one-offs on a percentage basis."

"We can line up jobs for you. We don't allow outside work."

"That works."

The waiter came back to the table, carrying the drinks on a serving tray he propped on his shoulder, like he was carrying food and not three drink orders. He put the rocks glasses of Canadian Club next to Ambrose and Finn, a bottle of Coors in front of me.

"Would you care for a glass?" he asked. He was holding a glass in his hand, the one I would get if I answered yes. It seemed like a present Enrique was willing to give if we became friends.

"I'm good."

"Very well," he sighed, and he walked away without saying anything else, moving slowly and quietly across the room until he disappeared through the swinging door where he first appeared.

Ambrose took a large sip from his rocks glass, put it down and said, "I can't get in touch with Jimmy right now. He's doing ninety days in the hole for punching out a guard."

I shook my head sadly. Jimmy Metcalfe. What a guy.

"Normally, that would end our conversation," he continued. "I don't know you and taking down four of my guys in the Spyglass—all that should get you is a trip to a salmon pen. Ever seen a man after he's been stripped bare and left in a salmon pen for a few days, Danny?"

I shifted my weight in the chair. Changed the angle of my legs at the same time, so if I had to push myself up in a hurry I would be heading straight toward the stomach of Ambrose Danby. It was a good, wide target, but I adjusted the angle anyway.

"Can't say that I have."

Ambrose narrowed his eyes and gave me a hard look. "You feel lucky right now, Danny?"

"Don't feel one way or the other."

"No . . . take your time. I'm interested in your answer."

"Why?"

"Because it will tell me something about you."

He looked at me and started tilting his head from side to side. He could have pulled out a magnifying glass right then and it wouldn't have surprised me. I felt like a dried butterfly about to be pinned to a board and used as part of a science fair project.

"I don't feel one way or the other about luck, Mr. Danby," I said. "What I'm feeling more than anything right now is thirsty. I should have ordered a Jack to go with my beer. How do we get that guy back here? Is there a hidden bell or something?"

Tess Danby turned away from the window and looked at me. I somehow knew she had done that, although I didn't see it. Just not surprised when I turned my head and saw her staring at me. For the first time since I had entered the room, there was curiosity in her eyes.

Ambrose started slapping the table. He did it slowly, the way people used to do it in beatnik clubs, when they weren't allowed to use
their hands and make noise. He slapped the table about a dozen times
before saying, "Nicely done, pal. Well, in case you didn't know it,
you're a lucky man. In a couple ways. We're light right now, and I can
use some help. At least until I talk to Jimmy, or his lawyer gets a message to him. Jimmy's going to remember you, right, Danny?"

Get a message to Jimmy Metcalfe through his lawyer? I tried to
remember if Gardner or Hart had mentioned that possibility.

"He'll remember me. But I don't want to cool my heels for ninety
days," I said.

"Don't worry, pal, I got work for you right now. Do you want to get
paid in cash, or is there an account?"

"There's an account. I'll give you the SWIFT codes. . . . What else
makes me lucky?"

"What?"

"You said I was lucky in a couple ways. What else?"

"Thought you could have figured it out, smart boy like you. You
brought down Jean the giant, and he ain't found you yet."

Ambrose laughed and shook his big shaggy head as gleefully as a
rutting bear. Finn laughed, with less hair, but just as much joy. Tess
Danby, when I looked over, had gone back to staring out the window.

I wasn't invited for dinner. I got one more Jack and one more beer.
Ambrose asked me questions about Beau Lafontaine and the Malee, a
few about Duluth, a city he'd never been to but with which I was familiar. I told him what a bad storm was like out on Lake Superior,
how it could creep up on you sudden, faster than in open seas because
land was nearby, hills and cliffs and chutes that could push the wind
out like a race car, and it might as well have been open sea when that
wind caught you. Five minutes after the storm story, he said, "We're
done here, Danny. Someone will fetch you in the morning."

9

HENRY CARTER AND the girl stay hidden in the woods for thirty-six hours. They should have brought food from the girl's cabin, and she offers to return, to bring some back, but Carter says no, it's best that she stays. They eat chokeberries growing on a nearby bush, drink water that falls in trickles down a rock face not far from the chokeberry bush. They cup their hands and let the water pool before drinking it. Bring the berries back to the red fir and eat them while keeping watch on the logging road.

As dusk falls on the first day, she tries talking to him. "You may still have metal in you, you know. It's a nasty wound you have there."

Carter takes the rind of a chokeberry from his teeth and flicks it away. "You know a lot about nasty wounds, do you?"

"No. Just know when a man's got a big hole in his back."

He smiles. "Fair enough."

"Just saying you might still have some metal in you. I ain't no doctor."

"You seem to be doing all right."

"You probably want to see one . . . a doctor."

"Don't see any around, do you?"

"Well, you might want to consider it. That wound looked nasty enough to me. Shotgun . . . close enough to burn you."

They sit on the trunk of a fallen pine. He can smell the soap in her hair, and the old campfire smoke in the fur trim of her parka.

"It was close enough, all right," he says.

"You must have known him . . . or her."

Carter spits out another chokeberry rind. "Why do you say that?"

"What?"

"Or her."

"'Cause it could be true, ain't it? I don't know. Just know whoever shot you was someone standing close to you. Or you was sleepin', but you don't seem to do that too often."

She takes another handful of chokeberries. Puts a few in her mouth and bites down, so the liquid shoots out. She uses her fingers to take out the rinds. Takes another handful of chokeberries, puts them in her mouth and bites down, chews for a while and says, "Also 'cause you talk in your sleep. You said the name Tess a few times."

She says it quickly, like it is something she doesn't want to say but thinks she must. "I shouldn't have said anythin'," she says in a quiet voice. "You should see a doctor. That's all I'm sayin'."

"Did I say anything else in my sleep?"

"No. Just that name a few times."

———

HE'D MET HER at his brother's wedding; most of Clayton County was there for the reception, along with anyone his dad ever did business with; Townes Carter bringing a train-car of wedding guests to Snow Corners from Chicago, another train-car from Seattle, another from Kansas City. Every room in the Commodore Hotel booked for the wedding, along with every motel room along County Road 7, where his father put the guests he didn't need to impress.

Ambrose Danby, his son and his daughter got three suites at the Commodore, got them because Ambrose was one of Townes Carter's oldest business associates, someone given to him upon birth, like an inheritance. The Danbys were the ones who ran the Carter liquor and then the Carter weed up and down the West Coast, something they had been doing faithfully, and profitably, for a hundred years.

Despite the long business relationship, it was Ambrose Danby's first visit to Snow Corners, the largest town in Clayton County. The Danbys didn't come all that often, and Townes Carter knew why, same way anyone from Snow Corners knew why. Clayton County was hillbilly country, the place where busted-out cash-crop farmers from down south—the ones who never bothered to cross the Mississippi River—washed up when they hit an international border and couldn't go any further. Clayton County was scrub pine and blunt-peak mountains, bush camps and gravel-road churches; uneven, unfriendly land on the back of the Kettle River Range, where Pretty Boy Floyd and Alvin "Old Creepy" Karpis hid out for a spell in the '30s, where you didn't have cell reception in a lot of places and cutting phone lines and racing down gravel roads was still a viable way to rob someone. The biggest employer in Clayton County was the state penitentiary, and unless you were doing hard time, there was no good reason to ever visit.

It took a wedding—with three days of free drink and food—to finally bring Ambrose Danby. If his brother had never got married, he never would have met Tess Danby. Strange and absurd, how you can track some things back, thinks Carter.

He'd noticed her in the church. He and every other man sitting in a pew. One of the last to arrive, she had to walk to the second row from the pulpit, where Ambrose had put the family. Her red hair was unbanded and she wore a white lace dress with shoes that had no heel, that looked like ballet slippers. He thought she'd done it because of her height, because she was a tall girl and self-conscious. But it had nothing to do with her height. Those were simply the shoes she liked.

He noticed her again at the reception, when he was standing in the parking lot of the Commodore having a cigarette. She was talking to some FBI agents who had shown up to photograph license plates, talking while some of his cousins slashed the tires of the agents' car, the agents not noticing because Tess Danby had them enthralled, asking them questions, telling them she was considering a career in law enforcement. She was nineteen years old. His cousins probably could have driven a backhoe up and down that car and the agents wouldn't have noticed.

She ran past him after telling the agents to turn around and look at their car; flashed him a smile and a peace sign as she went past, heading back into the wedding reception. She held the hem of her dress in one hand, her shoes in the other. Running barefoot.

How could you not follow a woman like that?

—————

WHEN DAWN COMES, they return to the chokeberry bush and collect more berries. Drink water from the stream falling down the rock face. Sit under the redwood and eat the berries they have collected.

The sun rises but is barely noticed for the first few hours. A glow upon the forest floor, some weak shafts of sunshine breaking through from time to time, nothing more. It is almost noon before there is light in this forest.

Even then, it is hard to spot the vehicle. A gold-colored Grand Cherokee that blends in with the brown pine needles on the road and the weak light coming through the trees. But there is enough chrome to see it, a slow-moving vehicle that starts to twinkle as it nears them.

Carter falls to the ground and motions for the girl to do the same.

They watch the Jeep come down the road, pass them, then stop a hundred yards farther down. It sits there a minute before the tail-lights come back on and then the Jeep backs up fifty yards.

The driver's door opens, and a man gets out. He is a middle-aged man, dressed in a camel hair overcoat, gray slacks, thick-soled black shoes that perfectly touch the hemline of his pants. He leaves the door open and looks around. Sniffs as though there is an unpleasant smell nearby.

He pats the pockets of his overcoat, then reaches in the left pocket and takes out a piece of paper. He unfolds the paper, and it grows to the size of a computer sheet. He stares at the paper, then up and down the road, eventually to the gully. He refolds the paper, hikes his pants—using a hand to pull up each leg—and heads toward the patch of fern moss.

"Running would be a bad idea," says Carter, as he rolls away into the forest.

———

THE MAN IN the camel hair coat stares at the dried blood. He scratches his head and starts walking around the fern moss, kicking at the undergrowth, kicking at nearby shrubs. He walks around a large tree. Then another.

He comes back to the fern moss and begins walking in circles, each circle a little larger than the last, working his way to the edge of the clearing. His collar is turned up, and a scarf is tied tightly around his neck.

He stands on the edge of the clearing, then comes back to the place on the fern moss where he began. He looks around. Begins unbuttoning his camel hair coat. Opens the coat wide and reaches for the gun that is there in a shoulder holster.

But he has spent too much time thinking about it.

"Leave it where it is, Billy."

The man turns and sees Carter walking toward him, a .22-caliber Winchester hunting rifle in his hands. "Henry," he says, and that's all he says for a few seconds, as the color washes from his face. "I thought you was . . ."

"Get your hand out of your coat, Billy."

The man leaves it there.

"A hunting rifle? What the fuck are you doing, Henry? Is this some sort of a joke?"

"What I'm doing is getting ready to shoot you, Billy, if you don't do exactly what I tell you. Hunting rifle will work just fine for that."

The man waits a few beats before taking his hand out of his jacket. When he does, he has his fingers spread wide, his palm facing Carter. "I never thought you was dead, Henry," he says. "Never thought you could be taken down that easy. God's truth."

"God's truth?"

"I had nothing to do with that play . . . you know that, right? You must know that. I got told what happened later. By Finn."

"Yet here you are."

"Ambrose sent me. To get something. That's all I know."

"You thought I was dead?"

"I had nothing to do with that, Henry, God's truth. You got to believe me. Finn was laughing about it. Ambrose too."

"You thought I was dead?"

"Henry . . . they're the ones you're mad at. Tess too, I guess. She's back on the island. . . . That's cold-assed, Henry. Can't blame you for being pissed."

"You thought I was dead?"

"Why the fuck do you keep asking me that? Yes, I thought you were dead, Henry. Glad you're not. I've got no skin in this fuckin' game."

"No skin? You came here to take something from me, a man you thought was dead. You didn't kill me. You merely wanted to rob my dead body. . . ."

"Henry . . ."

". . . You are merely a graverobber."

"God's truth . . ."

"Stop saying that. You don't understand either word."

———

THE FIRST SCREAM is the hardest for the girl to hear. She was expecting the sounds of violence—men arguing, some cursing, maybe running feet or a gunshot—none of that would have surprised her.

The screams surprised her. Unlike anything she'd heard before, high-pitched and otherworldly, pain and terror heard in equal measure. The pain of a catastrophic wound recently inflicted. The terror of anticipation, knowing more pain was coming. Her body winces every time a new scream begins, goes slack when it ends; her body contracting and releasing so often she begins to perspire, sweat falling onto her cotton T-shirt, onto her jeans.

The forest is silent a long time after the last scream. The birds that had flown away when the screaming began do not return right away. She hears no animal moving through the woods. There is a silence and stillness that seems to fill the physical world, leaves no room for anything else. It only ends when the girl hears footsteps coming up behind her.

She turns and sees Carter walking toward the Jeep. He opens the hatch and takes out a suitcase, then another. He motions for the girl to come to him, and when she gets there he has a suitcase open and is rooting through the clothes.

"What are you doing?" she asks.

"Billy was about the same size as me."

Her dad's jeans and flannel shirt are covered in blood. And Carter is wearing a shoulder holster now. She stares at the butt of the gun.

"You knew him?"

"Yeah, I knew him."

"You . . . you had to do that?"

"Only way to be sure Billy was telling me the truth. Always had trouble with that. First time I had a chance to solve the problem."

He looks up from the suitcase and smiles at the girl—a leer, it seems to her, and she takes a couple steps back. Carter's smile disappears.

"I had to do it that way," he says, opening the second suitcase. One of Carter's hands has a cloth wrapped around it. The girl thinks at first it is because of a wound, but soon sees it is simply to keep blood off the clothes he is inspecting.

"Was he the one who shot you?"

"No."

"But he knew who done it?"

"He worked for them."

"There was more than one?"

Carter holds up a white shirt, turns it around so he can see front and back. "You ask a lot of questions."

"Yeah . . . I do that when I'm nervous. I gotta stop it, I know. . . . So he worked for the people who shot you in the back? . . . Hard to feel sorry for a man like that, ain't it?"

Carter's smile returns. "You find that necessary?"

"What?"

"That he be a bad man? To accept what just happened, in those woods over there, you find that necessary?"

"Well . . . sure, he deserved it, right?"

"Because he was a bad man? Just like you, a good person, will get the fate you deserve. . . . Is that how it works?

The girl doesn't answer, and Carter continues: "Life is easy when people get what they deserve, isn't that right, girl? Easy when things connect up the way they should, and you can feel good about what you're doing. That's a sunny day. It's harder when it's just something you need to do, and it don't connect up right with anything."

Carter stands. His right arm stretches across his chest, reaching for the shoulder holster.

"I won't say anything, mister," the girl says quickly. "I'll go back to my cabin and forget about you. Why would I want to get involved with you? I don't even know your name. I don't ever *want* to know your name."

Carter looks at the girl with eyes that have grown dark and still. "I almost believe you."

"You can believe me."

"But I don't need to."

He unclasps the metal snap on the holster.

"You haven't thought this through," the girl says, more quietly than before. "That dressing of yours is going to need changing. Who's going to do that for you?"

Carter lets her talk.

"There's going to be more people coming to look for you. Am I right 'bout that? Anyone going to be looking for you and a girl? . . . I know how to cook, and track, I can play cards, I'm not that good at it, but maybe that's a good thing for you. I can take care of just 'bout any wound, you've seen that yourself . . . there's all sorts of—"

"What are you doing?" he asks.

"Giving you reasons for not killing me."

"That's what you're doing?"

"That's what I *hope* I'm doing."

Carter lowers his arm. Soon his expression changes, not an obvious change, but the muscles around his jaw go slack, his lips part slightly.

"Maybe you're right," he says. "You can be useful. I believe that. Are you the kind of person who can keep a promise too?"

"I am."

"What about me? Am I that kind of person?"

The girl thinks about the question. It seems wise to do that. Not rush her answer. Let him know it has been considered: weighed and measured, as her daddy used to say. Although, to her surprise, she is never in doubt about her answer.

"I think you are."

"Then let's make a promise to each other. You promise to come with me, do as I ask, and I promise to bring you back here, when I'm done."

". . . What will I have to do?"

"Nothing you're not doing already . . . nothing illegal."

"Then I promise."

Carter nods and they stand there a few seconds, until the girl says, "That Jeep's got Washington plates. That where we're going?"

"You always ask this many questions?"

"I'm sorry. I'll try to stop. . . . *Is* that where we're going?"

Carter says, "We need to go somewhere else first. You'll need to pack a bag."

10

WHEN I AWOKE the next morning, I stared up in surprise at a cedar-plank ceiling. Over at a dark wood dresser with a cracked oval mirror. A nightstand with a framed photo on top of it showing a mean-looking boy standing in front of a Christmas tree.

It came back to me.

I didn't get up right away but stayed in bed, listening for sounds outside my door, listening the way you do when you awake in a strange bed and forget for a minute where you are. I heard every sound. Didn't move on from the sound until I'd identified it. Water running through pipes. Fluorescent lights buzzing. Wooden beams creaking. I listened to the creaking until I was sure it came from outside, a good wind blowing broadside against the bunkhouse.

When I had identified and categorized every sound, I got out of bed, walked to the door and stuck out my head. No one in the hallway. No one standing outside the exit doors at either end of the hallway, both doors propped open, tall fir showing through the openings.

I closed the door, went to the closet and got out my duffel bag.

When I checked it last night, I'd found everything tossed around, the toiletry bag was a shambles, but it wasn't the rudest search I'd ever seen. Nothing was damaged. Nothing was missing.

I didn't bother taking the clothes out but tossed the toiletry bag on the bed, took a nail clipper from the bag, then fetched a belt from the bottom of the duffel. I picked away at the belt until I got a thread loose. Unraveled some cross stitching and the belt popped open, like a pouch. I squeezed the belt and a watch face squirted out. It was black, rectangular, an exact copy of the watch that had been returned to me along with the duffel bag.

I switched out the watch faces, slipped the old one into the belt and restitched the threads with a needle I'd taken from the toiletry bag. I hit the side button on the new watch a few times and a small keyboard appeared. I sent Gardner a message—"*will call this a.m.*"

Then I got dressed, opened the blinds in the room and looked outside. It was another clear day. I could see well past the buoy marker showing the entrance to the west-arm shipping channel, past that even, to a reef that was showing at low tide, peppered with quartz so it was blinking like fairy lights. I made the bed, turned down the Christmas photo and left the room.

There was an eagle drifting on a high current above the island when I got outside, and a boat was leaving the wharf, almost past the break wall, whitecaps rolling it from side to side, a flock of seagulls already trailing. An ATV was starting down the switchback road to the wharf. The garage doors were open, and I could hear a grinder running.

Ambrose Danby had told me to wait in my room until someone came for me, but I was hungry and the workday on the island had obviously begun. Kitchens in camps like this don't stay open all day. I started walking toward the old hotel. In the light of day, I could see that the building had almost as much iron as wood. There were iron fences and iron gates, iron railings on the wraparound porch, iron hinges on the shutters, iron weather vanes and iron widow's walks surrounding all four turrets. Four widow's walks seemed a lot of tragedy for one house to be expecting, but I'm not an architect.

At the back of the house, I found a side door with a sign above it that read Service Entrance. It was an old sign. The paint was chipping, and the wood had turned porous. It looked like it had been hanging there for a hundred years.

I walked through the door and found myself in a kitchen. There were two commercial-sized stoves against the left wall, steel cupboards and a long steel counter in front of me. To my right was a buffet table set up with warming trays and cereal bowls, dishes and cutlery, coffee cups stacked at one end.

None of which I noticed right away, for when I walked into the room my gaze settled on the four dining tables in the middle of the room. At the table closest to the door sat Jean the giant.

When he looked up from his plate of scrambled eggs and saw me, he broke into one of the happiest smiles I'd ever seen.

"Look who crawled out of bed, boys," he said.

THREE OTHER MEN sat with him. One was the kid from the Spyglass that I'd fought with two nights earlier. The other two were men I soon learned were called Skipjack and Obie.

Skipjack looked to be in his midfifties, a short man with a bony chest and lantern chin too large for his face, a chin that made him look like an elf, or a goblin. He also had a bad leg, his left one, that he dragged behind him when he walked, always throwing his right foot forward, then dragging the left one, planting it, throwing forward the right one.

Obie looked to be in his seventies, although his health was bad and I could have been off by decades. He had the tremors and the red-veined face of a bad drunk, wore a discolored white T-shirt that hung loose on his frail body, along with green factory pants he cinched with a leather strap.

I hadn't paid that much attention to the kid when we were at the Spyglass, but I took a good look at him now. He was tall and lanky with peach-fuzz hair on his cheeks, and zits that he was picking at right then, a trickle of blood running down his chin. When he noticed the blood he wiped it away with the back of a hand, then wiped his hand on his jeans.

The giant hadn't stopped smiling, but I turned my back on him and headed to a coffee urn set up with cups and spoons at the end of a buffet table. I took my time about making a cup, letting him stare at my back for a while. When I was finished with the cream and the sugar, I went to their table and sat down.

"Who the fuck said you could sit here?"

I took a long sip, blinked my eyes a few times, like I was just waking up, and then I said, "You still upset about the other night?"

"What the fuck do you think, asshole?"

Now that I was sitting across the table from him, I could see the bruising around his eyes, the cuts on his nose. The nose didn't look broken, and I couldn't understand that.

"We're working together now. You need to get over it." I took another sip of coffee. "Anyway, it was a lucky punch. Everyone there could see that."

This seemed to cheer the giant. "Damn right it was a lucky punch."

"It was."

"Damn right."

"Damn right."

The giant gave me a nasty look but seemed to have run out of things to say. The kid opened his mouth to fill in the silence, then changed his mind about it and stayed quiet. Skipjack was staring hard at me, trying his best to look mean, but only managing to look like a disgruntled elf.

"And it wasn't a punch," said the giant, a new thought coming to him. "It was a kick . . . when I was down."

"We were both down."

"So what?"

"So, it's not cheating if we're both down. It's the same as both of us being up."

The giant looked at me as though I had coffee running from my nose. With great solemnity, he said, "Down ain't up."

Skipjack and the kid started laughing. "Down ain't up. You tell him, Jean," said Skipjack. The giant shoved a large forkful of eggs into his mouth and chewed with a smile so broad he had food splatting onto the table.

I was an idiot, and everyone had just seen it. The giant's day was turning joyful. "He won't get a chance to fool me again," he said, shoving two more forkfuls of egg into his mouth, back to back, quick, like he was in a race. "Can't see him lasting on this island too long either."

"Yeah . . . lot of cliffs on this island," said the kid. "People have accidents *all the time.*"

He started cackling and gave me what he thought was a nasty look, but it's hard to pull that off when you're a kid with a face full of bleeding zits. Skipjack glared and thrust out his chin, trying again to look mean. It was a better job. Angry elf now, maybe.

"I'm careful around cliffs," I said.

"Hard to be careful twenty-four seven," answered the giant.

"That's what careful is, Jean,"

I thought there'd be a few more rounds in the game, but just then Finn Danby walked into the kitchen.

"There the fuck you are," he yelled. "Thought you were going to be in your room."

"Needed coffee."

"And what the fuck are you guys doing? Aren't you getting a boat ready?"

Obie and the kid were already standing, dishes in their hands. Skipjack was ahead of them, dishes in his hand and already walking to the dirty-dish bin at the end of the buffet table.

"Waiting for a part. Jacques is milling it right now," said the giant.

"Takes four of you to do that?"

"Fuck, Finn, it's barely nine. Boat will head out on time."

"We don't pay you to eat in the kitchen all day."

The giant opened his mouth to say something, then didn't. There were still eggs on his plate, a few strips of bacon as well when he brought the dish to the bin. It looked like he wanted to cry.

He still had time to slap me on the back though before leaving, tell me one last time—in a friendly, helping-the-new-guy sort of way—to be careful around the cliffs.

——————

UNDER THE FLUORESCENT lighting of the kitchen, it was easy to tell Finn Danby was a bad drunk. He had busted blood vessels under his half beard and circles around his eyes you only get from years of poor sleep. His hands trembled when he poured himself a coffee. He sat down and drank his coffee while I ate a quick breakfast of scrambled eggs and pancakes.

"How are the eggs?"

"Pretty good," I answered.

"They should be. We pay the fucker enough. When did you see Jimmy last?"

"Two years ago. I was working for him when he got popped."

"Piracy," snorted Danby. "Jimmy was always a lucky bastard. When he gets back here, he'll crow 'bout that for the rest of his fuckin' life. It's going to be made-in-the-shade time for that asshole."

I cut my pancakes and nodded. The social and economic benefits of being a real-life, sent-to-prison pirate in a place like Cape Rage? Jimmy Metcalfe was probably going to be parade marshal one day.

"He's got a bit of time to do, before that happens," I said.

"Yeah," said Danby. "Lucky bastard."

I didn't know what to say to that, so I finished my breakfast in silence, put away the dishes and followed him outside.

"I'll warn you right now," he said, as we started down a trail that would take us to the west side of the island, "this is a shit detail."

Danby Island was different from most of the large islands in the Georgia Strait, as it was never logged in the nineteenth century. It had been bought by the Blaine-Tacoma Railway Company in 1879 and the hotel was built the following year. It was meant to lure sportsmen of the day to Blaine, where the railway company had its main terminus. The island had an indigenous population of black bear, elk and white-tail deer.

It only took twenty years to kill off the animals. The black bear went first, then the elk, then the deer. The railway company tried to repopulate but none of the animals took, not even the deer. The sportsmen the company had hoped to attract stopped coming long before the Great War, disgusted by shooting pen-raised game. Hunters who cared nothing about such things—drunks and dandies, roustabouts, and day-catch-rich fishermen—came for a few years after that. The scarring of their practice bullets could still be seen on the north wall of the house.

It wasn't until the Danbys bought the island that the first trees were felled, and there were still some old-growth stands of red fir on the island. The land that was cleared back in the '40s and '50s was now heathered fields and moss-covered rock, with vistas onto the Pacific that went so far the horizon didn't fade away but seemed to slip over the curvature of the planet.

After twenty minutes of walking, we came to a hut. It was the sort of hut you would find a security guard sitting in, or a child waiting for a school bus. It sat on the edge of a cliff face that rose more than five hundred feet from the waterline at low tide. There was a switchback path down the escarpment leading to the ruins of an old wharf and an abandoned cannery. The roof of the cannery had sunk and most of the windows were broken. When the wind came in off the ocean it blew through the windows and gave off a metallic wail so lonely it made you feel sorry for the old building.

"This is where you're going to be," said Danby.

I looked around. "Doing what?"

"Manning the perimeter line."

"Why?"

"So we don't get raided."

"Are you serious?"

"I wouldn't be asking my dad that," said Finn, and he handed me a walkie-talkie. "It's already turned to channel sixteen. Leave it there."

I took the walkie-talkie from him. Then a pair of binoculars.

"What am I looking for?"

"Any signs of trouble."

I didn't say anything. Danby started laughing. "Told you it was a shit detail."

"Why am I doing this?"

"Something else you shouldn't ask my dad. There's been a perimeter line since 1954. See that reef out there?"

I looked to where he was pointing.

"ATF agents tried to raid us in 1954. Their boat hit that reef. My granddad wouldn't let the boat be salvaged, kept a blockade around it for nine days, until it sank. There were agents on the boat when it went down."

"They drowned?"

"No, they had life jackets. They bobbed around out there until my granddad let them get rescued. But the perimeter line went up right after the boat sank."

"It's always been manned?"

"Always. My dad thinks it would be bad luck if it wasn't."

"What do you think?"

"Already told you. . . . I think it's a shit detail."

———

I USED THE binoculars for an hour, training the optical lenses on distant fishing boats and slow-moving tankers, minke whales and rising schools of mackerel. Once, I tracked an albatross that flew in and out of streaks of sunshine until it disappeared in an instant, no fade, like a magic trick.

Midmorning, I pushed a side button on my watch in the sequence I'd had no trouble memorizing—three short, three long, three short. SOS. Some FBI agent back in Seattle had a sense of humor. When I finished the sequence a telephone keyboard appeared on the watch face. I punched in a number and a few seconds later heard Gardner's voice.

"Barrett?"

"I'm here."

"Congratulations, you made it onto the island. You know you're the first cop to do that? Have I mentioned that?"

"You have."

"Thought so. Well, that was good work. Where you phoning from?"

"West side of the island, in a hut that's supposed to be part of a perimeter line."

"I know the place. Can you see a reef, northwest from there?"

"I can. I just heard a story from Finn Danby about that reef."

"The ATF agents?"

"That's the one."

"Did he tell you his family tried to drown a boatload of federal agents on that reef?"

"He led with that."

"They're bastards, the Danbys. The Carters are no better."

"Henry Carter? Didn't know there was a family there too."

"Hell, the Carters are Danbys without the boats."

Gardner spent the next few minutes telling me about the Carters. How they came from Clayton County, which would have been the poorest county in Washington State if Ferry County wasn't right next door. The largest town in the county was Snow Corners, the other side of the Cascade Mountains, up near the Canadian border. The Danbys and Carters were business partners going back generations, the Carters having more stills in Clayton County in the '20s and '30s than there were cars. The Carters took most of what they brewed to Cape Rage, where the Danbys shipped it up and down the West Coast, going as far north as Prince George, as far south as San Diego.

But the families weren't friendly. Didn't behave in similar ways, or hold similar values; the Danbys, starting with Artemis, intent on building a criminal dynasty; the Carters more intent on making easy money and spending it fast, ripping up every juke joint they ever walked into, road-tripping with people like Pretty Boy Floyd and Alvin Karpis.

Henry Carter's great-grandfather was Clayton Carter, a legendary bootlegger who walked off a bridge in 1934 with thirteen bullets in him after the local sheriff and some FBI agents right out of the academy botched an ambush. He died in his bed, forty years later.

Henry's grandfather was Townes Carter, one of the few men to ever escape from San Quentin and stay out. He was on the run thirty-one years, although you could have found him in Clayton County every one of those years. He turned himself in one day after his seventy-first birthday. He had fourth-stage lung cancer by then and needed the healthcare.

Henry's father was Townes Carter Jr., who continued the family tradition by doing a fourteen-year stint at San Quentin, going in the year after Henry was born. "One of the first things Townes did when he got out was rob the Peabody mail train for the last time," said

Gardner. "He took Henry with him. Kid wasn't sixteen yet. Yeah, you caught a lucky break when the Danbys took out Carter. So . . . give me your sit-rep."

I told him about the fight at the Spyglass and meeting Finn Danby; about the boat ride to Danby Island and the bunkhouse I was now living in; the layout of the island, from what I'd seen so far, and the people living there.

"One of these guys is a giant. Not exaggerating when I say that."

"Jean Levesque," said Gardner. "Get him to bench-press an ATV for you. I hear he can do that. How many people are on the island, you figure?"

"Bunkhouse has twelve rooms, and they all look used. I've met six men so far, besides the Danbys, so I'm missing a few. I'm in someone's room who's not here right now. Name's Billy."

"Billy Walker. He left the island last week."

"They're expecting him back any day."

"He has a son in Portland. He goes to visit him sometimes."

"That's where he is?"

"Don't know. That's usually where he is. Give me the layout of the island."

"There's a main house and a garage, a big garage, looks more like a warehouse. There are six cottages I've seen so far, along the cliff beside the house. The house is set up like it's still a hotel, has a lobby, a bunch of tables in the dining room, guy serving drinks dressed in a busboy jacket. The whole place seems like a stage set. Ambrose helps with that. Guy dresses like he pulled his clothes out of a kid's play chest, like he's some Saturday-morning pirate. He told me he saw Hélio Gracie fight in Mexico City and didn't think much of it. I'd double-check a story like that. Also said he would have shot me if he'd been the one fighting me at the Spyglass. I wouldn't bother double-checking that one."

"Have you seen any guns?"

"Finn Danby is carrying, but I haven't seen anyone else. Ambrose must have one. Don't think anyone is allowed to have a gun when they're on the island."

"Sit-rep on the family."

"Ambrose lives up to his billing. He's a massive guy, enough hair on him to open a string of wig factories. He scares his children. Cunning, self-entitled, aggressive as hell."

"Mean bastard."

"Yeah . . . mean bastard."

"Finn?"

"A bad drunk. Probably a coward. He acts tough but avoids confrontation, happy to let his father take charge, looks at his sister like she frightens him. Can't see Ambrose trusting him much, and I can't see him having any real power. That probably eats at him day and night."

"There could be a play there," said Gardner.

"There could."

"The daughter?"

"Hard to get a read on her. She didn't say much when I was there. Only spoke to the waiter."

"There's really a waiter?"

"There's a guy who owns a busboy jacket."

Gardner laughed. "She never spoke to her father or brother?"

"No."

"That's interesting. Maybe Tess Danby wasn't a willing participant in her divorce."

"You thought she was?"

"I think that young woman is capable of just about anything. Did you know she was charged with extortion?"

"I didn't read that in her file."

"Sealed juvenile record. A Seattle city cop told me about it. She was fifteen and there was a jewelry store on her walk to school. She shoplifted so many things from that store, she went in one day and told the owner it would be cheaper, and a lot easier for everyone, if he just let her pick out something nice from time to time. She suggested once a month."

"That's extortion?"

"Yeah, it is. It's also more gall than a fifteen-year-old girl should be allowed to have. Be careful around her. . . . Anything else worth reporting?"

"Ambrose said something that might be a problem. He wants to get Jimmy Metcalfe's lawyer in to see him, to vouch for me. Can Metcalfe get legal visits?"

"We'll make sure no one gets in."

"Can you stop a lawyer?"

"Depends how good the lawyer is."

Gardner had another little laugh. When I didn't join in, he said, "Relax, that was a joke. We'll make sure no one gets in to see Metcalfe. What about the other people you've met?"

I gave him a sit-rep on the other men: Skipjack, the two cousins, the kid. I described their appearances and Gardner had proper names for each of them. He asked a few more questions, and that was the end of the sit-rep: I'd made it onto the island. Ambrose was mean and confident. Finn was drunk and weak. Tess was an unknown. I was manning a perimeter line with no gun, on a short leash, living in a sad room recently vacated, in a camp with men who hated me, and if Jimmy Metcalfe's lawyer got in to see him, I was a dead man.

That was about it. Early days.

"When will you be able to contact us again?" he asked.

"Communications won't be a problem. I'm going to be in this hut most of the day. I'll check in tomorrow, same time."

"Good . . . you know, now that you're on that island, this case isn't all that complicated. Have you thought about that?"

"I've thought about that."

"Hard part might be behind you. Creep around and find something linking the Danbys to that bank job in San Francisco and you're done. We'll be over there the same day."

Gardner made it sound simple, but he was right. There was nothing clever about what needed to be done now. Nothing that needed much planning or long-term thinking.

"Go out tonight if you can, Barrett," he said. "Maybe we can all be home by the weekend."

11

THE GIRL WATCHES Henry Carter as he searches the Jeep. He finds another handgun, and a Mac-10 machine pistol, a toiletry bag with what looks like an ounce of cocaine inside, along with two bundles of hundred-dollar bills tucked under the toothpaste. The bank wrappers are still on. Ten thousand dollars to a bundle. Carter puts the money in the glove compartment, throws the cocaine into the woods, motions for the girl to get in and drives to her cabin.

He starts to gather his things. Not that there is much to gather: what had been in his pants pockets when he was shot, the black Florsheims and socks he is wearing. He takes the shoes off his feet and cleans them in the girl's sink, after first pouring in water from a plastic jug. He rinses out his socks as well.

The rest of his clothes aren't worth taking. He starts a fire in the airtight stove and burns them. Thinks of burning his shoulder holster as well—he has a new one—but then burns the new holster and cleans his old one, scrubbing at the bloodstains until they are worn down to what looks like an imperfection in the leather. He gets dressed in the clothes he has taken from the suitcases: a white shirt and gray suit.

The girl packs a pink suitcase covered with images of mermaids and underwater castles. Two pairs of jeans. Some T-shirts, panties, two small white bras, a hoodie with more mermaids. She has no jewelry to pack, no notebooks or toys or books.

When the girl closes the suitcase, Carter asks if she needs to do anything to close up the cabin. The girl says they can throw some water on the coals in the airtight; but other than that, she can't think of anything.

———

IT IS LATE afternoon, almost dusk, when they head out. There is a copper-red glow in the forest, the needles on the pine and red fir lit up like a million flashing matchsticks. It is the way that forest always looks in late afternoon of a clear summer day.

It has been many years since this forest was logged, but there was a time when logging trucks and bush camps were the norm, and the system of abandoned roads and trails is vast, and intricate. Carter drives for long stretches at no more than ten miles per hour, to make sure he stays on the main road, doesn't veer the wrong way down a road that dead-ends at a lake or the rotten-timber remains of an old camp.

Eventually they reach a gravel road and Carter turns east. The gravel road isn't in much better shape than the logging road, still the crazy dips and hills, still the washed-out shoulders and blindside turns, but the ruts in the middle of the road are gone, and the forest has thinned, no longer seems to be pressing in on them.

It is dark when they leave the gravel road and finally turn onto asphalt, a darkness so complete it has pooled into something total, Carter surprised by the reflective road sign his headlights catch when he turns onto the asphalt of the county road, by the sign's unnatural brilliance, its denoting of human activity. It comes as almost a shock. There are people out there.

━━━━

HE DANCED WITH her at his brother's wedding. Walked to her table after the meal, after the speeches and the glass-tapping, after the tossing of a bouquet and the cutting of a cake. She had been sitting with her father and brother, an uncle and some cousins, but she was already standing by the time he reached the table, like she knew why he was coming. He didn't even speak, just took her hand and they walked onto the dance floor.

She let him hold her tight as they danced to three songs, two of them being ridiculous songs to slow-dance to, but they did it anyway, never letting go, holding on to each other like they had finally found what they were meant to hold—the child, the tool, the musical instrument—holding on to what they already knew was their future.

"You're Henry Carter," she said, halfway through their first dance, the first words they'd said to each other.

"You're Tess Danby."

"I've heard of you."

"I've heard of you too."

"What have you heard?"

"I asked around tonight. . . ."

"Just tonight?"

"Yes."

"I've been hearing stories about you my whole life."

Carter smiled. "How many years would your whole life be?"

"Nineteen. And you?"

"Twenty-eight."

"Those are nice ages. Neither of us are a child, neither of us are old. . . . So, what have you found out about me?"

"You go to a private school in Eugene. Your fifth. You live on Danby

Island when you're not in school. You're Ambrose Danby's daughter, which means you haven't had a lot of boyfriends. Your dad tends to scare people. And, oh yes, this was a good one. You were charged once with extortion."

"Charges were dropped."

"Heard that too. That's a big-time charge for a teenage girl."

"I thought someone had a sense of humour. Turned out, I was wrong."

Carter laughed, and when they finished dancing they went outside. She had a joint rolled, took it from a pocket of her dress, lit it while they walked toward the river.

"Your dress has pockets?" he asked.

"I love pockets. Hate wearing anything that doesn't have pockets."

"Not many dresses have pockets," he said.

"I know. Why you won't see me in one all that often."

They stood by the river. It was a clear night, mid-July and the temperature was warm, but not hot, late enough in the evening so the gnats and mosquitoes had gone away. The mountains to the west showed as shadowy, bas-relief sculptures under a star-filled sky. They passed the joint back and forth. She smoked while holding the burning ember turned to the sky, tilting her head and taking short puffs, smoking the way a nonsmoker would smoke.

"So, I won't be seeing you wearing a dress all that often," said Carter. "That's what you're telling me?"

"That's right."

"What might I see you wearing?"

"*Might* you?"

"Yes."

"You talk funny. Anyone ever tell you that?"

"From time to time. And your answer is?"

"I guess it *might* depend on what we do after we smoke this joint."

When they went back inside it was only to return to their tables, gather their things and leave. His father said to him, as he left, pulling his son down to the height of his seated position so he could whisper in his ear: "She looks like a lovely girl, Henry. Just remember she's a Danby."

"So what?"

"So . . . never trust a Danby. You just need to look at that girl to know she ain't no hand-upper."

He asked his dad what that meant.

═══

WHEN DAWN COMES, Carter and the girl are no longer in a forest but driving across a land turned flat, the horizon broad and getting broader as the sun rises in front of them. They pass a sign welcoming them to Nevada. Thirty minutes later, Carter turns off the road and heads north, down another county road, this one running beside the interstate. It is the time of morning when objects appear briefly in relief, with sharp edges and a depth that will weaken and disappear as the sun rises. They are driving beside buttes now, and red-sand foothills, Joshua trees and four-limbed cacti.

Carter takes a turn off the county road that leads to a four-corner truck stop, and nothing else. No other buildings anywhere near it. As though the truck stop had fallen from the sky. A mile past the truck stop, he turns onto a gravel road that quickly turns into a twisting hard-pack trail running beside a small creek already dried up for the season. The trail cuts through a line of buttes, turning and curving back on itself, almost going in circles at times, and Carter is back down to ten miles per hour for some stretches. It is almost noon and there are heat rays sitting in front of the horizon.

They are on the hard-pack trail for nearly an hour when Carter rounds a butte and in the distance sits a ranch. It has a T-shaped main house and many outbuildings. There is a fenced yard with what look like chickens and pigs, and longhorn bulls graze in a pasture behind the house, near the creek that doesn't look dried up anymore.

Another fence line runs east down the bank of the creek, until you can't see it anymore.

"Strange place to have a ranch," says the girl.

"They don't think so," says Carter.

There is a locked gate that Carter parks in front of. He walks to a clump of stones, lifts a rock and comes back with a key. He unlocks the gate and drives through, returns the key and closes the gate. When they reach the ranch ten minutes later, a woman is waiting for them. She stands in the shade of a front porch, one hand shielding her eyes, looking at the Jeep as it drives into the courtyard. She looks to be in her fifties, plump, with red hair, wears a yellow summer dress with a white apron cinched tightly around her waist.

When Carter steps out of the Jeep, she starts laughing.

"Should have figured it was you. I was standing here trying to remember who all knows about that key."

"Hi, Ruby," he says.

"Huey ain't here right now."

"Know when's he coming back?"

"Left yesterday morning. Said he'd be back tonight. Want to come in and wait for him?"

"Appreciate that."

"Come on. You look tired."

"Been driving all night."

"You say that 'bout every time you come here. Do you know that?"

"Do I?"

"Yeah, you do. And how you doing, girl? You look tired *and* hungry. When did Henry feed you last?"

"Last night . . . late last night. Weren't that long ago."

"My lord, the sun's going down, child. Get yourself in here."

The woman holds the screen door open for them. As they walk past, she says, "Just cause you're runnin', Henry, don't give you no cause to be starving a child. My lord, what are you thinkin'?"

12

FRANK GARDNER MAY have wanted to be home by the weekend, but it wasn't going to happen for him. Before I did any sort of reconnaissance, I needed to know the routine on Danby Island. Needed to know who was living here, and where I could expect to find them, day or night.

The Danbys lived in the main house; everyone else was in the bunkhouse. Enrique and the cook, an old man named Hank who I never once heard speak, lived in the two rooms by the bunkhouse's front entrance. There was a boat mechanic named Barry in a room next to them, a fat man who never put in his dentures and always spoke to the world through a concave mouth. A boat captain named Peter lived next to the mechanic. He had a master's license, foreign going with no restrictions, which meant he could have been piloting anything: from Norwegian cruise ships to supertankers going through the Panama Canal. He was a small man who wore thick glasses and checkered shirts and went to his quarters whenever the unregistered contents of his boat changed hands on open sea, always making sure he was the last to embark a ship, the first to disembark, so Peter did nothing more than guide the vessel.

I found out later he was from Miami and had done twelve years in Coleman for killing his second wife. A felony conviction meant he could never be bonded and never do legitimate mariner work again. Maybe the bond didn't matter much. Job opportunities for convicted murderers are rare and Peter seemed to know this. He never seemed bitter or sad. I remember him being rather happy. He just needed to pretend he was somewhere else, doing something different. A lot of people are like that.

The men who had driven me over to Danby Island and then up the road to the camp were not brothers but cousins. Fenton and Leslie Cooper, and what their story was I'm not sure. They never did talk much more than they did the day I met them, and no one ever talked about them. Not that I can recall.

There was the giant, the kid and Skipjack, who along with the cousins were the crew on any illegal boat run. Two men were missing. Billy Walker, the man whose room I was in, and Henry Carter, who lived in one of the cottages with Tess Danby. Both men were expected back any day. That's what the men believed.

Within three days, I had a good sense of the routine on Danby Island. If they weren't out on a boat, the crew was in the common room in the bunkhouse or drinking over in Cape Rage. The kitchen staff and the mechanic had regular shifts, as did Obie, who trudged out every morning to another hut, on the south side of the island, so he could man the perimeter line down there. The "southern flank," Finn Danby called it.

It was absurd. After three days on Danby Island, I was getting a good sense of that as well.

―――

ON DAY FOUR, I walked into the kitchen and the only one sitting there was Obie. He was wearing one of his yellowed T-shirts, this one with fresh milk stains on the front. I watched his hands shake as he brought a spoonful of cereal to his mouth.

"Where is everyone?"

"Went out at first light," he answered. "Headed to Prince Rupert. They'll be gone a couple days."

I went to get a cup of coffee. Took my time about it, so Obie would have a chance to finish his cereal before I sat down. The tremors of a bad drunk always put me on edge. Sitting next to a bad drunk was like sitting next to bad luck.

"Finn go with them?" I shouted over my shoulder. Finn Danby also had a captain's license.

"No, Pete's captain. Barry went too. We'll be the only hands in the bunkhouse for a couple days."

Obie wasn't counting Enrique and the cook. Sailors didn't consider kitchen staff to be working men. But that still meant the bunkhouse would only have four men tonight, Obie being one—who, when I turned around, had his cereal bowl tipped to his mouth, milk running down his chin, splashing onto his T-shirt, splashing onto the table.

I might never get a better night.

A HOT SUPPER was set out in the kitchen every day at five, but with most of the men gone, it was cold-cut sandwiches and coleslaw that night. I made a sandwich and brought it to my room, nodding to Hank, who nodded back. He seemed a bigger version of Obie.

I waited until eleven, when I knew Ambrose would be in bed. He drank in the dining room most nights after he had his meal and was passed out by ten. Some nights, it was closer to nine. I was giving myself four hours for the reconnaissance, which would have me back by three. Hank, an old cook, was used to getting up early. He wouldn't be awake at three in the morning, but he could be sleeping lightly.

Dressed in black jeans and a black T-shirt, black mackinaw to keep out the chill, I crept down the hallway, stopping briefly at Obie's room. Merle Haggard was singing on the other side of the door. Something about someone singing someone else back home before they died. I could hear Obie snoring out harmony. I went down the hallway and outside.

I headed toward the garage first. The building had intrigued me since I arrived on the island, an Adirondacks-style garage with Tudor framing and large, double-gated wooden doors. Three of those bay doors, with an outside staircase leading to a side door into a loft. A building that size needed a back door. I found it at the northeast corner.

It wasn't locked and I wasn't surprised. Other than the perimeter line, and the check of my gear and phone when I arrived, there had been few signs of security on Danby Island. Living on an island can give people a better sense of security than a company of armed bodyguards. A mistake, as I was about to prove.

I stepped inside and took a good long sniff of oil and diesel, gas and wood shavings, the sweet smells of an old-time working garage.

I peered at shadowy, misshapen objects sitting atop the benches and waited for my eyes to adjust. I didn't need to find a pirate's treasure to close the Danby case. That would be nice—if fantasies came true, I was about to find every penny they stole in San Francisco—but the CCTV tape, magnified a thousand times, had given partial serial numbers on Henry Carter's Glock. The camo he and Tess Danby were wearing was made by a Norwegian company with limited distribution in the United States. There were a few things I could find that would bring boatloads of feds racing over to Danby Island.

I went through the garage in under an hour. I wasn't doing a thorough inspection. Didn't have time for it. There were plenty of cabinets, quite a few storage containers, but none of them held anything more than boat parts, mechanic's overalls, ropes and bumpers, cans of oil and other fluids. The loft was an office, with steel filing cabinets, desks, computers—no doubt material in there that Hart could use in his RICO investigation. After twenty minutes of searching the office, I found nothing I could use.

I left the garage and went down some trails I had seen on my walks back and forth to my hut. The trails were wide, the terrain open, and I had no trouble making my way around the island without a flashlight. One trail took me to what must have been Obie's observation hut on the southwest cliff. It was more forlorn than mine, not even an abandoned cannery to keep him company. Another trail took me back to where I had started, a meandering loop that seemed to have no purpose.

It was coming up on one in the morning when I started circling the house. I'd always suspected I would end up there. What I was looking for would be inside that house, where Ambrose Danby could grab it anytime he wanted. I should have started with the house. Given myself more time. I was heading to the back, thinking I could get in through a window in the dining room, when I suddenly heard voices.

"What if it's not there?"

"It'll be there."

"We should have heard from Billy by now."

"We'll hear from him. Sit the fuck down, Finn."

———

AMBROSE AND FINN Danby were sitting at a table by an open window not more than twenty feet away. I fell to the ground and rolled to the side of the house.

"We should have heard from Billy by now," I heard Finn Danby say. "What if he's decided to play the same game Henry was playing?"

"You're drunk. Go to your room."

"Not too drunk to see this is a rat-fuck. What did Henry steal? And when are you going to tell me what the fuck we were doing in San Francisco?"

"When you need to know."

"I'm your fuckin' son."

"Not a good time to remind me, Finn."

"This isn't right. . . . *It isn't fair.*"

Ambrose didn't bother answering. Or maybe he did. He laughed for about thirty seconds. Then he hit his son.

It was a hard slap that I had no trouble hearing. Maybe it was a punch. Although I suspect it was a slap, a big, open-palm slap on the face, father to son.

"What the fuck!" I heard Finn yell, and then I heard another slap. Louder this time. Chairs were being pushed back; dinnerware was falling. There was loud slap after loud slap, surprised scream after surprised scream. *He's giving him a beating*, I thought, *right at the table.*

"We're in this rat-fuck because of that fuckin' tear gas, Finn," he yelled. "Have you forgotten that? *Have you fuckin' forgotten that?*"

It was punches now. And kicks. A lot of kicks. The beating lasted about a minute and when it was finished Ambrose was panting like a Kentucky Derby winner. His son was whimpering on the ground, like the horse that busted its leg on the stretch. I imagined Finn Danby lying at the feet of his father. I suppose he could have been lying anywhere. He wouldn't have been standing.

"Get the fuck back to your room," Ambrose snarled, his voice hollow sounding now, the anger spent. "We'll hear from Billy. And when we have what Henry stole from us, I'll tell you what you need to know. . . . Go clean yourself the fuck up. You look like shit."

There may have been more whimpering after that. I'm not sure. I like to give a man his dignity, even those who never earned it, and it may have been the wind I heard, an unsteady brackish wind that blew across the cliff in fits and starts, low and barely audible, almost secretive, a wind that only managed to sound from time to time like the ragged cries of a beaten man.

13

I WAS DONE for the night. I backed into the shadows and made my way to the bunkhouse. When I got to my room, I was too hopped up to sleep. Merle Haggard was still singing down the hallway. The only other sounds in the bunkhouse were ones I was now familiar with—running water, creaking wood, Obie's dry-rattle cough.

I opened the blinds and looked outside. Pitch black. The light in the dining room had been turned off. The bedrooms were on the opposite side of the house, and I couldn't see if lights were on there. I turned from the window and opened the drawer of the nightstand. Shook the box of ammo. Empty. I crumpled the box and did a sky-hook toward the wastebasket. It bounced off the rim.

I started thinking it through. That bank robbery in San Francisco—already a little screwy, already seeming like the FBI had more than enough evidence to arrest the Danbys and why weren't they doing that?—just got screwier. Henry Carter had stolen something from Ambrose Danby and that must have been why he was killed.

Gardner and Hart hadn't mentioned anything about that. Strange.

Ambrose Danby had killed a thief without getting back what was stolen. Stranger.

What did Carter steal? It had to have something to do with that bank robbery. And unless this island was crawling with men named Billy, the man living in this room had been sent to get it back. He'd never gone to Portland. If his son was the boy standing in front of the Christmas tree, and if Billy were a smart man, he'd *never* go to Portland.

It was valuable, whatever had been stolen. That much seemed certain as well. People had been dispatched to get it back. The Danbys were fighting about it. I made four hook shots in a row before missing again. I was walking to retrieve the crunched-up ammo box when I heard a knock.

I stopped walking. Stopped breathing and stared at the door—two seconds, three seconds—maybe I hadn't heard anything—six seconds, seven. . . . And then I heard it again. Not a knock. A tapping.

I turned and there was Tess Danby's face, staring at me from the darkness the other side of my window.

———

I TOOK MY mackinaw from the hook and went back outside. I found her crouched beside my window, her back pushed up against the wall of the bunkhouse. I crouched beside her. It was a clear night, nearly two weeks now without rain. There were a lot of stars to look at and she took her time looking at them before saying, "It's Danny, is that right?"

"It's Danny."

"Still no clouds in the sky. Been a while now since it rained."

"I suppose."

"You didn't notice? Thought you would have. You been out here long enough."

I took a deep breath. "Couldn't sleep. Went for a walk. What did you want to see me about?"

"Thought we should have a talk."

"About what?"

"About you."

I turned away from her. Took my own turn looking at the stars. "That doesn't sound too interesting. You're the crime-boss princess. You'd be a better story. Why don't we talk about you?"

"Danny, Danny, Danny . . ." As she spoke she started patting my knee. "Danny . . . as much fun as that might be, I'm not the one who just got caught spying. No, you're the better story tonight. Let's talk about you."

"I was out having a walk—just told you that."

"While spying on my father and brother . . . you're leaving out the best parts." She chuckled and I thought she was going to start the sad Dannys one more time, but she spared me the embarrassment. "What were they talking about?" she asked.

"Why do you want to know?"

"Always want to know what I don't know, Danny. Lifelong learner."

"Not sure I should be answering a question like that. I work for your father."

"Are you serious? You were just *spying* on my father. Do you have any idea what he would . . . fuck, do you have a cigarette?"

The smile came back. She stuck out her hand. You needed to know how to handle sharp turns if you were going to spend time around Tess Danby. And I *did* have a cigarette. I usually return to being a smoker when I'm working a case—you can go anywhere these days if you have a cigarette in your hand and a guilty look on your face. I took out my package of Winston Lights, shook a cigarette free and gave it to her. I lit it and she took a long drag, tilting her head and sending the smoke skyward.

"I couldn't hear them very well," I said.

"You were beside their window. They were *yelling*. I heard part of it."

"Then you know as much as me. They're looking for something they think your husband stole from them. Henry Carter. You're married to him, right?"

She didn't answer, and I continued. "Your dad is pretty upset with him. Upset with your brother too, because of something he did in San Francisco. Maybe you should stop asking me questions and talk to your husband. Sounds like he'd have your answers."

"Stop asking . . . are you fuckin' with me? I catch you creeping around, spying on my father, *the new guy*, and you think I shouldn't be asking you questions?"

"Not the ones you're asking me."

That stopped her. She looked annoyed and took another long drag from her cigarette, perched delicately between her fore and middle fingers, the glowing tip pointing skyward, smoking in the affected way occasional smokers have about them. For the first time, I wondered if she was nervous. I hadn't considered it until then. Tess Danby wasn't acting the way nervous people should act. Didn't seem uncertain, didn't seem weak; but there was something there, some sort of unease.

I decided to risk it. "What's going on here? What happened in San Francisco?"

"I left my heart . . . know the song?"

"I know the song."

"It's the Danby version, I'm afraid. I betrayed my husband. Same thing . . . maybe."

Her cigarette was almost finished, the glowing tip much longer than it should have been because of her deep inhalations. It lit her face as though she were sitting beside a campfire.

"You're no coincidence," she continued, almost dreamily. "Finn is too drunk to see it. Dad is too arrogant . . . but you're no coincidence.

You're here because of San Francisco . . . because of Henry and what we did to him. You're part of the ripple."

I stayed silent a long while, not wanting to talk, wanting to take as much time as possible to assess how much danger I was in. I wasn't sure where this was going, but one thing was certain—Tess Danby wasn't buying my cover story.

"I'm here because I need work," I said quietly. "Nothing more to it than that."

"I love stories. Tell me another one."

"Ms. Danby, maybe you like playing games with the hired help but I don't care for it much. I was out having a cigarette when I heard your father and brother arguing. I listened. Most people would have done the same thing. They weren't trying very hard to be quiet. If you want to tell your dad about it, go ahead. I'm tired and I'm going back to bed."

"Tell my dad about you?" she said, and she started laughing. It was a loud laugh, louder than it should have been at two in the morning, laughing like she didn't care where she was, what she was doing or who might be listening. "Danny, why would I *ever* want to do something like that? You're going to be my little secret. Same way I'm going to be *your* little secret."

"What are you talking about?"

"I'm talking about you and me helping each other."

"To do what?"

"Same thing you were planning on doing—robbing my dad."

She said it quickly, for effect, to see how I would react, and she must have been happy with her work because she started giggling. "Come on, you can't *really* be surprised. Do you think you're the first one to come over here looking for my dad's treasure? Let me help you. Do you *want* the help?"

It was hard not to join her in laughing. I had been waiting for Tess Danby to accuse me of being a cop; waiting for her to turn and run to the main house while I ran to the wharf hoping you hotwire a boat the same way you hotwire a car. Or near enough.

I hadn't considered there was another plausible explanation for what I had been doing that night. I was a thief. Come to rob them.

"Do you want my help?" she repeated, and this time I smiled. She smiled back. We sat crouched beside the bunkhouse smiling at each other.

I was going to leave it at that, but after some time had passed and it seemed like something more needed to be said, I told her, "You're wrong about your husband. I've never met him. Can't remember meeting *anyone* named Henry, now that I think about it."

She blew a last entrail of smoke toward the sky, stood and dropped the cigarette, ground it out with the heel of her boot. Before she walked away she said, "You would have remembered this one, Danny."

14

HENRY CARTER AND the girl sit in a kitchen and watch the plump woman with red hair and a flour-powdered apron make them sandwiches. It is a country-style kitchen, with large wooden cupboards and pantries, windows over the sink with a view of the back meadow, a chrome-legged, Formica-topped table in the middle of the room.

"Which way you headin'?" the woman asks. Her back is to them as she cuts strips of ham off the large hind of what would have been a freshly cured pig.

"West."

"How far?"

"Far as we can go."

"What you goin' to do when you get there?"

"Have some business to take care of."

"Already know that—you're here to see Huey. I'm asking what you and this girl plan on doing."

"We'll see when we get there."

"That's what you're doing these days?"

"Pretty much."

"You're headin' west . . . far as you can go . . . goin' to run that Jeep into the ground, drive it till the seat covers explode, till there's water moccasins coming up from the engine . . . but first, you got to see Huey, take care of some business. . . . That pretty much it?"

"Yeah."

The woman is laughing when she places the ham-and-cheese sandwiches in front of them. She tousles Carter's hair, like she knows him well, like she might have known him when he was a child, says, "Some babies never learn, Lord, ain't that the truth?"

When they finish their sandwiches, they go to the parlor. That is what the woman calls the room, although she seems too young to remember rooms ever being called that. The girl wonders if this is a house that has been lived in by generations of the same family, and if Ruby has grown up here with a parent, or grandparent.

It seems possible. All the furniture in the room looks like it could have been purchased by a grandparent. Dark wood furniture uphol-stered in fabric darker than the wood, patterns of periwinkles and acanthus leaves. A tea table with bone-china cups and lace doilies. Wool drapes with two backings of dark muslin. It is a room decorated for open-casket wakes.

"Do you mind if I do crosswords while we wait, Henry?" the woman asks.

"It's your house, Ruby."

"Would you like me to turn on the television for you?"

Carter shrugs. She gets up from her chair and walks to a wooden, Electrohome television. It has rabbit-ear antennas sitting on top and when it is turned on there is a pastel fog on the screen for several seconds before it clears, and there is Vanna White spinning a wheel.

"Clear night, so we can probably get all five channels," the woman says. "This is ABC. Want me to go through the channels for you while I'm standing here?"

"There's no remote?"

"Talk to Huey."

"This is good."

"You sure? What 'bout you, girl? You want to see Vanna turn them letters?"

"If you like."

"I'm going to be doing my crossword, so I don't have a like."

"Sure."

The woman nods and waddles back to her chair. She isn't that overweight but has the penguin walk of a much heavier person. She sits down with a loud exhale, straightens her dress, reaches into the side compartment of her chair for a crossword book. It is an old Morris chair, with the magazine rack built in. She opens to a page already marked, takes a pencil from the side table next to her chair and sticks it in her mouth. Occasionally, she takes the pencil out and writes something in the book. Mostly, it stays in her mouth.

———

A WEEK AFTER his brother's wedding, he was in Cape Rage for the first time. Tess Danby met him at the wharf, driving a cherry-red cigar boat. She didn't take him to Danby Island right away but went far out into the Georgia Strait, making turns around the navigation buoys so tight he could have slapped the bifurcation lights. Harbor seals barked at them as they passed, but the boat was gone before the seals knew what they were barking at. She made a long, banking turn in front of a cruise ship, the deck filled with people in Bermuda shorts and beach wraps cheering her as she flew down the port side. Watching a comet. Watching sheet lightning in front of a sinking sun. The passengers wouldn't have known exactly what they were cheering.

She didn't slow until they reached the western channel of Danby Island. The sky went dark as she drove beside it. Atop the cliffs Carter saw a large white house with gables and widow's walks. Dotted along the escarpment were huts, and in front of one hut was a man with a pair of binoculars, watching them all the way into the harbor.

Fast, dangerous, suspicious—you didn't need to spend a lot of time on Danby Island to get a sense of the place.

They'd had a family dinner. Just the four of them. Finn was drunk and passed out before dessert was served. Ambrose did most of the talking, asking the sort of questions a father might ask a man who had started dating his teenage daughter. Questions about his occupation. His prospects. His intentions.

"I never took down a mail train," said Ambrose. "Guess I'll never get a chance. How many did your granddaddy take down, Henry?"

"Four. The Peabody twice."

"Old man Peabody hated your family."

"We hated him."

"I heard your granddaddy bought rounds in the Commodore Hotel after one of those robberies, for the men whose pay he'd just stolen."

"True story. The coal miners asked him to rob Peabody the next week too, so they could come back to the Commodore. Most of them had never seen the inside of the place."

Ambrose laughed. "Money went through your granddaddy's hands faster than shit through a goose, didn't it, Henry?"

"I suppose," answered Carter, not liking the question much. He stared at Ambrose, then around the dining room, at the crystal chandeliers, the waiter with the busboy jacket, standing silent in a corner. "Your granddaddy clung onto his, didn't he?"

"Yeah, he did," said Ambrose, and his smile went away. Ask a man who covets money a question about his money and he's never happy. It's a personal, intimate relationship they have, and a third wheel is always a third wheel.

"Hear you have a crew now, Henry."

"That's right."

"Hear you like jewelry stores."

"Not particular. I like shopping malls. Go in through the roof. Most shopping malls have a jewelry store."

"Where do you move the stuff? I might be able to help with that."

"I've got a cousin, in Chicago. No complaints."

"Well, there you go. Keep it in the family."

Tess looked at him and smiled. He was doing well. As dessert was being served, Ambrose said, "My daughter has done nothing but talk about you since we came back from Snow Corners. The girl's crazy about you. Driving the rest of us crazy."

"I've spent a lot of time thinking about her as well. Tess is . . . remarkable."

"Yeah, she's that all right," snorted Ambrose. "A remarkable lot of trouble when she gets carried away. You can't let that happen. Just comes back on the rest of us."

Carter nodded.

"She's not part of your crew, Henry. She don't run with you."

"I know that."

"She can't get popped. I can't have my daughter sitting in jail, getting squeezed by the feds. Just can't have that, Henry."

"I understand," said Carter, and he left it at that. Ambrose didn't care about his daughter getting arrested and sitting in jail. Cared only that it might come back on him. Tess heard him say it. He didn't need to point it out.

They ate the rest of the meal while telling family stories about old bank robberies and moonshine runs through the mountains of Washington State. When they were finished, Tess asked if she could borrow the cigar boat.

———

CARTER AND THE girl watch two episodes of *Wheel of Fortune*; an episode of *Friends* with Brad Pitt; an episode of *Friends* without Brad

Pitt. They are watching the opening scene to an episode of *Seinfeld*, Kramer coming through a door with his head bobbing like a water duck, when headlights appear on the windows of the parlor.

The woman puts her crossword book down and says, "Huey might want some coffee. Want any, Henry?"

Carter doesn't answer. Instead, he takes a gun from his shoulder holster and points it at her. "Sit back down, Ruby. Coffee can wait."

The woman sighs, shakes her head sadly and sits down. A minute later a man comes through the front door. He walks to the parlor and stands in the doorway.

"Henry."

"Huey."

"Been a while."

"It has."

The man looks to be in his early sixties, has long gray hair with strands of black running through it, a half beard the opposite of his hair—more black than gray. He wears a black T-shirt and Lee jeans, Tony Lama cowboy boots with silver tips. Has a full-sleeve tattoo of a dragon on his left arm, Cerberus on his right. He is tall and slim, but his arms are muscular, and his shoulders are broad. He stands in the doorway and looks around.

"Why the gun, Henry?"

"Thought it'd be best to have one when we said hello."

"Any reason for you to be thinking that way?"

"No particular reason; just thought it best."

The man nods. Looks at the woman with the red hair and the yellow apron.

"Ruby been lookin' after ya all right?"

"She has."

"When did you get here?"

"Midafternoon."

"I've been on the road most of the day, Henry. Mighty thirsty. I'm going to get a beer. You already checked the fridge, right?"

"You're good. Better take out anything you've got in your boots though. No . . . better take off your boots."

The man starts taking off his boots. He doesn't seem angry.

"You should empty your pockets too," says Carter. "Got anything in your waistband?"

"No."

The man assembles a little pile on the tea table: a Glock 19 with thirty-three-round magazine, one extra magazine, one French stiletto, one single-shot Bond Snake Slayer, smaller than the stiletto. When he is done, he walks into the kitchen, gets a beer and comes back to the parlor, sits down. He has brought a kitchen chair into the room with him, so he can sit closer to Carter.

He opens the beer, takes a long swallow, looks at the girl and says, "Who's she?"

"She's with me."

"Not what I asked you, Henry. I've never seen this girl."

"That's not saying much, Huey. I wouldn't expect you to have seen everyone that I know. You do? Why would you be expecting something like that?"

"Don't start with the questions, Henry, you're not going to rattle me. Gun ain't going to do much for you either. I've had plenty of guns pointed at me. It's part of the business. Pointing a gun makes some men feel more comfortable. Never took you for one of those men, but there you go, live and learn."

The man takes another sip of beer. "No . . . I can live with guns. What bothers me is having someone sitting in my house that I ain't *never fuckin' seen before.*"

His jaw clinches and his eyes bug out from their sockets. The knuckles on the hand holding the beer bottle turn pinch white.

"You need to get over that, Huey."

"You bring a fuckin' witness into my house, and *I'm* the one who's going to have to get over it? You know the rules, Henry. You've known them your whole fuckin' life."

"She's with me. That changes the rules."

The man puts his beer bottle on the tea table, cranes his neck back, tilts his chair at the same time so he can stretch out his back, so he can hear some bones crack. He brings the chair back down and says, "Who the fuck is she, Henry?"

"She doesn't matter to you. She's not here."

The man shakes his head in disgust. The woman hangs hers in what seems like shame, the domestic embarrassment of a spouse who has accidentally invited in an obnoxious dinner guest. The silence continues until the girl speaks.

"I found your friend shot in the back in the woods near my home. I saved his life. Now I'm traveling with him to see if he's going to keep his promise and save mine."

They stare at her. It is a long time before anyone speaks. When someone does, it is the man with the silver-tipped boots, who drains the last of his beer, puts it on the tea table and says, "Well, I wish you the best, miss." Then he turns to Carter and says, "Henry, let's go into my office and talk about why you're here."

As they leave the room the man asks what's for dinner. Pot roast, the woman answers. Half an hour.

———

HENRY CARTER AND Huey Dalton sit in a room in the basement of the ranch house. It is a room they have entered through a steel door the height and thickness of a bank vault. Dalton had to punch in a combination and have his retina scanned before he could push open the door. On the walls of the room, hung like shoes in a Foot Locker, are guns. There are several models of 9 mm handguns—Glock,

Beretta, Sig Sauer—more models of machine pistols—Uzi, Mac-10, Heckler and Koch—a Carl Gustav bunker buster. There are even two old-model General Dynamics stinger missiles, and—for the nostalgia buffs among Huey Dalton's clientele—three vintage models of a Colt .45, including an SAA from 1907.

They sit at a steel table in the middle of the room. Dalton lights a cigarette and opens one of the beer bottles he took from the fridge on his way to the basement. He passes it to Carter. Opens another one.

"So that girl found you shot in the woods, that right, Henry?"

"That's right."

"Where?"

"San Francisco . . . just north of there."

"Wells Fargo? . . . I heard about that one. Two guards dead on that one, brother."

Carter drinks his beer and doesn't say anything.

"Who shot *you*?"

"The Danbys."

"Tess?"

"She was there."

"That mean she shot you?"

"Just told you she was there."

"And now you're heading to Danby Island?"

"That's where she'll be. . . . I have money on account, Huey."

"I know that."

"Why are we talking?"

"Really? There's some girl sitting upstairs I ain't never *fuckin' seen before*. In my house—someone I don't *fuckin' know*. You tell me the Danbys have tried to kill you, for some reason you haven't told me. I have no *fuckin' idea* how many people might be chasing you right now, and you had a gun on me ten minutes ago. . . . Why are we talking? I don't know, Henry—*why the fuck* might we be talking?"

"Lot of noise, Huey. Money on account. Customer in front of you."

"Always simple with you, eh? You're a freak, Henry. Anyone ever tell you that?"

"Because I don't believe in distractions?"

"No . . . because you're a freak. Do you at least know *why* you were shot?"

"Got an idea."

"Is it anything I need to worry about, when you pull out of here?"

"You're good."

The man runs his fingers through his hair and lets out a loud sigh. "Man, betrayal like that—it's cold, Henry, I don't blame you for wanting to settle things. I'd want to do the same thing." He keeps running his fingers through his hair. "Sure, I'll kit you up. You can take what you need, if you go over you can settle the account later. What do you figure you *do* need?"

"Little bit of everything."

The man starts laughing and just then the woman yells down the stairs, "Roast is ready, Huey. Should I take it out or turn everything down?"

"We're coming up," he yells back.

———

IT IS A good cut of beef, and the woman knew how to cook it, served it on a silver tray surrounded by potatoes and carrots and yams that were seasoned with fresh herbs and had been roasted in the oven beside the beef. The gravy is thick enough to stand up a sterling-silver fork. There is homemade horseradish.

The two men talk about the ranch, and the longhorn cattle on the back pasture. Carter seems to know something about livestock, and the girl is surprised to hear the conversation.

"You're still wearing suits and fancy shirts, I see," says the man.

"It's a shirt that has buttons, Huey."

"What I just said. Why you always dress up fancy like that?"

"It ain't fancy."

"Whatever. Why you do it?"

"I guess because I don't like wasting time."

"What's that supposed to mean?"

"Means when you put on a white shirt, Huey, a nice one, you're not getting ready to watch *Wheel of Fortune*. You're getting ready to go out and do something. . . . I like that feeling."

The man looks at Carter a few seconds before shaking his head and saying jovially, "You're a fuckin' freak." He goes back to eating. Before long, he says, "I have to go to the bathroom. That all right, Henry?"

"The one on this floor, over there," Carter says, pointing toward the parlor.

"That's the one. You've already checked it, right?"

"You're good."

The man stands, wipes his lips with a linen napkin and heads toward the parlor. Carter goes back to eating. As the man is walking past Carter, he trips. It looks like he is about to fall, and he throws his arms wide, trying to catch his balance. The outstretched arm nearest to Carter pulls the handgun from his shoulder holster.

"Stay where you are, Henry," the man says quietly, as he backs away from the table. "Ruby, get that bitch down on her knees."

═══

THE WOMAN STANDS and slaps the girl in the head. Then she pulls her from her chair, grabbing a full hand's worth of hair to do it. The girl screams and tries to twist free, but the woman slaps her in the head again and pushes her to her knees. The man laughs.

"You are so fuckin' dead, Henry," he says. "You and this fuckin' skank. Think you can come into *my house*, talk to me and Ruby the way you been talking? Just because you're *Henry fuckin' Carter*. That it? Think you're better than us, Henry, with your fuckin' white shirts and your fuckin' questions, like some fuckin' lawyer—I'm glad this happened. Hear that, Henry? I'm fuckin' *glad*."

Carter is still eating his meal. The girl had screamed when the woman yanked her from the chair, but she hasn't done much more than that since. She doesn't even look scared, keeps her head up, her eyes on Carter, as the man keeps talking.

". . . I don't blame the Danbys for shooting you. They were probably sick of ya too. You really thought you was something, didn't you, boy? But you ain't your granddaddy, Henry. Weren't you that went over the wall at San Quentin. Weren't you that walked off some goddamn bridge with thirteen bullets in your chest. Should have showed some respect, boy. That was your undoing. Remember that. With the time you have left . . . remember how fuckin' high and mighty you were and what brought you down."

The man stops to take a breath, a deep, long breath, and as he does that he looks at Henry Carter and a puzzled look comes to his face.

"Why the fuck are you still eating?"

"Because I'm still hungry."

Carter slices another piece of beef. Twirls it in gravy. Brings it slowly to his mouth, chews and pats his lips with a napkin, puts the fork down. After he has done all this he bends down and pulls a Glock 40 from a holster strapped to his ankle.

"Also, because I have this, Huey. A loaded gun. Much more useful than the gun you have."

It takes him a few seconds to put it together. You can see the process play out across his face: surprise, confusion, the first twitch of understanding, a new world glimpsed; getting closer, closer, then the shock of seeing the shoreline: the unpassable reefs, the spiraling eddies, the approaching falls.

He still pulls the trigger. When the pneumatic hiss fades away, he says, "You had an unloaded gun on me the whole time?"

"And you, the arms dealer. Bit embarrassing I'd say."

"Why?"

"I wanted to give you a chance to show me what kind of man you are, before I drove away from here. Wanted to know whether you could be trusted."

"What the fuck are you doing, Henry?"

"Telling your wife to let go of that girl before I shoot her in the head. Unless you want to tell Ruby that yourself."

The woman lets go of the girl's hair and steps back. She puts her arms above her head.

"Good idea, Ruby. Keep them there. Huey, sit back down. You haven't finished your meal."

━━━━

THEY EAT IN silence. The man uses a butter knife to cut his roast and it looks a few times like he is considering doing something else with the knife, but it is a butter knife, and he never does. The woman stands with her arms raised. The girl stands next to her. When they finish eating, both men push away their plates. The man asks if he can have a cigarette and Carter tells him it is time to quit.

"So . . . where do we go from here, Henry?"

Carter doesn't answer.

"You can drive away, son. Take that girl and go. You can do that. You're under a lot of stress. I get that."

"You do?"

"Think you're the only man who's ever been shot? Or ever been on the run? Yeah, I get it, Henry. Drive away and good luck to you. That's how this can end."

"You were going to kill me a minute ago. Remember that?"

"Henry . . ."

"Yeah, you remember. And just how long, do you figure, have you known Ambrose Danby?"

". . . You're getting distracted."

"Would it be your whole fuckin' life, Huey?"

"Henry, I keep that crazy bastard as far away from me as possible. You can have him. This is your deal."

"And your wife pulled the girl's hair. Looked like it hurt."

The man turns to look at the girl. "Are you shitting me? Who the fuck *is this* girl?"

"She already told you who she is, Huey. You got to listen better."

Carter picks up the Glock 9 mm he's put on the table next to the gravy boat. He tosses the gun from hand to hand and keeps talking. "As you can see, Huey, we got a few problems. Now, we can argue and talk about 'em, but that probably won't get us too far. You'll always think you're right. I'll always think different about it. Back and forth we'll go. Drive each other crazy."

The man watches the gun. Watches it pass from hand to hand, then watches as Carter flips it, so it lies broadside in the palm of one hand. Then places the gun in the middle of the table.

"That looks about halfway to me. . . . What do you think?"

Dalton stares at the gun but doesn't answer.

"Yeah . . . that's halfway. So, this is how we're going to solve our problem. We're going to sit here, like this." Carter places his hands palms down on the table, nods his head, indicating the man should do the same. "That's right . . . just like that, Huey. Now, we're going to sit here like this, and what we're going to do . . . well, it's simple. Whoever gets to that gun first . . . that man doesn't have any more problems."

"You're fuckin' crazy, you know that?"

"No, I don't know that. Come on, don't you ever get tired of it, Huey? What's right, what's wrong, what should I do next? How much time you figure we waste on questions like that? *That's* crazy. Sometimes, you got to have faith. There's no substitute for it; you got to have faith that things will turn out all right for you. Got any faith, Huey?"

"Crazy as fuckin' batshit."

The woman and the girl look at the men as they talk, staring at them like they're witnessing galaxies being formed, stars coalescing, something of that primacy and import. Everything that matters in the world has been distilled down and shoved into this kitchen, where two men sit across from each other at an old-fashioned, chrome-legged table, one gun between them.

It is a static scene. No air circulates. No foreground, no background, and when Huey Dalton lunges for the gun it is like a long-paused movie has started up again.

But Henry Carter doesn't move. He sits still and calm, even as a smile comes to Dalton's face, one that grows as his fingers touch the metal grip of the gun, as they fold around the sleek, polished curvature, as they feel a weight being transferred to his hand, the gun rising from the table.

And right then Carter punches him.

Punches him with a powerful, two-foot jab that lands on a face moving in speed from the opposite direction. When the blow lands bones crack, blood flies, and Huey Dalton goes reeling backward. He is tottering, about to fall, when Carter reaches across the table, picks up the gun and shoots him in the head.

After that he turns, still seated, and shoots Ruby Dalton as she runs toward a pantry where Carter later finds a sawed-off shotgun hidden beneath some flour bags. He stands and walks to both bodies, kneels and fires one more bullet into each head. There is a pneumatic-sounding thud after each shot is fired. Not loud. Barely heard.

When he is done, he tells the girl to wait in the Jeep. He'll be a few minutes.

————

HENRY CARTER KNEW something about revenge long before he was shot in the back and left for dead; already knew it was the ugliest and most toxic of emotions, one capable of revealing itself in dead bodies even, so easy was it to spot those who had died by act of vengeance. Those bodies were the hardest to look upon. The most damaged. The least human.

He knew also that it is the most useless of emotions, the one that gives no reward. Greed gives comfort. Sex gives pleasure. Revenge gives nothing tangible; it is a hollow, end-of-the-road emotion that cannot be sustained without the fantasies of a vengeful person.

Which also makes revenge the falsest of emotions, the one that puts us in opposition to the natural world, for we are the only animal that kills for revenge—sex, greed, power, we share those—only revenge is ours. No other animal understands it.

We are the only creature on the planet that will kill because of story—because of narrative—and if it were required of a vengeful person to attain retribution they would gladly gouge out their eyes, burn down their house, tear down the stars. There are no half steps with revenge. No uncompleted journeys.

Henry Carter knows this when he walks out of that ranch. Has always known. He carries a duffel bag with him and the girl hears the bag clang and ping when he puts it in the back of the Jeep. He needs both hands to lift it.

When he is behind the steering wheel he adjusts the crease in his pants, the line of his collar, and starts the Jeep. Neither of them speaks for many miles, although eventually, wanting to say something, but not wanting to ask questions about what has happened at the ranch, the girl asks, "Where we goin' now?"

"Go see my wife," he answers.

15

A POD OF minke whales was feeding below the cliffs. I didn't know that much about whales, but it seemed they fed at the same time each day, midmorning, with the sun behind me casting long shadows off the cliffs that just managed to reach them. The whales rose and dove in near tandem, as though choreographed, the slick black humps looking not that different from the rock spits and small islands that appeared at low tide. Between the tide and the whales, there was always something appearing and disappearing off these cliffs, something black and cold and distant.

"Do you believe her?" I heard Gardner say.

"Too early to say."

I turned away from the whales and looked up the trail leading to the house. In eight days of manning the Danby perimeter, I had yet to see anyone come down that trail.

"Could be a trap," he said.

"Could be a lot of things, but I don't know what the game would be. If Tess Danby wanted to trap me, I was already trapped. She could have gone to her father last night and told him what she'd seen. What does she gain by waiting?"

"Maybe she wants to catch you red-handed. Turn you over to her father tied up in a red-ribbon bow."

"She doesn't seem the gift-giving type."

I had just given Gardner my sit-rep, talking into my watch and no longer feeling like a foolish, castaway Dick Tracy. Getting used to it. It had been a busy night and a long report: a three-hour reconnaissance of the island, Ambrose and Finn going at it in the dining room, Tess Danby knocking on my window and asking if I wanted to come out and play.

He hadn't spoken right away, and I was left wondering what he would ask me. I wasn't surprised when his first question was about Tess Danby. She was the most direct route to finishing his case. Everything else in my report was a dead end, or a problem.

"She seems nervous," I continued. "That may be part of some con she's running—she's quite the actress—but it didn't feel that way. She wanted to know what her father and brother were talking about. That seemed genuine. There's something she doesn't know, and it's worrying her."

"I thought it would be the brother we'd have a chance of turning."

"Still could happen. That was a nasty beating he took last night. He drinks too much. There are a couple things he might want to get out from under."

"He might be the more straight-ahead play."

"He might be. But it was Tess Danby that made the first move."

"Yeah, she did." A few seconds later, Gardner said, "You know, instead of worrying about this, do you want to look at it a different way? This could be a fuckin' gift, Barrett. Tess Danby is offering to convict herself. She might as well have tapped on your window and said, 'Arrest me.'"

"What about Ambrose and Finn?"

"What about them?"

"What were they fighting about?"

"No idea. You were the one who heard them."

"Ambrose was upset because Henry Carter had stolen something from him. He blamed Finn for it. What did he steal?"

"Same answer. You heard them, not me."

"Don't you *want* to know? The guy whose room I'm in—his clothes and stuff are still here—Ambrose sent him to get it back. . . . Whatever was stolen, it's valuable."

"So what?"

"So, why would you kill a thief and not get back what he'd stolen? Carter's dead, right?"

"He's dead, Barrett. We've had it confirmed on two more wiretaps since you were in Seattle. We got mutts everywhere talking about it. Big underground news, my friend."

"So, Ambrose sent this guy to get something from a dead man? Does that make any sense to you?"

"Doesn't have to make any sense. It's some disagreement between mutts that has nothing to do with the case, one of the mutts being a dead mutt. You're overthinking it, Barrett. Sounds like you've got Tess Danby begging to put herself and the rest of her family into hand-cuffs. When do you see her next?"

"We didn't put anything in a Daytimer," I said, and felt foolish as soon as I said it, realizing it sounded more peevish than annoyed, more childish than cavalier. I'd been trying to strike a balance between the last two.

I knew Frank Gardner didn't want to talk about the fight between Ambrose and Finn because that was a confusing fact, one that offered no direct line or fast action, a confusing fact that would meander and grow and probably have no bearing on the case, although it would surely consume hours of manpower.

There comes a point in the career of any senior law enforcement official when they become a bureaucrat. It sounded like Frank Gardner reached his a long time ago.

"I'll be seeing her later today," I said, making my voice sound as neutral as possible. "I'm not that hard to find."

"She'll come see you?"

"I suspect."

"All right, then go ahead, Barrett. You've got a green light to proceed with Tess Danby. It's the full operational range so long as you stay on that island. Any illegal activity the little girl wants to dream up—you're game. Fuck, you're a lucky son of a bitch."

———

TESS DANBY CAME down the trail just as the sun was starting to slide down toward the western horizon, touching the highest point of land on Gilmore Island from the back side. The island was ten miles further out in the Strait and pelicans flew in front of the sinking sun, casting crooked, dinosaur-winged shadows across the island's hills.

It was a long pathway to the hut, with no trees, no turns on the last stretch, and I watched her coming toward me for a long time, walking at a steady pace, not pausing to look around, not stopping and staring at the sinking sun. Walking with purpose.

She didn't enter the hut when she got here, but stopped and looked at the sinking sun, as though noticing it for the first time. I went outside and stood beside her.

"Busy day?" she asked.

"A pelican tried to come ashore earlier," I answered. "That whale out there has been acting suspicious for a few hours now. Busy enough."

"Glad you're here to protect us. Have time to talk?"

"Think I can squeeze you in."

"Have you thought about my offer?"

"I have."

"So, are we doing this?"

"I'd like to know a few things first."

"So would I. Let me go first. I'll pout if I don't."

"All right, what would you like to know?"

"Do you really know Jimmy Metcalfe?"

"I do," I lied.

"And he told you about my dad's hidey-hole."

"He did."

"I don't think Jimmy ever saw it. I'm sure he never did. I've only seen it once. My sixteenth birthday. Dad brought me down and showed me. He'd been drinking. Said it was all going to be mine one day. Mine and Finn's. We could figure it out between us . . . he laughed after he said that. He thought that was funny. I really should get more, you know, fifty-fifty don't seem right. You're just going to be carrying stuff out . . . bit more than that . . . but I'm going to get us in there and get us off this island. Should be more like seventy-thirty."

We seemed to be negotiating. "Fifty-fifty sounds more right to me," I said.

She laughed and tossed her hair back, flashed me a scamp-who-just-got-caught smile. "All right, can't blame a girl for trying . . . but you're getting a hell of a deal, Danny. My dad's got stuff down in his hidey-hole that my great-granddaddy stole. Hell, he's got gold bars down there with Treasury stamps from the Mexican-American War."

It took me a few seconds to figure it out. When I did, I tried to hide my surprise. "Your family has been hiding away stuff they've stolen?"

"A pirate's treasure, Danny. My dad told me once that he wanted to make Blackbeard look like a piker. . . . I thought Jimmy told you all this?"

". . . He may have left out some details."

"Yeah, he probably did. I always thought Jimmy had plans on coming after it one day . . . then he got popped. Finn thinks he's one of his best friends. Can't tell you how many times I've seen Jimmy Metcalfe laughing at my brother behind his back."

Laughing at her brother seemed to bother Tess Danby and she puckered her lips as if she had just tasted something sour. She was dressed in jeans and a Cowichan sweater, had her red hair pulled back in a ponytail. Looked a bit like Amy Adams. I knew from reading her criminal file that she was twenty-four years old. She looked to be exactly that old.

"Doesn't your dad fence what he's stolen?"

"'Course he does. He just keeps what he likes . . . he likes gold."

I started to visualize what Tess Danby was talking about: A hidey-hole somewhere on Danby Island filled with gold—bars, coins, jewelry—stolen by her family for the past one hundred years. An Ali Baba cave, a Scrooge McDuck vault, a secret, happy place for Ambrose Danby to gaze upon the Danby family's looted fortune, so tangible he could pick it up and roll it through his fingers if he wished.

"He really thinks he's a pirate, doesn't he?"

"No argument there," she answered. "He had a boat once with a gangplank. Not really a gangplank . . . my dad's was a surfboard with a bracket you slipped over a transom. He used to joke about it. When he was out drinking, he'd ask men if they wanted to go surfing."

"You saw this?"

"Saw the surfboard. . . . Never saw it being used. I know it was used a few times and I know it was a lawyer who told him to get rid of it. My dad wasn't too happy with the lawyer."

She bit her lip, then went back to smiling. I wondered if it had been a continuous motion, the brief display of nervousness meant to give greater effect to the smile.

"Your dad's a dangerous man," I said. "Why do you want to rob him?"

"I think it's time I left home."

"Why? You've lived here your whole life. Do this, and you don't have a home anymore; don't have a family."

"What difference does that make to you, Danny? Maybe this is just what pirates do."

I got the full-blown scamp smile. Like I had just passed a club initiation and secret festivities were about to begin. It was a great smile.

"Not buying it, Tess. If you wanted to rob your father, why didn't you do it a long time ago? Why didn't you do it with your husband?"

"You see Henry around here anywhere?"

"Good point. What did you mean the other night when you said you betrayed him?"

"Meant I betrayed him."

"How?"

"In the worst way, I would think."

"That's not an answer."

"You don't think so? I thought it was."

It looked like she was about to pout. Then she laughed, as though admitting she couldn't go through with it.

"Stop being cute, Tess," I said. "How do I know you're not setting me up, walking me right to your dad's hidey-hole, where he'll be waiting for me? Maybe that passes for entertainment on this island. Maybe you're bored and a stunt like that is more fun than anything else you have planned for the next few days."

"In the next few days, I'm planning on getting off this island and becoming rich. Thought you had the same plan."

"Not until I know what's going on here. You're not telling me the whole story."

"The whole story? That's a big ask, Danny. Who gets that?"

"I'm not doing this blind."

She bit her lip again. But there was no smile this time. "I've got family problems, Danny. It's time I left this island. That a good enough answer for you?"

"Lots of families have problems. They don't start stealing from each other."

"My problems are unique."

"Probably not."

"Don't think so?"

"Just told you that. Lot of people think their problems are one-of-a-kind things. They never are."

She gave another sigh, not quite as theatrical this time, not quite as long. "All right, you win. My father killed my husband after we robbed a bank in San Francisco eight days ago. I've got to leave before he starts thinking he should do the same thing to me."

She raised her chin and looked right at me when she said it. Defiant. Determined. But her eyes couldn't pull off the same trick. There was panic and fear in those eyes; the eyes of someone who is trapped and has just realized they're trapped, that exact second, when they know with certainty bad things are coming and there's no chance of ever jumping out of the way.

"Unique enough for you?" she asked.

16

FOR THE NEXT hour I stood outside the hut and listened to Tess Danby talk. I was uncomfortable long before she finished, a feeling I often get when someone has decided to befriend me and is in the process of sending themselves to prison.

I wished I could have stopped her, but confessing to the bank robbery and the murder of her husband—committing one crime, witnessing the other—seemed a cathartic release for Tess Danby. I couldn't have stopped her if I tried. A lot of the hour was spent talking about Henry Carter, and it was easy to tell she was guilt-ridden about what had happened to him. Burning up with guilt; running a fever with it, telling me stories she shouldn't have been telling someone she'd known for only a week.

She told me how she'd met her husband at a wedding in Snow Corners, after she'd been hearing stories about him and his family since she was a child; stories about the Peabody mail train, and the shootout at Stone Quarry Bridge, the armed robbery of the cashiers' cages at a Seahawks playoff game. She told me how she helped some boys slash the tires of an FBI car at the wedding reception, and how she did it not to help the boys but so Carter could see her doing it, so he would know, from the first day he saw her, that she would be willing to do most anything, that risk didn't bother her and consequences were for people not as fast, not as daring.

She talked about Henry Carter holding the record in Washington State for the largest unsolved robbery, a UPS truck he took down in a service alley at the Seattle airport. He was twenty. Had his own crew. She talked like the boastful spouse of a professional athlete. Told me Henry Carter was her first love. Her only love. She actually said that, and the more she talked, the more uncomfortable I became. Most of the people I betray deserve everything they're about to get; but even then, it's hard to watch someone destroy their life, watch bad fate slip over someone as surely and certainly as a shroud, without them knowing it.

Knowing a person's fate before they do seems tawdry and shameful to me. I know that makes no sense, given what I do, but knowing this has rarely stopped me from feeling bad about it. I finally had to turn away from Tess Danby, unable to watch anymore.

"I wanted Henry in my life so bad," she was saying by then. "What do you think that says about me?"

I told her it meant she was crazy about the guy. "What happened in San Francisco?" I asked.

"I still don't know," she answered. "It was my dad's score. He asked me and Henry to help him. He said it was a big score and he wanted to keep it in the family. We had never worked with him before."

"Did you believe him?"

"Yeah, I did. Henry was good with safe deposit boxes. Probably no one better in the entire state. No one I ever heard about, anyway."

"Safe deposit boxes?"

"Yeah, Henry could pop a box and have it emptied in fifteen seconds. Any box, even the big commercial ones they have in the bonded warehouses."

"You stole the safe deposit boxes? Why didn't you go after the money in the vault?"

"No idea," she said, and when she said it she sounded annoyed, like a child irritated by a parent's habit. Every once in a while, Tess Danby said or did something that reminded me of how young she was. "We could have been out of that bank a lot quicker if we'd hit the vault. Finn was feeling rushed. My brother screws up when he's feeling rushed, when he's under stress."

"Not a good habit for a bank robber."

"Don't need to tell me. But it wasn't just Finn. I screwed up. Henry screwed up. . . . It was a freakin' *Gong Show* at that bank."

"How did you screw up?"

"By taking my hood off on the front steps of the bank. Man, I was choking. I didn't know where I was. Just knew I was outside, and I needed to get that thing off my head."

"How did your husband screw up?"

"By trying to protect me."

She didn't say anything after that, and I decided it was the wrong time to push it. Or maybe I just didn't want images I had been trying to forget to come barnstorming back into my head: A security guard so young he has acne on his cheeks, cowering under an armored truck. A man in black camo tilting his head back and sniffing the air.

"Why did your dad shoot your husband?"

"Because of what Henry did in front of the bank. That's what he said, anyway. Henry was going to become the world's biggest heat score. He said there'd be cops everywhere looking for him, they'd come right onto the island looking for him; they'd never stop looking for Henry and I'd thank him one day, for what he did."

The sun was sitting directly over Gilmore Island now and the dinosaur-winged shadows disappeared whenever the pelicans flew over the island. The shadows were there when the birds flew over open water but vanished when they soared over the hills. Like they'd been shot down.

"What did you do after your husband was killed?"

"I came home," she said. And then she started crying. I was surprised to see the tears, didn't believe them at first, but a few minutes later I wasn't as sure. The panic I'd seen in her eyes was real. It's hard to fake something like that. I was probably the first person—I couldn't think of anyone else—she had spoken to about the death of her husband.

"I was talking to Henry when it ha . . . happened . . . my dad came up behind him. If Henry heard the shotgun being pumped . . . I think he heard it . . . if he'd heard it . . . he would have thought I knew . . . that I was part of it. That would have been the last thought he ever had."

I had an almost uncontrollable urge to comfort her, to put my arms around Tess Danby and wipe away a tear. But that would have been way over a line I shouldn't get anywhere near. I didn't say anything, and she continued.

"It all just blew up, Danny. Ever have that happen to you? Your whole life blows up and you had nothing to do with it, you were just standing there, watching it, a by . . . bystander to your own freakin' life. You're left with the pieces. But you can't put them back together. That's not an option. So . . . what do you do? . . . You keep going. That's the answer, right?"

"I suppose."

"That *has to be* the answer."

She steadied herself after saying that, like a decision had been made, or she was suddenly standing on familiar ground, no longer blown away. When I knew she had cried herself out, I asked, "Robbing your dad, do you have a plan?"

She dabbed her eyes a few times, before saying: "I do."

17

Henry Carter and the girl leave Nevada under a night sky filled with space. No horizon. No edge. Room for a million stars. He had thought briefly about switching vehicles, taking the chromed-up Chevy Avalanche that was parked next to the Jeep when he walked out of the ranch. It's always smart to switch out vehicles, as a general, not-to-be-messed-with rule of survival when you're on the run.

Billy Walker and Huey Dalton were men who could go missing a long time before anyone reported them missing. If anyone ever did. Both vehicles were probably safe. But despite the rule, a chromed-up Avalanche is flashier than a Grand Cherokee, and it would be stupid and inexcusable if that caused him problems, if he overthought his way into making a mistake. He stayed with the Jeep.

They travel down the hard-packed trail, and at night it seems a land without reference points. Or, more accurately, only one: a red-sand hill with a blunt peak, circular in form but having four distinct corners, rising to the height of about a twelve-story building, roughly a hundred paces in breadth and width. A butte that is always the same shape and the same mass, and how Carter makes it through without once needing to back up, without once stopping—it doesn't make any sense to the girl. There is starting to be a list of things like that.

When dawn breaks, they are back on the county road and Carter is racing down the asphalt, heading true north, trying to stay ahead of the dawn it seems, stay under a night sky. The stars disappear as he drives until only one remains, a high northern star that seems to move in tandem with the Jeep, that seems to have the same idea Carter has—outrun the coming of the day—then that star too is gone, and the road stretches out in front of them, clear and hot and endless.

The towns they drive through that morning are towns the interstate never touched and so they became forgotten towns. They see the towns from miles away—low and flat, a black line beneath the rays of heat—but they drive through them in minutes. Desert towns with a wooden-cactus welcome sign, a gas station, some adobe stores with tables out front piled high with brightly colored blankets. Fast-food restaurants. A Walmart. String of mobile trailers. When you pass the last trailer, you've left town.

To Carter, there is a depressing similarity about the desert, not just the land, not just the geography, everything—the squat, one-color buildings, the straight highways, the circling birds, the cloudless horizon. People who live in the desert call it big and open, gush about vistas and horizons, but Carter figures that is an excuse people use when they don't have a choice about where they live. He thinks big and open is just allowing one thing to take over. Like an invasive species. He prefers trees and lakes and rivers that change with the seasons, horizons that go back and forth and even disappear on you some days. Living in the desert would be like living in a glass house with no curtains.

Tess was the same way. But for different reasons. It wouldn't be trees or rivers for her. It would be islands and coastlines, salt and fir.

That's what she'd miss, the reason she would never live in a desert. They'd end up feeling the same way about it, but they'd come at it from different directions. He stares down the highway. That's right. That's how it works.

═══

THEY DID THEIR first job together the week after he left Danby Island. A jewelry store at a shopping mall in Butte. Her idea. Carter may have told Ambrose Danby she'd never be part of his crew, but after Tess Danby heard about stealing diamonds by going in through the roof of a shopping mall, well—try and stop her.

Strange thing about parents giving advice. Kids usually only hear what they want to hear.

She could have done any job in the crew—even been the driver, she was that good behind a steering wheel—but the natural job for her was scout. Tess Danby could walk into any jewelry store and practically be given the combination to the safe and the blueprints for the building. She never aroused suspicion. Was never once doubted, when she asked a clerk if she could see something a little bit more, what's the right word—at this stage of the grift she would bite her lips and look mischievous; she was, after all, shopping with Daddy's money—a little "classier."

Tess Danby cut in half the time needed inside a jewelry store. When Carter broke in later that night, he knew where the best gems were located. Knew the location of every camera. Knew the walking distance from the entry point on the roof to the first display case he would smash. If he was going to try and air-winch a safe onto the roof, she would know the model number, and whether it was bolted to the floor.

A month after he first came to Danby Island, Tess Danby turned twenty and Carter threw a party for her at the Four Seasons in Seattle. Friends of hers from the private school Ambrose had sent her to—the last one, in Portland—came, and he put them up in suites. They seemed like children to him, the girls talking through dinner about some reality show on an island, the boys drinking Southern bourbon and talking about golf. He wondered why Tess bothered with them. But she seemed glad they were there. Made sure each one met him, and some of them must have heard stories, because there were boys who had trouble holding his eyes, and girls who seemed nervous and laughed too much around him.

He never saw any of them again. Neither did Tess. Their lives were about to change, and he thinks they both knew it. There had been the time before, and now there was this time, a new time, and where it would take them—what had changed, what had been gained and lost—these were questions for another day. He thinks of that party as the before and after mark.

It was possible—he cannot recall the day it didn't happen—that he had spent every day with Tess Danby from the day they robbed that jewelry store in Blaine to the day he was shot in the woods outside San Francisco.

Obsession? He'd like to argue. But it seemed the right word.

=====

THEY DRIVE THROUGH Nevada and into Idaho, the land around them changed again, no longer desert but foothills running in a blunt line to mountain ranges tall enough to have peaks lost in the clouds. There are trees now, hemlock and spruce, and rivers that run fast and white off the foothills. The windows of the Jeep are down, and they can hear blue jays and magpies, the burbling rush of a river they cannot see.

There is more traffic on the highway now and the towns they pass through are larger, with water towers and redbrick main streets, car dealerships and Target stores. They drive through Twin Falls—the Niagara of the West—then through Boise. In early afternoon, north of Boise, they pass a town big enough to have a community college and a strip of motels. You can see the motels from the highway. Carter passes them, takes the next exit, comes back on the highway.

He has not slept in two nights. Is halfway to where he needs to go. It is time to stop. He drives down the service road off the highway that has the motels, six of them, not far from the community college. Most of the motels are part of a chain—Red Roof, Comfort Inn, Quality Inn—but two are local. One is the last motel on the strip, a two-story rectangular box with a flat roof, no trim, fading paint and dumpsters at either end of the building, sitting there like design features. There is a neon sign missing letters—w ite pin In, and beneath that, another sign flashing the cryptic message: Voted be t Inn in Me id an. The motel looks like something that has been left beside the highway for recycling.

Carter drives past each motel, turns around and comes back. The service road is wide, with a median running down the middle. On his third pass, he turns into the circular driveway of the last motel on the strip.

<hr />

THE MOTEL CLERK is tall and lanky, in his late twenties or early thirties, ribs sticking out from underneath a too-tight Hawaiian shirt, but his pants need a belt. Has a chin so weak it seems to fade off his face. Dilated eyes and oily black hair that falls to the collar of his shirt and there pools like a garage-floor slick.

"Evenin'," he says when Carter walks into the office, at the same time hitting a button on a remote and the TV playing on a shelf behind him goes mute. The office has posters tacked to the wall: a mountain lake in fall foliage, a hunting lodge near Twin Falls. There are flowerless plants in macrame baskets, and by the cash register a wicker basket with foil-wrapped mints.

"You'll be needing a room?"

"Just for the night," says Carter.

"Well, we should have some rooms available. Let me see. Just yourself?"

"Traveling with my sister. I'll need two beds."

There is a computer next to the cash register, but the clerk doesn't use it. He opens a leather-bound ledger and starts flipping pages. "We have a breakfast special going with the truck stop up the highway. Sixty-five dollars for the night and you get any two meals from their breakfast menu. If you're heading west, lot of people like that deal."

"I'm good."

"Forty-nine dollars then."

The clerk stares outside. The front windshield of the Jeep is refracting the midafternoon sun, but the girl can be seen well enough.

"How old is your sister?"

Carter turns and looks at the Jeep. "Why do you ask?"

"We have coupons. . . . There's a petting zoo, next to the truck stop . . . if you're heading west, lot of people like the coupons."

"I don't need any coupons."

"No, I guess not. Your sister looks a little old for a petting zoo."

He smiles at Carter. Takes a pair of glasses from his shirt pocket and looks at the ledger. "Just the one night?"

Carter doesn't answer, and the clerk says, "Right, you already told me that. Two beds." A bony finger moves down the page. "Looks like I can put you up in room twelve. That's a corner unit, so it's a bit bigger, and you got windows on two sides. No extra charge. How would you like to pay?"

Carter turns away from the clerk one more time, to look outside. There is traffic on the highway, but it is moving fast. There are no houses nearby. There is a gas station next to the motel, but the next building after that is a quarter mile. On the way in, he counted four cars in the parking lot.

"You're not very busy today."

"Come back at high season," says the clerk. "You'd be lucky to get a room this time of day, I tell you."

"Does someone man the desk all night?"

"I live here."

"In back?"

A curtain hangs from a doorway next to the television. Not quite closed, it shows a littered kitchen table, a distant sink.

"That's right. Emergencies only after midnight. Don't come knocking on my door looking for ice."

He laughs. It sounds like it is going to be a big laugh, but when Carter doesn't join in, it becomes a short laugh. "The ice machine works," he says quietly. "Don't need to worry about that. How would you like to pay?"

"Cash."

"We ask for a security deposit when someone's paying cash. Do you have a credit card I can run through?"

"No," says Carter, and he puts five twenties on the counter. "Will this cover it?"

The clerk looks at the bills a second, then scoops them up and opens his till without ringing through a transaction. "I'll have you sign in, sir," he says, and turns the ledger around, takes a pen from his shirt pocket, places it atop the page. "It's the room at the far end, bottom floor. You can park right out front. Without a security deposit I can't turn the phones on for long distance. You probably have a cell, anyway, right? No one uses the room phones anymore."

He holds out the key and takes a quick look at the ledger. Gives Carter one last smile and says, "You and your sister have a good night, Mr. Danby."

THE ROOM HAS the smell of a motel room that hasn't been rented in a long time: trapped air and moldy carpeting, moist heat and dank water. There are juice glasses atop an apartment-sized fridge with paper lid-covers coated in dust. The television has a UHF cable taped to the wall and the two beds have mattresses so badly sunken they look bowed. There is a wooden nightstand between the beds and a rotary-dial phone atop the stand. Tourism brochures for Twin Falls and a nature preserve called Craters of the Moon are stacked next to the phone.

Carter puts down the duffel and takes off his jacket. He starts to unbutton his shirt and when he is done, he hangs it carefully over the back of the one chair in the room. A metal desk chair without the desk. He hangs his jacket over the shirt. The gauze around his chest has turned a tallow color.

"I should change that dressing," the girl says.

"All right," he says and sits on the bed. She takes a cloth bag from her suitcase and heats a washcloth in the sink. She pulls out six strips of bark, looks at what is left and wishes she had brought more. Cedar may not be easy to find anymore. She doesn't know. She closes the bag, gets the washcloth and begins peeling off the tape holding the gauze. She works slowly, quarter inch by quarter inch, stopping whenever there is too much resistance, rubs again with the cloth.

When the dressing is off, she heats the cloth again and cleans the wound. It has started to close, new skin growing along the black ridge of burned flesh. The new skin looks white and fragile. Ringing the hole the way it does, it looks to the girl like a skiff of ice on the shore-line of a lake.

"Looks like it's healing all right."

"It feels better. Cedar, is that what you're using?"

"It's a wonder tree."

She takes out the roll of gauze and tape that had been in a first aid kit in the Jeep and begins redressing the wound. After a time, Carter asks, "What is it you want to ask me?"

"Why do you think I want to ask you something?"

"Because you bite your lip when you want to ask a question. If you haven't asked it yet, you bite your lip."

"I didn't know that."

"I suspect it's not just about asking questions. I think you do it when you're impatient. . . . Haven't spent enough time with you to know for sure."

The girl doesn't answer. Carter continues. "You want to ask me a question about the ranch, about what I needed to do back there?"

"That how you see it?"

"That's how it was. Do you know what Huey would have done to you? Ruby wouldn't have been able to stop him. She wouldn't have even tried. . . . Billy would have been worse. He would have found you too. Closest cabin to where I'd been shot? He would have gone looking, and he would have found you."

"What am I supposed to do, thank you for what you done?"

"Yes."

"How can killing someone be the right thing to do? . . . Tell me how that works."

"I don't need to tell you what you already know. You just need to accept it."

The girl finishes her work in silence. She has proper pins now and can pull the gauze tight across his chest. When she is done she says, "That gun trick you did back there . . . it ain't the first time you've done that, is it?"

"You want a number?"

". . . Works like a magic trick, don't it? You trick people into looking the wrong way. . . . He should have been looking at you, not the gun . . . and the way you were moving that gun around in your hands before you put it on the table . . . you were doing that on purpose, weren't you? Like hypnotizing him."

"Why do you want to know?"

"I'm not sure . . . just so I know."

Carter gives her a strange look. "I wouldn't call it a trick."

"What would you call it, then?"

"Human nature . . . people are used to looking at the wrong thing, it's no trick getting them to do it one more time. Maybe I hurry people along a bit. That's all I do."

The girl doesn't ask any more questions. She packs the gauze and tape back into the first aid kit, returns the washcloth to the bathroom and lies down. Carter has closed the drapes in the room and is already lying on a bed.

She turns her back to him, her eyes focused on the front door and the framed piece of paper next to the light switch. It has seasonal rates and shows an evacuation route in the event of an emergency. It doesn't say what kind of emergency. There is a dot-dot arrow showing a path from the front door of their ground-floor room to a "rescue pick-up site," which is the neon sign missing half its letters.

The girl wonders if it's an intentional joke, or something that just happened.

18

THE DANBY CASE was finished.

I didn't need to hear the plan Tess Danby had to rob her father. She had already confessed enough crime to put her away for years; certainly she had said enough to make any plea deal dangled by Hart look too good to pass up. That *would be* too good to pass up.

The case was finished. I just needed to tell Gardner and Hart the news.

But I listened anyway. It was a good plan, thorough, inventive, some of the pieces coming together on a balance-of-probability argument I had no trouble accepting. It was a little bit *too good*, and she blushed when I asked how long she'd been planning to rob her father.

"Why do you ask?"

"You came up with this plan in a week?"

"Did I say that?" And she laughed, blushed again. I wondered if blushing was the sort of thing you could control, could turn off and on. It didn't seem likely, but it was convenient, being able to blush like that.

"You said what happened to your husband is the reason you're doing this. From what you've told me, that happened ten days ago. The stuff we're going to need to pull this off—you just *happened* to have it lying around?"

"It was Henry's stuff. Well . . . not the money. That was ours. Pretty much the end of our stash, but it needs to be enough money to make my dad move right away."

"When were you planning on using this stuff?"

"Ask Henry. It was part of his useful-things collection. Henry used to say everything that was truly useful in this world, if you were smart about it, if you thought about it long enough, you should be able to get it into a shoebox. Some of the things Henry had in his box . . . well . . . you needed to know Henry."

Pelicans and gulls were following a fishing boat making its way down the east-arm channel of the island, heading toward Cape Rage. You could just make out the cape, sitting at the far end of the channel, rising from the sea like a string of marble columns. The setting sun sent shafts of light down the channel that lit up the cape and backlit the birds so that they lost distinction, even the pelicans, no longer casting dinosaur-winged shadows over the water, but glinting like gemstones, like something hard and bloodless; that didn't look like animals anymore.

"You only saw your dad's hidey-hole that one time?" I asked.

"My sixteenth birthday."

"Describe it."

"A big room. Twenty by twenty, maybe. All sorts of shelving down there, cargo bins, old wooden chests. I didn't see it all. We stood on the stairs."

"I thought you saw gold bars."

"He went and brought them to me. He was cradling them. He was drunk and they kept falling out of his hands."

"He kept you on the stairs?"

"Yeah. I'm surprised I got that far. I didn't even know about the door until that night."

The Danby family fortune was kept in the basement of the main house, in a sealed room with only one entrance that was hidden in the back of a closet in Ambrose's study. The room was built shortly after the Danbys bought the island, in the '30s, and kept under lock and key for decades, although fifteen years ago—she was guessing it was around then—her dad hired a security company in Blaine to put in an electronic security system. It came with a steel door and a keypad.

The company wanted to put in cameras too, but Ambrose wouldn't let them. Not in his study. The technician who did the job argued with him about it but stopped when Ambrose said if a steel door and electronic lock wasn't enough security, the technician should look for an honest way to make a living.

The technician disappeared the day after the job was finished. He was never found. The security company's invoice was paid upon receipt.

"That's the only way in?" I asked. "You can't get into the basement another way? It'd be easier if you didn't have to go through your dad."

"The walls are stone. There shouldn't even be a basement in this house, or anywhere on the island. It's built right into the bedrock. The railway company dynamited the hole. Maybe they left some around. You might get in that way."

The fishing boat was almost at Cape Rage, about to disappear, more birds now, no longer diving in sequence, somehow knowing they were entering the final stretch and time was limited. They looked like birds again. Nothing I saw off these cliffs ever stayed the way it was for long.

"Run it down for me one more time," I said.

As she explained her plan a second time, I tried to imagine what it would have been like growing up on this island. How could Tess

Danby have become anything *but* a criminal? That didn't make her innocent. There's free will in this world. In my line of work, you need to believe that, believe that the people you're betraying have made conscious, legally culpable decisions and deserve every badass thing about to happen to them. If you didn't believe in free will, I don't know how you could do this job.

But it was easy to feel sorry for Tess Danby, for what had happened to her and the way she was now trapped. But that was another thing I needed to resist, seeing her as a helpless victim, the way Dirty-'30s molls were portrayed back in the day, as girls who fell in love with the wrong men and ended up riding shotgun with Pretty Boy Floyd, or John Dillinger, or Clyde Barrow.

That story was never right. Bonnie Parker, Ma Barker—they weren't women who hooked up with the wrong men. They were women who'd been *raised* with the wrong men. They'd kept six when the boys started doing break-and-enters at the back of the five-and-dime; drove flatbed trucks up switchback roads to moonshine stills, to help with the packing and distribution. They weren't victims. They were just who they were meant to be.

So how should I feel about this criminal who had just confessed, and that I would be arresting soon? It's a question that gets asked every case. Sometimes I get a quick answer. Sometimes I don't. Tess Danby was taking some time.

She had taken a notebook from her pocket and was drawing a map. "This is so you can find the spot," she said. "Don't hang on to it."

Although I know of no better way to do it, it was still odd, seemed slightly absurd, to watch Ambrose Danby's daughter drawing a map with a large X to mark where the money would be found. A pirate's daughter, drawing an X-marks-the-treasure map.

"This is setting someone up for a big fall," I said, as I watched her work.

"You can't just *find the money*, Danny," she said. "My dad would never believe that. Someone stealing it from him, he'll believe that story."

"How did you get the passport?" I asked.

"Henry's shoebox. He has passport blanks in there. I found the photo online. It's a mug shot from six years ago. Mug shots look just like passport photos. Lot of them look better."

"The guy we're setting up—I'm sleeping in his room, right? It's Billy somebody."

"Billy Walker. But we're not setting him up. I just told you that."

"Your dad thinks he's coming back."

"Billy should have been back days ago. Something's about to blow on this island and Billy must have figured it out. He's run." She showed me the map she'd drawn. "This is where you're going to say you found the bag. You should have a look at the place before you go see my dad. He'll ask you questions about it."

I looked at the map. The trail I walked down every morning had been drawn almost to scale. The X she had drawn looked to be about fifty feet off the trail, midway from the cliff to the main house.

"There's already a hole there?" I asked.

"Been a hidey-hole there for a long time. Finn and I found it when we were kids. Say you found it while you were walking back." She started to fold the paper. "You should show the money to Jean and the other men before bringing it to my dad . . . to protect yourself."

Just as Tess Danby could surprise me sometimes by acting young, she could do the same trick going the other way. She had learned a thing or two about people, and how they would react in certain situations. I knew what she meant when she said I should see the giant before I saw her father. They needed some skin in the game we were about to play.

"All right," I said, and didn't say anything else because we were done, and it didn't matter. I was never going to see her father. Never going to go ahead with her plan. I just needed to contact Gardner and Hart and wait for my ride home.

She had confessed, and the Danby case was finished. When I put her carefully folded paper into my shirt pocket, I was putting away a piece of courtroom evidence.

That's what I was thinking as I watched her walk down the trail that would bring her back to her cottage. My only thought. She never looked back. Was well down the trail, nearing the turn that would send her over a knoll and out of view and I was wondering how quickly Gardner and his team could land on the island, was already tapping my phone, getting ready to phone him, when another thought finally entered my head.

Why safe deposit boxes?

19

FORTY-FIVE MINUTES LATER I had finished giving Frank Gardner my sit-rep, and he had given me new orders. I asked him to repeat them.

"Go ahead with the robbery, Barrett."

"Why? She's just confessed. She witnessed the murder of Henry Carter. She was part of the robbery in San Francisco. You can pick her up today."

"A good defense lawyer will say that you coerced her, or you bullied her. It's not on tape, is it?"

"Doesn't have to be. You can get me recognized as an expert witness by the judge. Been that way for years. Last trial, there wasn't even a defense motion to have me excluded."

"I've seen your file, Barrett. I already know this."

"Then why aren't you coming over here to arrest Tess Danby?"

Gardner didn't answer right away, and I stared out the window of my hut. For the first time since I had been on the West Coast, I was looking at clouds. Not many, and not close, high stratus clouds that looked like trails of camp smoke. But they were drifting over Cape Rage and it was early enough in the day to shade the sun from time to time.

"She's a Danby, Barrett. Five minutes with a lawyer, five minutes with her *father*, and she'll be telling everyone a different story. I don't trust her. Our lawyers don't trust her. *You* shouldn't trust her."

"You can turn her in five minutes," I answered. "She wants off this island. She has *good reason* to want off this island. You know what will happen to her if we get caught?"

"So . . . don't get caught."

"Why are you taking this risk? What aren't you telling me?"

There was a long silence. Long enough for my heart to break a little, the way a casino loser's heart gets broken when he decides to give it one more try, only to walk out of the casino the next morning with his head down, muttering, "Yeah, that's what I thought."

Why is it always muddy? Why do people running undercover operations always think the job requires more secrets than what are needed? Why do operational commanders hate straight lines, clear days, and only think a job is well done if someone gets played?

The work attracts a certain personality type. Best answer I've come up with so far.

"There's operational security around this investigation, Barrett," Gardner finally said. "Thought you would have known that."

I wasn't buying it. "Why did the Danbys go after the safe deposit boxes?"

"Who the fuck knows? Who the fuck cares?"

"I'm betting you know."

Another silence. Longer this time. When Gardner's voice came back it was flat and pinched, like every word was being pulled through his teeth. "Nothing that affects your *operational safety* is being held back. Your job remains *exactly* as described in our meeting, *Barrett.*

Find what the Danbys stole in San Francisco, notify us when you have it, and we'll come rolling over there with the warrants. Sounds to me like you're getting cold feet."

"Just asking questions."

"Not good ones."

"Never thought there were bad ones."

He went silent again. When it dragged on a while, I knew what was coming. Frank Gardner would stonewall and flat out ignore me until I hit him with something he couldn't control. Three times he had been given an opportunity to provide a logical reason for not arresting Tess Danby, and three times he'd whiffed.

It was time to get serious.

"I need to know why the Danbys hit the safe deposit boxes and not the vault. I'm getting an answer or I'm bugging out of here."

"You're *what*?" screamed Gardner.

"You heard me."

"How do you think you're buggin' out of there? You're on a fuckin' island."

"Thinking of taking a boat."

"What the fuck . . . are you serious?"

"I'm tired of being played, so yeah, I'm serious. If you need to talk to Hart, go find him. I'm off this island today if I don't get told what's really going on here."

He didn't say anything. The silence went on a long time and once or twice I almost asked, "Are you still there?" but that's the last thing you want to say when you're pretending you don't care about something one way or the other. Finally, Gardner said, "Give me a minute," and then there was a loud click on the phone. After that came some barely audible white noise, some mechanical beeping, and a minute later I heard Jason Hart say, "Barrett?"

"I'm here."

"Frank's just given me your sit-rep. He tells me there's a problem."

"Don't know yet. I do know it's time you told me what that bank robbery in San Francisco was all about."

"What are you referring to?"

"Could be referring to a few things. Let's start with me referring to why you're not over here arresting Tess Danby."

"Our lawyers—"

"Don't . . . don't say it again."

". . . You know, Barrett, everyone had misgivings about bringing you into this case. I'm the one who put in the requisition. I'm the one who stood up for you."

"Don't recall asking you to do that."

"Why are you pushing this? You've been told everything you need to know to complete your assignment. Those safety deposit boxes— it's bullshit. You should thank me for not telling you about those boxes. I was doing you a kindness."

"Don't recall asking for that either."

"Fuck Barrett, it's politics. Nothing but bullshit politics. You should trust me."

"Bit hard to do that at the moment."

Hart gave a long, sad-sounding sigh. I imagined him sitting behind the desk with the brightly colored file folders, his head down and his fingers running their way through the long blond hair.

"All right . . . all right . . . you win. Some of the people who had boxes at that bank—you wouldn't believe the names, Barrett. You really wouldn't—some of these people have contacted my superiors and my superiors have made it abundantly clear to me, and to Frank, that those boxes need to be in our possession before any arrests are made. They cannot be left unfound."

"*Unfound?*"

"*Unfound,*" he repeated.

"I don't believe this. Why wasn't I told?"

"Why should you be? It's a distraction that doesn't affect your assignment in any operational way. Come on, Barrett, you know what we'll find in those boxes. Some guy's got photos of his buddy in a bikini. Some rich wife shot a porn film once. It's background noise, political fuckin' bullshit. We're here for the bad guys. Nothing else."

He said it like he was being heroic, keeping secrets from his agent in the field. "Why did the Danbys want the boxes and not the vault?" I asked.

"Probably more money in the boxes. A bank like that—main branch in San Francisco—there could have been a lot more. One bearer bond could have blown away whatever was in the vault."

"That's what the Danbys were after . . . bearer bonds?"

"No idea . . . look, Barrett, I'm sorry for not telling you about the boxes, but honestly, I didn't think it made a difference. I *still* don't. Your assignment remains exactly as described—locate what the Danbys stole in San Francisco, let us know, and you're done here."

"That's why you want Tess Danby to go through with the robbery."

"I got to tell you, Barrett . . . it's a gift. Why don't you keep things simple? Go ahead with the robbery. It's the quickest way to end this case."

The broken hearted feeling came back. Whenever someone tells me to keep things simple, I'm sure of two things. One, I'm in trouble. I don't need to debate that, don't need to look around to see where I'm standing. Keeping things simple is never a suggestion that gets made when things are going well.

The second thing I know is that I'm being played. Someone has decided the complete, complicated story is too much for me; I can't handle it, or I don't need it, and it's best for everyone, including me, a kindness, as Hart put it, that I be treated like a mushroom.

I didn't know yet what that story was—Hart wasn't telling me—but Tess Danby was right. Something was rippling in this case. And the ripple seemed to start with Henry Carter.

20

WITH THE WOOL drapes closed it is cool and dark inside the motel room and Henry Carter and the girl are asleep within minutes. The girl dreams again of her father, but no longer driving, living with him in the cabin in Northern California. Her father teaching her how to hunt, how to dress what you kill, how to build a stand using trees you find near a deer path. He wasn't drinking for a few years in that cabin, and it is a happy dream.

Then it becomes a different dream; alone in that cabin, waiting for him to come back, and when he does, he is drunk. Drunk every time now when he comes back, leering at her, and punching her when she asks if he's sold the golden root and dried fiddleheads she gave him before going into town. Both of them crying about it the next day. The first real sadness in her life. Not knowing any better until then. Loving him until then. If not for the beatings, she would have hung on until the end of time. Then her father disappears, at the same time as she disappears, and her dream becomes an abyss without narrative or sequence.

Carter's dreams are just as fitful. Images of Tess Danby flashing in his head like a video on slow fast-forward. Tess sitting at a blackjack table in Las Vegas. Tess peering through a jewelry case, her blue eyes misty and dreamlike through the glass. Tess gunning a cherry-red cigar boat through the Georgia Strait, the boat turning as smoothly and effortlessly around the islands as the tide. Tess standing in front of her cottage on Danby Island, laughing and saying she would never live anyplace else. "Never been a cop here, Henry. Where am I ever going to find another place like this?"

Then the lights of Dallas as seen from the cabin of a Lear 70. Dozens of black-velvet jewelry boards shoved into an Adidas gym bag. Tess Danby's body in black lace. The images keep rolling, faster and faster, until it seems they're going to roll out of focus and then suddenly they stop.

He is still on Danby Island but no longer standing with Tess Danby. Ambrose is now in his dream, standing beside him where Tess had been. In front of her cottage, looking out on the strait. His long black hair is blowing out, so much hair it looks like streams of smoke coming from his head. There is sheet lightning in the distance. The sound of a foghorn.

Neither of them moves and it is such a change of pace from the quick-cut dreams Carter had been having that he is struck with vertigo. He starts to wobble, and Ambrose says, "I'm doing a job in San Francisco, Henry. I could use some help."

Still wobbling and the sheet lightning is closer now. The foghorn is closer too. Suddenly, the lightning turns red and begins to spin. The foghorn changes too, becomes high pitched and tremulous. Carter's eyes snap open.

There is light bleeding through the drapes in the motel room. A darkish, two-tone light. In the distance is the fading echo of a siren.

He sits up. The girl is already sitting. They listen to a car door open and shut. Footsteps make their way to the door, slow-moving, leisurely footsteps. When the knock comes, Carter is already on his feet, buttoning his shirt, motioning for the girl to stay seated.

CARTER DOESN'T BOTHER peering through the drapes or through the peephole in the motel room door. Doesn't open the door slowly either, but swings it wide, and the cop standing the other side looks surprised, looks almost comical, his right hand raised, getting ready to knock on a door that has disappeared on him.

He is a fat cop. The third button on his blue shirt is almost popped, the shirt is stretched so tight. On the left pocket of the shirt is some municipal crest, and beneath the crest the word "sheriff," all in capital letters. On his hips are a can of mace, a set of good-quality handcuffs and a Sig Sauer 226 in leather holster.

"Evenin'," he says.

Carter doesn't answer. He rises on his toes to look over the cop's head at his patrol car. The warning lights have been turned off, but the headlights are still on. Carter needs to shield his eyes to see the car. There is no one sitting there.

"Sorry to bother you," the cop continues. "We're searching for some inmates that broke out of the state prison farm earlier today. That's about ten miles from here. We've been keeping an eye on the motels in the area, and . . ."

"Why?"

"Why?" says the cop, and again he looks surprised. "Well . . . to catch the bastards, of course."

"You think they'd want to check into a motel ten miles from the prison?" asks Carter.

The cop closes his mouth, and the sorry-to-bother-you good humor drains from his eyes. "I'll need to see some ID, sir. You and anyone else you have in the room. There *is* someone else in the room with you, isn't there?"

Carter doesn't think the cop will be so obvious as to smile after he says that, but he does. A dopey, got-you smile, which spreads across his face like a teenage blush.

"Why don't you come in and I'll get my ID," he says.

"That sounds like a good idea."

The cop walks into the room and Carter closes the door behind him.

"How you doin' this evenin'?" the cop says to the girl sitting on the bed, but she doesn't answer. "I was just saying there's been a prison break not far from here. Nothin' to worry about. The state farm ain't no max pen, no one's going to come and bother you."

The cop laughs at something he has found funny. "Yeah, no one's goin' to come and bother you . . . but we're checkin' the motels along the highway, just to be sure. This won't take long. How you doin' tonight?"

The girl's gaze drifts over his face, but she doesn't answer.

". . . Where you comin' from?"

"East," says Carter. "We live near Chicago."

"And you're headin'?"

"Los Angeles."

"Well, that don't surprise me. This here girl's pretty enough to be in the movies. . . . Cat got your tongue, miss?"

"Sorry," she says.

"I asked how you were doin' tonight. Asked you a couple times. You still ain't answered."

"I'm doin' fine."

"There you go. Everyone's doin' fine. It's a fine night. Well, if I can just see some ID for you and your sister, sir, I'll be on my way."

The cop has taken off his hat. Put it on the nightstand. Stands with his knees bent and his legs slack, arms by his side, the casual posture of someone who isn't leaving a room anytime soon.

"How did you know she's my sister?" asks Carter.

"Gosh, she *better* be your sister. How old is this girl?" he says, and then the cop laughs a dirty little laugh. "Just kidding. Just kidding . . . the desk clerk told me. We asked the motels to contact us if anyone checked in today. Johnny phoned right after you got here. I've been busy, so I couldn't make it out till now."

"Until it was dark."

"Yeah, that's how it worked out. I need to see government ID, by the way. Driver's license. Birth certificate. Is your sister old enough to have government ID?"

"That would be a problem, wouldn't it?"

"Sorry?"

"If she didn't have government ID. That would be a problem. You'd need to make some phone calls, to verify her identity. Phone my home, probably. Just doing your job. . . . You normally say that, right?"

"Mr. Danby, we seem to be getting a little off topic here. I just need . . ."

"To see my ID."

"That's right . . . your sister's too."

"I have it in my jacket. I'll get it."

"You don't carry your own ID, miss?" The cop's posture has become even more casual, almost insolent, his shoulders slouching forward, his fat tongue licking his lips. He gives his groin a scratch and adjusts his pants. "Just how old *are* you?"

He keeps staring at the girl, his back turned to Carter, so it is a few seconds before he sees what Carter has taken from the breast pocket of his jacket; has to pull himself away from the girl, remind himself where he is in his grift, not quite there yet, turning around and saying, "I'll take those. . . ."

And then he stops. Stares at the handgun in Carter's hand. It is aimed at the third-from-the-top, almost-popped button on his shirt.

"What the fuck are you doing?"

"Showing you my ID."

21

AFTER MY CONVERSATION with Gardner and Hart I sat in my hut, thinking about what I'd just been told. I was becoming fond of my hut. What seemed like a penance only days ago now seemed a refuge, the perfect place to think—a hut on the edge of a cliff on the edge of the continent.

From where I sat the horizon was an unwavering line and every color had born witness to the physical world; been worn down a little, bled out a bit. There were no bright colors or anything false around me; any sound was muted from having traveled a great distance upon the wind. If the mindfulness industry could find a way to package and ship my hut, fortunes could be made.

I was thinking of the explanation I had been given for stealing those safe deposit boxes—best friends in bikinis, bearer bonds—having a hard time buying it. Ambrose Danby would always prefer bundles of American cash to bearer bonds. He kept the family fortune in a basement. Might as well have buried it. He'd have as much interest in bearer bonds as he had in hip-hop.

So, why steal the safe deposit boxes? The only one who knew was Ambrose. Or maybe Henry Carter. Brought on because of the boxes, killed right after the boxes were stolen. He might have known something.

Think it through—Henry Carter had gone to San Francisco because he was good at robbing safe deposit boxes. That made sense. He never came back. That made no sense. Nothing I'd been told about his killing made any sense. He'd stolen something from Ambrose Danby, and maybe that was the reason he'd been killed. But why would Ambrose kill a thief and not get back what had been stolen?

And what *did* Henry Carter steal? These were questions I'd been asking for days now and getting nowhere with them. I wished now I could have seen Carter's criminal file. It hadn't been one of the files Hart sent to Detroit. He'd only sent files for Tess, Finn and Ambrose Danby, explaining Carter was dead and no longer a factor in the case. The explanation made sense at the time. Did it now?

Although there was no file on him, Carter was part of the file on Tess Danby, an addendum put in after she was married: Henry Carter, person of interest in scores of unsolved robberies in the Northwest; as well as three homicides in Clayton County, all of them related to a feud the Carters had with another bootlegging family that went back generations, had died down but flared up again at the start of the millennium. Someone must have been feeling nostalgic.

The Carter-Kaminski War—or the Snow Corners War, as it was referenced a couple of places in the addendum—sounded brutal. Twenty-three people killed in eight years, eleven in the winter of '08 alone, when things got so bad around Snow Corners the town was shut down for a week by the state police, every road barricaded, dogs on the river, helicopters in the air and cops going door to door looking for illegal guns.

Henry Carter was twenty years old that winter and a Carter the cops were hoping to find when they shut down the town. Person of interest in three homicides, as well as car bombings that had destroyed a Kaminski trucking yard, a Kaminski meth lab and the Kabasha Goodwill Center, which the Kaminskis more or less ran.

But they couldn't find him. Not for six years, until he was picked up in Seattle a few hours after the cashier cages at Lumen Field were robbed during a Seahawks playoff game. When his name was put into the computer by the traffic cop who pulled him over doing six miles per hour over the posted speed limit—*that kind of a traffic cop*—he must have thought a slot machine had hit.

The cop didn't know what to do and basically hid in his car until a tactical team showed up. Carter was smart and never tried to take off or resist arrest. Maybe he already knew how it was going to play out. One of the top criminal lawyers in Seattle was waiting in the lobby of the police detachment when Carter was brought in. The cops held him for five days and the lawyer was there, or another named partner in his firm was there, for every minute of it.

The lawyers seemed to know the evidence against Carter better than the cops did, and after five days, the district attorney told the cops to release him. They didn't have a case. Not for anything that happened in the Snow Corners War. Not for the cashiers' cages at Lumen Field. Only thing they had him for—and they had him dead to rights on this one—was six miles over the posted speed limit.

It seemed the cops didn't even know where Carter was after that until he showed up in Cape Rage one day with Tess Danby. When they were married four years later and the addendum was added to her file, an FBI agent with a sense of humor had added, in a handwritten margin note: "Check wedding ring against stolen-goods flyers."

How did Ambrose get the jump on someone like Henry Carter? I sat in my hut on the edge of a cliff on the edge of the continent thinking about it, but never came up with a good answer. Never came up with a good reason to disobey Jason Hart either. He wasn't being completely truthful with me, but what's that great line in *Apocalypse*

Now?—"Like handing out speeding tickets at the Indy 500." That's what it would have been like, walking away from this case with that being my reason. A less-than-truthful FBI agent.

Also, what Hart was telling me made sense. The quickest way to end this case was to deliver Tess Danby to him. She had a good plan. It was time to start it.

———

THERE WERE TWO rooms in the bunkhouse that had been converted into a common room, the adjoining wall ripped out, couches, fridge and large-screen television put in. It was where men played cards and drank in the evening. I walked in after my shift that day and Skipjack, the giant and the two cousins were there, watching a college basketball game.

"Found this on my way back here," I said, putting a dirty gym bag on a table by the door. "It was buried in some sort of a hidey-hole, 'bout fifty feet off the trail."

The men turned away from the television to look at me. Then at the bag.

"Buried?" said the giant.

"Yeah."

All four men stood and walked to the table. The giant unzipped the bag and looked inside.

"Holy fuck."

"Yeah," I answered.

They stood there a few seconds and then the giant lifted the bag and turned it upside down. Bundles of cash fell onto the table. Along with a passport and a Sig Sauer handgun. When the giant stopped shaking the bag, there were seventeen bundles on the table. "Holy fuck," he said one more time.

Skipjack picked up the passport, opened it and laughed. He showed it to the other men.

"Fuckin' Billy," said one of the cousins, shaking his head.

No one said anything for a while. "If the bank wrappers are right, that's a hundred and seventy grand," said the giant.

"They ain't been ripped," said Skipjack, picking up one of the bundles. "Wrappers look good, Jean."

"Fuckin' Billy," said the other cousin.

"That's the guy whose room I'm in, isn't it?" I said.

"Yeah."

"The one that never came back."

"Yeah," and the giant scratched his chin.

Seeing this, Skipjack rubbed his chin. They rubbed for about a minute and then Skipjack asked, "Why wouldn't he come back, if he had this stashed?"

"Maybe he had more," said the giant. "Billy could have hidey-holes all over this island. He's been here long enough."

"Did you know he was skimming?"

"No," said the giant. "But Billy'd be the kind of guy to skim. Could be some of our money there."

"Holy fuck," said the two cousins in unison.

There was more silence.

"I guess I should bring it to Ambrose," I said. "His island—it belongs to him, right?"

As Tess Danby predicted, this turned out to be a difficult question to answer. One that seemed to stump the men around the table, as they scratched their heads, looked at each other, shuffled their feet, settled in to give it some serious thought.

"You *could* do that," said the giant.

"You *could*," agreed Skipjack.

"Although it's Billy's money . . . and Billy ain't here."

"Billy ain't here," repeated Skipjack, while the cousins rocked their heads back and forth in gentle contemplation of what had been said. Billy wasn't here. This was true.

"Don't know if you should be giving Billy's money to Ambrose," said the giant, more certainty in his voice now. "The old man sure don't need any more money. And we haven't had an outside job in a long time."

"Weren't even asked to go to San Francisco," complained Skipjack, who was also speaking with more confidence. "The good jobs get kept as a family affair these days. You're right, Jean—the Danbys sure don't need any more money."

I listened as the four men repeated and strengthened their argument: it might not be a skim, might have been Billy tucking away part of his freelance work, a saver that boy was, and sure, that might seem surprising, given how Billy plowed through money after most jobs, buying clothes he never got much of a chance to wear on Danby Island, sending money to an ex-wife, buying cases of forty-year-old single malt scotch and passing around the bottles.

But how well do you truly know a person? And Billy had been thieving with Ambrose a long time. One hundred and seventy grand—sure, he could have saved that for a rainy day. Billy never seemed to care much about rainy days, but he was smart, Billy was, and this just showed you how smart—keeping a thing like that a secret. Maybe they'd ask him questions about it when he came back, but that wouldn't be easy, because Billy wasn't coming back. Maybe that had been debatable a few minutes ago, but the four men seemed certain of that fact now.

Billy wasn't coming back.

So, what to do with his money? Money that was so unimportant to Billy that he left it behind. He must have had a lot more stashed somewhere else, a saver like Billy, to not care about this money, to leave it behind the way he did. Maybe . . . and within a few minutes, this didn't seem as crazy an idea as it first seemed—Billy had left the money behind so his friends could find it. Maybe that had been his plan all along. It would be just the sort of thing scotch-bottle-giving Billy would do.

I listened, making sure no one moved in behind me, making sure the money stayed on the table next to the bag. Listened until the argument for keeping the money was as polished and refined as it was ever going to be, until the men started repeating themselves and it dawned on them that they were repeating themselves. Then they turned to me with happy, expectant faces.

When that happened, I started returning the money to the bag. I didn't speak while I did it, and because I didn't speak, they didn't do anything. Unsure what I was doing. Still with gleeful, be-my-buddy smiles on their faces. When the money and passport were back in the bag, I zipped it closed.

"Still think I should give it to Ambrose," I said. "It's his island."

I left the room so quickly the four men didn't have time to move, let alone change the expressions on their faces. They stood huddled together with those dopey, happy smiles, although I'm sure in a few seconds those smiles disappeared. Just as I'm sure a few seconds after that—when it occurred to each man, in his own time, what they had done; conspired in front of the new guy to pocket money found on Ambrose Danby's island—their expressions would have been as different from expectant and happy as an expression can become.

22

AMBROSE LOOKED AT the gym bag and motioned for me to put it on the table. He sat in the dining room, a rocks glass of CC in front of him.

"Where did you find it?"

"On the path to the hut . . . little off it, 'bout fifty feet. It was buried, had a false lid on it, covered with turf."

"What were you doing off the path?"

"I saw it."

"How'd you see it? Thought you said it was covered?"

"It was, but the grass wasn't right."

"What the fuck does that mean?"

"The hole was covered with a lid that had turf on it. Perfect grass. How much perfect grass you got on this island?"

"You got good eyes."

"I do."

"You looked inside?"

"Yes."

"Put it on the table."

I took the bag, unlatched it and turned it upside down. Ambrose leaned over and grabbed one of the bundles of money. He flipped the edges of the bills, then threw the stack in the air a few times. He looked back at the piles of money and, using his finger, counted them.

"That's a hundred and sixty thousand." He stared at me until it became more than awkward, became combative, a game that would have winners and losers.

"I didn't think it would be the smart play," I said.

"You considered it?"

"Like you said—a hundred and sixty thousand."

"So why didn't you hang on to it?"

"Your island, your boats. How would it work? I also don't know if the guy in the passport is coming back. He's the guy whose room I'm in, isn't he?"

Ambrose reached for the passport and flipped it open. He stared at the photo and his knuckles turned pinch white. He looked like he wanted to rip the passport in half. He could have.

"Yeah, you're in his room. Billy Walker. He's been with me twenty years."

Staring at Ambrose Danby's face right then was like staring at a windstorm coming down a river, a bad one, just starting to take physical shape, just starting to rip off tree limbs and cut whatever it touched.

"I'd rather be kicked in the balls than be cheated," he said. "That's direct. That's something I understand. But lying to a man, sneaking around behind his back, stealing his money, betraying a man like that . . . I don't understand it."

I sat there and didn't say anything while I made a mental list of people who were, right then, betraying Ambrose Danby.

The men in the bunkhouse had all wanted that bag of money.

Whenever his back was turned, Finn looked at his father like he wanted to kill him.

His daughter wanted to rob him.

I was an undercover cop.

I wasn't sure about the kitchen staff.

"Anyone who betrays me deserves every fuckin' bad thing that's ever going to happen to 'em," Danby continued. "I'll make it my mission in life to fuck 'em up, fuck up their family. Not even a second fuckin' cousin gets a walk." When Ambrose noticed I hadn't said anything in a while, he added, "What . . . you don't think that?"

"I maybe haven't thought about it as much as you," I answered.

THE FIRST PERSON I betrayed was my brother. I set him up for a life term in the Marion Pen, no possibility of parole for thirty years. That's the sentence a crooked cop gets when he's convicted of homicide. The judge told my brother he wished it could have been more, but he was prohibited by sentencing guidelines.

I went to see my brother before the trial, to tell him I was going to be testifying. It seemed the sort of thing you should tell a brother. He was being held at a federal detention center near Dearborn and it was one of the saddest buildings I've ever been inside. Worse than a max pen, and I've been inside a few of those. A max pen might as well be a library. It's dead time and dead weight, a hushed, flatline place for people whose tragedy had come and gone.

A federal detention center is a whole different beast. Nothing has been decided yet, nothing is fixed; the mania inside the building is so thick and choking it feels like humidity on an unbearable day. A federal detention center is a crazy frontier waystation for people moving on to greater tragedies.

There were three security checks to get into the visitors' room, and at each check I was surrounded by people wailing and arguing and shouting at the guards, speaking in different languages, an old couple always on the edge of the crowd, the woman holding a paper bag with grease stains on the bottom. The bag of food was taken away at the third security station and the couple accepted the loss without complaint or murmur, never asking why they had been allowed to get so far. They looked like people accustomed to not asking questions like that.

The guard at the first station looked at my Detroit police identification, noticed I had the same last name as the detainee I was visiting—his head snapped up as soon as my brother's Corrections file appeared on his computer screen—but he didn't say anything about it. Same for the second security station, the guard there repeating the first guard's actions so perfectly it may as well have been an act they'd rehearsed. The third guard, the one who took away the falafels, said something.

"He a relation?"

"Brother."

"Really. Ummm . . . he's in the secure wing. Not sure if he's down yet. You may have to wait."

I didn't say anything. Behind the guard were large, steel-mesh-reinforced windows, the visitors' room behind the windows, a large room about the size of a basketball court, with plastic tables and chairs set up like the room was being used for a high school exam. Four rows of eight tables, each table with a plexiglass divider down the middle. There was an open area in the corner, with four tables that didn't have shields. There were children's toys around these tables. Prayer mats lined the nearest wall. The toys were the only bright color in the room and looked marooned.

I followed the guard to one of the tables. It was the last table in the first row. Furthest one from the door at the end of the room where my brother would come in, and the one nearest the guards at the security station.

"Anyone from the secure wing, I'm supposed to put here," the guard said. "Not the most private table, but those are the rules. Your brother's going to be cuffed and chained too. Did you know that?"

"No, I didn't know that."

"Yeah, even if you were his lawyer, that's the way he'd have to come in. . . . What's he here for?"

"Bad career choices."

"That's funny."

"Wasn't trying to be."

The guard looked startled. I sat down and turned my back to him. He left without saying anything else. Gossipy jail guard trying to chat up a city cop while stealing falafels from old people—I didn't have any more time for that guard.

I was feeling mean, out of sorts, starting to wish I hadn't come—my brother wasn't expecting me, no one had told me to come—and that guard was sublimation. A place to briefly unload some of my anger. I knew that. He was also the only guard who'd asked about the last name, so screw him.

Twenty minutes later, my brother walked through the door at the far end of the room. He was wearing an orange jumpsuit and his hair had grown out, ran down past his collar. My kid brother always had short hair. Some years, it was a buzz cut. It was strange to see his face framed by hair. Almost as strange as the handcuffs on his wrists, and the manacles on his ankles. A guard led him by the arm, holding it at the elbow, to the table where I sat.

My brother stood awhile before he sat down. Long enough for the guard who brought him in to stop walking toward the exit door, turn around and look at my brother, wondering if it would be a short visit. Then my brother sat down, and the guard continued walking toward the exit, shaking his head, and chuckling, it looked like.

"What are you doing here?" he asked.

"Thought I should come and see you."

"You wouldn't call that gloating?"

"I'm not gloating, Bobby."

"Don't know any other reason you'd come, big brother. You want to see what you killed, is that it?"

"I tried to stop you, Bobby. You know I did."

"Stop what?"

"Are you kidding? Stop fuckin' everything. What do you think I'm talking about?"

"You were always a Boy Scout. Guess I shouldn't be surprised."

"Not a Boy Scout, Bobby, just not a bent cop."

"You're not even a cop."

"What does that mean?"

"Think you're going back to patrol?"

I must have looked surprised because my brother laughed at me. I *would have* looked surprised because I hadn't thought about it until then.

"I'm going back to the twenty-two after the trial."

"You're a dead man if you do. They won't let you."

He glared at me, a hard look coming from a hard-looking felon, but I remembered another time, and another Bobby, when I was trying to explain why things had turned bad for him; a teenage Bobby who had just been kicked out of the house because our dad was frightened of him. Long story made short, that's what it was. Bobby full of bluster and I'll-show-him bravado until he broke down crying and I had to hold him in my arms until he calmed down, him asking the whole time why Dad had done it.

I couldn't hold him this time. Didn't look like he wanted me to try.

"If there's a problem at the twenty-two, I'll transfer out," I said.

"There's no place for you in Detroit. And I can't see any other police force wanting to touch a rat-fink bastard like you."

"Bobby . . . this isn't about me. You've got to stand up for what you've done. Some of the shit that you did for that mutt, what you did for money . . . it was way over the line, Bobby. You didn't leave anyone a choice."

"Was it Carson who told you that? Sounds like something he'd say."

"Nobody told me that, Bobby. It's how it is."

"You're telling me how it is, big brother? I think you're the one who's about to find out how it is."

I still don't want to admit Bobby had a better sit-rep than I did that day, but it's the truth. He couldn't have seen the dime my life was about to turn on after I testified against him, but no one could have seen that. But the broad brushstrokes—he had those.

"I'm going to be testifying at the trial," I said.

"I need to be there too. Guess I'll see you."

"Mom and Dad won't be coming. It would be too much for them."

"Message delivered."

"Do you need anything?"

"Yeah—for you to die before the trial starts."

We stared at each other after he said that. I don't know how long, but long enough for men to show up and kneel on the prayer mats, begin chanting before the concrete wall and two perimeter lines of barbed fencing that faced Mecca; long enough for a young boy and girl to show up and start playing with the marooned toys; long enough for the guard who brought my kid brother into the room to come walking toward us while looking at his wristwatch.

"Should I be getting protection, Bobby?"

"Don't know. Ask Carson."

"Nothing's going to change by threatening me. I'm still going to testify."

"Not expecting anything to change. Too late for that."

"Wish things had worked out different, Bobby."

"But they didn't. Don't ever come back here. There's nothing left now but the doing."

And that's what I did. I walked out of that visitors' room and out of Bobby's life, out of my own too, which was about to change so completely most days I don't recognize the beat cop who visited the Dearborn Federal Detention Center twelve years ago. He's some distant relative.

I don't feel bad knowing I will never see my brother again. I don't think he feels bad about it either. It's one of those situations where good and bad almost don't apply, where something has started, and you don't have any choice about finishing it.

Some things in life are like that. My brother understands that. I understand that. Henry Carter—although I only met him once, talked to him for no more than an hour, I've been upfront about that—he understood that.

23

THE FLASHING NEON sign in front of the motel lights up the brocade drapes every few seconds, turns the fabric from dark brown to vermillion, then back to brown. Like watching a lava lamp. Like watching skin burn.

The headlights on the patrol car were on a timer and have shut off. The only other light in the room comes from the partially opened bathroom door, a shaft of weak yellow light that the cop is standing in. His gun and cuffs are on one of the beds. There is nothing left around his waist but a belt with two extra holes punched at the end.

"Are you fuckin' insane? I'm here on a routine fuckin' call."

"No, you're not," says Carter. "You're here because you're a crooked cop trying to shake us down. Now is not the time to lie."

"What the fuck, mister . . . Mister Danby, you gotta put that gun down. There's been a misunderstanding."

"I agree. You, thinking you can prey on people unfortunate enough to have to stay in this motel; thinking you can do this with no consequence because you're a cop, because someone made you a cop—that was a misunderstanding."

The cop takes a step back. He had looked surprised when he saw the handgun, fearful, now he looks panicked.

"I really think we need to settle down here. I'm sorry if I startled you. Maybe you thought I was coming on too strong. It's just the way I am sometimes, but if you—"

"I wasn't startled. I was expecting you."

The cop takes another step back. He is standing by the bathroom now; can't back up any further.

"What the fuck are you talking about?"

"The desk clerk was too obvious. He's been popping suitcases since the day he started working here. It's his nature. You can smell a low-rent hustler. It's the same smell you get when you walk past plates of food that have been left in a hotel hallway too long. Stale, half-used, going bad—that's how your friend smells.

"When you meet a man with that smell, you start thinking of how he's going to try and hustle you. Your clerk asked too many questions about the girl. Didn't ask what I did, or where I was going. Only asked about the girl."

The cop stares around the room, at the travel brochures atop the side table, the rotary dial telephone covered in dust, the badly sunken mattresses on both beds. He has never paid much attention before to the details of these rooms.

"This is crazy . . . you're *both* crazy."

"If I hadn't been so tired, I wouldn't have stopped," continues Carter. "But I knew you'd be coming at night, and that would give me enough time to rest. I didn't know it would be a cop. Thought it would be some of the clerk's friends, waking me up and telling me what it would take to get out of this motel without my wife getting a phone call. Or the cops getting a phone call. . . . I should have thought about that."

"Mister, you're making a big mistake."

"Could be. I'm on a roll."

"I'm a *cop*. You know what's going to happen to you if you keep this up?"

"You think you're safe because you're a cop? . . . What do you usually do to the girls you trap in these rooms?"

"Mister . . ."

"Do you make videos of them? No . . . don't tell me. I already know. People like you running the world, getting to be boss over other people. . . . I should be used to it by now, but every time I get up close to one of you bastards I want to throw up."

"Mister, you don't even know me. You don't . . ."

"I know you. Quit pretending I don't know you."

Carter stops talking and motions for the cop to sit on one of the beds. It takes him a while to move, and when he does, it is like his legs weigh thousands of pounds; plodding, weight-of-the-world legs that take shorter and shorter steps the closer he comes to the bed. As he walks, Carter sweeps the travel brochures for Craters of the Moon off the nightstand and turns to the girl.

"You should gather our stuff and wait in the Jeep," he says.

The girl goes about the room putting clothes in suitcases, grabbing jackets off the tarnished metal hooks next to the light switches, makes two trips to get the bags into the Jeep, closing the door quietly when she walks out the second time.

The cop stares at the closed door for a while before saying, "I have a wife. Two young boys."

"Let's find out if that matters."

The cop turns away from the door and sees Carter moving a handgun from hand to hand. The gun travels and twirls and ends up lying broadside in the palm of one hand, then is placed carefully on the nightstand.

"That looks about halfway to me," says Carter. "What do you think?"

———

THE GIRL WATCHES Henry Carter walk out of the motel room and head to the office. Watches him walk inside, and a few seconds later she sees a flash of light through the curtained windows. After that she watches him walk back, climb into the police cruiser and drive it to the back of the motel. Then he comes back, gets in the Jeep, and they drive away.

It is a long time before either of them speaks. When Carter turns onto the highway the Jeep is one of the few vehicles traveling. They can track the headlights on the road ahead of them, watch the lights curve and follow the line of a river that cuts through the mountains. It looks like there are six cars between them and the Montana border.

"You could see a flash," the girl says finally. "Through the windows in the motel office . . . I saw a flash."

"You would have been the only one."

"I suppose . . . so the clerk . . . he's . . ."

"That's right."

"Why?"

"So we have time to get out of this town."

"Both of them?"

"That's right."

"Don't that bother you?"

"Don't what bother me?"

"What you just did."

"Not as much."

"What does that mean?"

"Not as much as it would bother me if I let them do what they wanted and I didn't kill them."

———————

HE KILLED HIS first man during the Kaminski Wars, the winter of '08, when eleven men got shot dead on the streets of Snow Corners. The man's name was Leon Kaminski, although he only knew that later. A big, barrel-chested man with more tattoos than Carter had thought possible, tattoos running up his neck, tattoos running beneath his eyes. Maybe it wouldn't strike him so strange today.

He shot Leon Kaminski in the parking lot of a 7-Eleven, after he and two cousins followed him there, waiting outside while Kaminski ordered a Slurpee, a large one, purple, drank about half of it after he paid, talking to the clerk, a teenage girl with blond hair tied in a ponytail. Carter getting impatient. Getting angry.

Then he's stepping out of the car as Kaminski comes through the door of the 7-Eleven, raising his Glock, Kaminski seeing him and the Slurpee falling, exploding when it hits the asphalt, a small, purple geyser at his feet when he dies. Strange, the things you remember.

He had wondered if it would bother him, but he was fine with it. Two days earlier, an uncle and two cousins had been murdered in their car when a bomb the Kaminskis put there exploded beneath them. Cops had told Carter's aunt if she wanted a quick funeral, she shouldn't be overly fussy about the provenance of the body parts. Revenge removes a lot of guilt. Family removes the rest. He'd never been anything but fine with murdering Leon Kaminski.

Same way he was fine with all his killings. What he was trying to tell the girl. He'd killed to protect himself, or protect his family. Self-defense? Maybe you couldn't go that far, but he'd tried, as often as possible, to give someone a say in how it turned out for them. That removed a lot of guilt too, knowing free will played a part, that the person who just died, they're lying in a bed they made. Leon Kaminski made his when he helped build that bomb. A cold, wet, strange-purple bed.

Never been anything but fine with it.

What he had to do when he got back to Cape Rage—he'd be fine with that too.

24

TWENTY MINUTES AFTER I gave him the money, Ambrose Danby was heading to his study to put it into his vault. He stayed in the basement fifteen minutes—more time than he would have needed to store the gym bag. He was looking around. Admiring his wealth. Tess Danby said he would probably do that.

When he came up from the basement, he left his study and returned to the dining room, where Enrique had a fresh glass of CC waiting for him. The study was never locked, and Tess Danby had no trouble returning to remove the cell phone she had hidden there while I was talking to her father.

That may have been the riskiest part of her plan. Ambrose had the eyes of someone who had spent his life at sea. He could spot the subtlest change in the line of any distant horizon. Could tell you the height and rise of any wave. The camera couldn't stay in his study for long.

As it turned out, less than an hour.

Henry Carter had the fingerprint spray. Not something that's easy to find, but her husband had it. A useful thing. She had the camera, an accessory to her iPhone. She had placed the camera on a high shelf, positioning and testing it so there would be an unobstructed view of the keypad.

She didn't know if the security system would allow for a wrong attempt when she tried later. Didn't know if it would shut down, or do something worse, like sound an alarm. There were number sequences that would be difficult to make out. Three numbers on the same line might scuttle the plan right there. Her husband's fingerprint spray would give her the number, the camera would give her the sequence, a little good luck would give her the rest.

Didn't even need good luck, she'd said when she first told me her plan. Just needed no bad luck. When she knocked on my window that night, I knew things had gone well. She was laughing like someone who had pulled off the world's greatest practical joke, and I was going to be the first to hear about it.

"Three numbers on three lines, you can see it clear as day," she said when I was crouched down beside her, our backs pushed against the bunkhouse wall. "Want to see it?"

She was waving her cell phone in front of my face.

"I don't need to see it."

"Three, five, nine," she said, and her laughter was so loud I worried someone might hear us. "It's his freakin' birth month and year."

═══

NOW THAT WE had the combination to the vault, Tess Danby's plan was about as straightforward as robbery plans get—grab the money and run.

The vault was in the east wing of the house, which had the study, bedrooms for Ambrose and Finn, and eleven empty rooms. No one came into the east wing except Ambrose and Finn, and Ambrose was passed out most nights by ten. We would go in at midnight and fill two duffel bags.

She'd have the key to a cigar boat, fueled and waiting at the wharf. A stand of ponderosa pine cast shadows right up to the veranda of the east wing, so it would be easy to slip into the darkness, then onto the service road to the wharf. She had already timed it out. Twelve minutes. That's what we needed to get from the east-wing veranda to the wharf. We could probably do it in ten if we ran, and the bags weren't too heavy.

There was no chance of sneaking away in a cigar boat. Soon as we started the engine, people would be awake and wondering what the hell was happening. We debated taking a quieter boat, one of the tugs, maybe, or a locked-oar skiff. I figured I could row across the channel in a little under two hours.

There's a good chance that plan would have worked. But if it didn't, we'd be on the western channel in a locked-oar skiff when the cigar boats caught up with us and we didn't want to look that stupid.

We were taking a cigar boat.

Henry Carter had cars stored at a garage in Cape Rage, two blocks from the wharf. She had keys to the garage and to each vehicle inside. She didn't bother telling me what model cars Carter had stored there, only said I would have a selection of cars "built for comfort or built for speed."

"That's a line from a Howlin' Wolf song," I said.

"Is it?" She looked surprised. "I didn't know that. Only ever heard Henry use it. 'Comfort or speed, Tess. What's it going to be?' He said that all the time."

I had no doubt the answer was always speed. Robbing her father and never having a family again—it was going to take her thirty-one minutes.

All we needed was to choose a night. There was a boat leaving for Anchorage in three days, and that meant half a dozen men would be gone. The number of people on the island didn't affect the plan in any way. We weren't sneaking past perimeter lines, weren't going to be confronting people. And on an island, getting caught by one person or getting caught by ten didn't make a lot of difference.

But it certainly didn't hurt the plan any if we waited. It would be a Monday too, the day the boat left, and maybe that was another good thing. There would be little chance of running into anyone at the Cape Rage wharf on a Monday night.

"I'm going to have a daypack and the duffels," she said. "Can't take more than a daypack. You got the right clothes?"

"I do."

"Right . . . I've seen them. I forgot."

I almost said I'd seen her working clothes too, then remembered it was on the CCTV tape in Jason Hart's office. A mistake like that is what trips up a lot of undercover cops, what ends careers. Forgetting what people know and don't know, what you told them and didn't tell them, what's real and what's been created. Sometimes, on a long, bad case, forgetting the differences.

"I'll meet you in the pines, nine o'clock Monday. We'll watch him pass out from there."

In the pines. That reminded me of another song, and I almost mentioned it, until I remembered how that song went, one of the oldest recorded songs on the continent, sung by the Carter Family at the Bristol Sessions, sung by Kurt Cobain a few months before his death, sung like he knew what was coming. A heartache foretold, that's what that song was all about. I wished she hadn't said it, but she was young and didn't know the song, and I decided it was silly to be bothered by something like that.

"In the pines," I said.

25

THE NEXT MORNING, I gave Gardner my sit-rep and there wasn't much to do after that. I would talk to him again on Monday. I wasn't going to see Tess Danby until then either.

It was Friday, and as the day wore on, it started to seem like the case was going to take a break for the weekend. Like everyone was about to check out, the good guys, the bad guys, like that old cartoon with the coyote and the sheepdog punching time clocks before starting a shift in the pasture attacking each other. Ralph and Fred. Like those two. Everyone going to clock off for the weekend and pick things up again on Monday.

I don't like breaks in a case. It gives a suspicious person time to become more suspicious, a secret the time it may need to be shared. An ideal case moves along at the speed of a Bo Diddley song, that sort of rhythm, that sort of tempo, frenzied and getting faster. It's good if the person you're chasing is a little bit rushed, a little out of control.

It was Fleming who taught me to hate breaks in a case. Maybe I was always going to hate them, but it was Fleming who taught me how deadly they could be, and why they should be avoided for professional reasons, if not personal.

"You want the person you're chasing to be spinning like a top," he'd told me, his voice carrying that soft Scottish burr that to this day I'm unsure is genuine. "The mutt not knowing what's up and what's down, that's a good thing for you."

"Not sure if poking some of these people is a good idea," I'd said, just to argue with him. I enjoyed arguing with Fleming.

"You care if they're upset? That surprises me."

"I'm asking from a tactical perspective. Why get them riled?"

"For several reasons. You always want motion. That's one. A case that isn't moving is a dead case. If you keep someone agitated, keep them off-balance, that person is going to move. They have no choice. You've convinced them that they're going to fall if they don't.

"Two, someone who's been poked puts their attention to where they've been poked. Think about it . . . if you get poked in the back, you turn. If you get poked in the face, you charge. Get poked on the top of the head, you look around. *You* decide where to poke someone. *You* decide where they go next. That's a jolly good tactical advantage."

"Jolly good?"

"Jolly fuckin' good. Third, and this is most important, when you keep people spinning, you haven't given them time to think. A thoughtful person is an undercover asset's worst enemy. Always remember that."

"Still seems like we're playing with fire."

"Of *course* we are. What did you *think* we were doing?"

That was Fleming. *What did you think we were doing?* Making near-suicidal missions sound easy and obvious; using a lot of words, anecdotes, stitched-together philosophies and made-up maxims to justify what was, more or less, Fleming's desire to create chaos. When in doubt, blow it up. He could have put that on a T-shirt and saved everyone a lot of time.

But he'd trained me well. Pausing a case was dangerous. It felt that way to me now without even thinking about the reasons. As the afternoon wore on, I became restless, walked up and down the cliffs, explored the inside of the abandoned cannery. A foul, coppery taste came to my mouth, like a dry hangover. The skin around my temples tightened and I had the dull throb of an early headache.

By the time my shift was finished, I was out of sorts with the world. Not looking forward to the next three days. Not sure if I was the coyote or the sheepdog but wishing I could punch whoever was standing next to me at the time clock.

Looking back, I'm not sure why I worried. With everything I had seen on Danby Island, everyone I had met—Jean the giant, Tess Danby, Ambrose Danby—why did I ever think there was going to be a pause? Why did I drive myself crazy in that hut all afternoon, not knowing I was on an island with people who stood still and punched out for the weekend about as often as they amputated limbs?

<hr>

I WALKED DOWN the hallway of the bunkhouse and saw that the door to my room was open. When I got there, I found Obie sitting on my bed. His head was cast down, and he was looking at the clasped hands resting in his lap. Standing in front of him, in the center of my room, was Ambrose Danby. I stared at Danby a few seconds before saying, "You need me for something?"

"Hired you, didn't I?"

I walked into the room. Obie looked up at me when I did that but went right back to looking at his hands.

"How can I help you?"

"Everything all right on the west shore?"

"Same as always."

"I hear Tess has been going out there to see you."

"She's come out a few times."

"Something going on between you two?"

"I hear she's a married woman."

"She is."

"There's your answer."

He tilted his head and stared at me. "Why would she come out to see you?"

"Maybe she thought I was bored."

"Why?"

"I'm sitting by myself in a guard hut on the edge of the planet. Maybe something to do with that."

"You feeling sorry for yourself? Thought you needed a job."

"Not feeling sorry about anything. Just taking a guess on why your daughter came out to see me."

"What did she talk to you about?"

"Not much. She asked me where I was from. I told her some stories about Detroit. Not much to it."

He cocked his head in the other direction and looked at me the way you look at something you've just seen outside a car window; but you were driving fast and couldn't make it out. Curious like that. Uncertain like that.

"Jimmy's lawyer can't get in to see him," he said. "His own fuckin' lawyer. Ever hear of something like that?"

My chest got a little tighter. "No."

"A lawyer can always see his client, right? How can the state turn him down?"

"Jimmy must have done something to really piss them off."

"National security. That's what the lawyer was told. He can't see Jimmy Metcalfe for reasons of *national security*, like he was a fuckin' spy or something. . . . That sound right to you? Jimmy fuckin' Metcalfe?"

I decided to stop answering questions. It was becoming a dangerous game. I shrugged my shoulders and started taking off my mackinaw.

"There probably isn't a bigger patriot in all of fuckin' Washington State than Jimmy Metcalfe," Ambrose continued. "If Jimmy *heard* you were a commie, he'd stomp your fuckin' head. If he *thought* you were pink, he'd stomp your fuckin' head. You know him, right?"

I kept my voice steady. "Doesn't sound like Jimmy."

Nothing was said for a while, but eventually Ambrose turned to Obie and said, "This old hand is Edwin Tupper, but everyone calls him Obie. Ain't that right, Obie?"

Obie lifted his head. A weak, don't-want-to-be-here smile appeared on his face. He was still smiling like that when Ambrose said, "You would have worked with his son, when you were on Jimmy's boats. Gordie Tupper—*remember him?*"

―――――

THERE ARE DIFFERENT ways of being scared in this world. There's the scared you get when you're being shot at, when you're in battle and you're defending yourself. That scared doesn't leave a lot of time to think about being scared.

There's the scared you get when someone has a gun pointed at your head, and that's a different scared. You're not moving. Barely breathing. But you have clarity, purpose. I'm normally talking in a situation like that, trying to stay ahead of the game, so again, scared in a way that doesn't leave a lot of time to think about being scared.

Then there's the scared you get when you're waiting for a bad thing to happen and that's all you're doing. The scared that came to me as I looked at Obie sitting on my bed.

"Gordie was with Jimmy a long time, ain't that right, Obie?"

"They grew up together," Obie answered.

"They did time together too, ain't that right?" asked Danby.

"Sixteen months at Burritts Rapids . . . when they were kids. It was the same beef . . . liquor store in Drayton. Gordie had the gun. . . . He was lucky on the sentence . . . 'cause of his age."

Ambrose was enjoying his conversation with Obie. He turned to smile at me. Turned back to Obie.

"I had Gordie as first mate, until Jimmy stole him off to Duluth. Remember that, Obie?"

"I remember."

"Yeah, Gordie Tupper . . . good man. You must have stories to tell about him, don't you, Danny?"

Ambrose had moved closer to me as he talked. I could feel his breath, the heat of it, the sour, rye-whiskey smell of it. He didn't need to be standing so close for me to know I had just been asked a question that needed an answer. I already knew that. He stood that close because he was having fun.

He'd made a mistake though. Shouldn't have talked to Obie. Shouldn't have dragged it out. I had been given just enough information about Gordie Tupper to fake an answer. Maybe two.

Couldn't see faking three.

"Gordie was captain on Jimmy's other boat, the *Drift Away*," I said. "He was a senior guy. I didn't work with him all that often. Mostly with Jimmy."

"But you knew him?"

"Sure, I knew him. He was a senior guy, like I said. Good friend of Jimmy's. The *Drift Away* was his boat."

I hoped repeating the name of the boat would get me something. I wasn't sure what, but it was a true fact, the name of one of Jimmy Metcalfe's boats, and I was going to use it as often as I could.

Ambrose moved a step closer, and I knew I hadn't given him enough of a story. Not near enough. I needed to take a risk.

"I went drinking with him a few times though," I continued. "He told me a story once about knocking off a pawnshop when he was a kid. Took the money from the cash register, and a guitar on his way out. When he couldn't learn how to play he went back, same pawnshop, same guy working behind the cash, stuck a gun at the guy's head and said he'd changed his mind. He wanted the television instead."

A look of doubt, the first one I'd seen, flashed across Ambrose's face. The story seemed to have details, although it really didn't. An unknown crime at an unknown pawnshop, committed by someone who had done prison time for the same sort of crime. And then I went out on a limb by betting someone like Gordie Tupper never hunkered down and learned how to play guitar. Wasn't the worst bet I ever made.

"Is that true?" Ambrose said, turning to look at Obie.

"Could be," said Obie. "Gordie was doing a lot of nonsense back then . . . tomcatting around with Jimmy, and Finn. A pawnshop, I can see that. . . . Can't *you* see that?"

Obie looked at Ambrose and then looked away. He got up from the bed, not fully, just enough to move his body a bit, then he settled back down, crossed his feet and said, "Gordie always had guns. Used to run them up from Mexico. You remember that. . . . He never played guitar."

He repositioned his body one more time on the bed, and added, "I told him to stay away from guns. Warned him so many times. . . . He's dead now. Got himself killed in Chicago . . . by a gun."

Ambrose looked annoyed, but Obie kept talking. He was talking to me now. "He promised his mother, before she died, that he'd stay away from guns. Only thing she ever asked that boy. . . . Is it wrong to blame a dead man for not keeping a promise?"

"I'm not sure," I said. "Seems like a question you'd want to think about awhile, to come up with a good answer."

"I've been thinking for two years now. . . . I've never been to Chicago. Have you?"

"A few times."

"Good town?"

"It's all right. . . . If you like that sort of town."

Obie nodded his head slowly, as though I had said something worth considering. "That's what I thought," he said eventually.

"What the fuck did Gordie look like?" Ambrose said impatiently. "Ask him that."

"He's standing right there."

It was a cheeky answer from Obie, but it was also an obvious one and Ambrose turned to me. "Fuck, I don't know," I said. "He wasn't that big. Dark hair. Tough as nails. He was a sailor . . . looked like a sailor."

Obie laughed. "Yeah, he did."

I could see the doubt growing on Ambrose's face. I had got it right. By describing the way Obie must have looked when he was a younger man.

"Ask him something else," said Ambrose.

"What?"

"Something only Gordie would know."

"You think they traded secrets?"

"*Think* of something!"

Obie opened his mouth, as though he were going to object again, then he closed it and gave me a pitying look. Obie feeling sorry for me. I remembered the number of times I'd seen him in the kitchen with milk splashing down the front of his T-shirt. I don't think I've ever felt more doomed.

"What did Gordie drink?" he asked eventually.

"Drink?"

"You said you went drinking with him. . . . What did he drink?"

Freefall. Nothing to work with on that question. Not even the scraps I'd been working with so far.

Not true. What he drank—had to be something unusual. The answer. Couldn't be beer. Couldn't be whiskey. You wouldn't ask that question if the answer was beer or whiskey.

Needed to be something different. Running out of time. What else? What else? . . . *Mexico.*

"Tequila," I said. "He always drank tequila."

"Is that right?" Ambrose almost yelled.

"Yeah, that's right," said Obie.

———————

AMBROSE TOLD OBIE he could get supper and we watched him through the window of my room, cutting across the courtyard to the main house. He walked as though he had the weight of the world on his shoulders, although that was the way Obie always walked. Except late at night, when he stumbled.

"Did I pass?"

"Think that was a test?" said Danby.

"'Course not. You must have thought Obie and I were going to hit it off, and we just hadn't met yet."

He looked annoyed. "Know what I think, Danny? I think you should be careful around my daughter. Tess spending time with you, maybe needing something from you—if you think that's a good thing, it ain't."

"Why would I think that? She's a married woman. That's right, isn't it, she's married to someone named Henry Carter?"

Not feeling scared anymore. Ride the win. That was another bit of Fleming-speak. Push the advantage, however small, however large; the best time to move forward is right after you've moved forward.

"She is," said Ambrose.

"Then I'd be staying away. When is he coming back?"

Ambrose gave me a dirty look. "Why the fuck do you care about Henry Carter?"

"I don't. Just haven't seen the guy. I'm curious."

"She's got you curious, eh, Danny? You're heading for trouble, and you don't even know it."

"Again, just sitting there doing my job when your daughter came down that trail."

"Wanting to know how you were settling in."

"That's right."

"Like she was the fuckin' Welcome Wagon."

I stood in front of him, returning his stare. He was wearing leather breeches and a dark-green slicker as large as a flag. He'd been working outside. His hair was wet and hung longer on his back than normal. "You know, most people, when I give them one hundred and sixty thousand dollars, they don't threaten me the next day," I said.

"Return money a lot, do you, Danny?"

"No. Another reason I'm wondering about the whole not-grateful thing."

"Funny, you finding that cash a week after you show up. I've got more'n a dozen men working for me, but you're the one that finds it . . . funny thing."

He hadn't asked a question, and I had no desire to talk, so we stood there awhile in silence. Eventually, I turned and took my mackinaw back off the hook on the door.

"You going somewhere?"

"Was thinking of going outside for a smoke."

"Well . . . don't let me fuckin' stop you."

Danby had positioned himself so that he was standing directly in front of the open door. I stepped around him without saying a word. There was nothing in the room for him to find if he wanted to toss it. I doubted he would. He just wanted me to feel his breath and walk his girth, listen to him laugh a dirty-sounding laugh as I walked past him. Men like Ambrose Danby always had time for games like that.

———

I KNOCKED ON the back window of Tess's cottage. It was one in the morning and there was no light on the island except the one-flood lamppost in the courtyard, almost two hundred yards away. When she came outside, we had to crouch close together to see our faces.

"Your dad came to see me this afternoon," I said. "He was in my room when I came back from my shift. He wanted to know what we'd been talking about out in the hut."

"What did you tell him?"

"The truth. We're planning on robbing him. Just needed to work out some details."

"Funny."

"He had Obie with him. His son worked on Jimmy's boats. Gordie Tupper, know him?"

"Sure I do. He hung around with Finn a few years. He and Jimmy Metcalfe did time together at Burritts Rapids. . . . My dad was testing you?"

"For some reason your dad hasn't been able to talk to Jimmy."

"What reason?"

"National security. That's what Jimmy's lawyer was told."

"Jimmy Metcalfe? What was he running on those boats?"

"Doesn't matter. What matters is Jimmy hasn't been able to vouch for me."

"That would worry my dad."

"I'd say you were right about that. He seems worried about you too."

"What are you telling me?"

"We don't have three days."

"We need to go sooner?"

"We need to go tomorrow night."

26

BECAUSE HE KILLED a crooked cop, Henry Carter figures he has more time. A good cop would be noticed right away. A crooked cop—one that clocked off regularly, like that cop would have been doing—it might take a few hours to notice him missing.

Night is turning to dawn and there is a murky horizon line in front of him now, a gray hump sitting out there in the semidarkness. He can sense low-hanging clouds, imagine songbirds flitting in and out of the sweetgrass, the haze of dust that will be trailing the car when the sun rises behind him. When he sees a turnoff sign for Idaho Falls, he puts on a blinker.

When he does that, the girl opens her eyes. She sits up quick, not bothering to stretch, not bothering to rub her eyes. "Where we headin'?"

Carter points to the "Welcome to Idaho Falls" sign.

"We headed east?"

"Uh-huh."

"Why east? I thought we were heading to Washington."

198 | RON CORBETT

"You ask a lot of questions. Anyone ever tell you that?"

"I know. I do it when I'm nervous."

"You're nervous now?"

"Yeah."

"And that's the question you want to ask—what direction we're going?"

"Useful thing to know, don't you think?"

Carter looked at her and almost laughed. "I do."

When they reach the Amtrak station, the parking lot is filled with a weak, predawn light. Shadows cling to the station. A street sweeper is rolling and hissing somewhere in the darkness. Carter circles the parking lot once, leaning over the steering wheel and looking up at the roofline of the station. Four cameras.

He leaves the parking lot, drives around the block and enters it again, this time parking the Jeep next to a cargo van with an illustration of a lock and key. He leaves the Jeep idling.

"I want you to do something."

The girl nods.

"I'm going to give you some money and you're going to go in there and buy two one-way tickets to Chicago. Then you're going to go to that street corner over there and wait for me."

The girl looks to where Carter is pointing. An intersection a block from the train station. The overhead light at one of the corners snaps off while she is looking.

"All right."

Carter takes a roll of bills from his pocket and gives the girl five hundred-dollar bills. She puts the money in a pocket of her jeans. An electronic door lock snaps open and he says: "Go on, now."

The girl gets out and he stares at her as she walks toward the train station. She wants to know direction, wants to know where she is and where she's going. A practical girl. A girl that can spot trouble coming because she sits with her back to the wall and her eyes on the door; a girl who knows how to survive. Her dad had been a fugitive, a bad drunk. That wasn't hard to figure out. She would have learned these lessons a long time ago.

He can't kill her. He realized that during the drive from the motel. He can't do that and ever feel good about anything he ever does again, no matter how he's been raised, no matter what he's been taught to believe.

He turns off the Jeep, gets out and opens the trunk. Takes out the duffel bag and a backpack and starts walking. He's set it up so that she won't slow him down any. No matter what happens now, people are going to think he's headed east. The direction he's been driving. The direction of the train tickets he told her to buy.

He looks over his shoulder a few times when the parking lot of the train station is still visible, but there isn't anything happening. No one has come running from the building. No one is walking toward the Jeep with a cell phone pushed against their ear.

He rounds a corner and walks past a Dunkin' Donuts. An elderly couple is standing outside, waiting for the shop to open. He adjusts the strap on the duffel bag, doing it as he passes the couple, so his arm is in front of his face. At the next corner he turns right and starts looking. It doesn't take long. He finds the sort of vehicle he needs—a late-model Hyundai Santa Fe with tinted windows, bad rust and good tires—one block over.

He pops the trunk, throws in the duffel bag and backpack. Pops the driver's door and gets behind the steering wheel. It's her choice now. Whether she comes or goes. Give people a choice, and you don't have to feel bad about what happens to them after that. No longer your responsibility. No longer your guilt.

He starts the vehicle. Hard to say what she'll do. She's a practical person. Keeping her promise might be the practical thing to do.

He drives around the corner, turns left, and she is where he told her to be standing. She gets in and hands him the tickets.

"You're heading west now, ain't ya?"

———

CARTER DOUBLES BACK on the highway and by early afternoon he is driving the northern tip of the Continental Divide. It is rugged country, the land gashed and torn, ravines dropping off the side of the highway by half a mile or more, rivers that twist and switchback and have white water showing on every stretch. The forest is mixed wood, with hardwood trees in late spring bloom, fir and pine growing between the hardwood, a many-shades-of-green forest that has never been cut, never been cleared. Eagles circle the highway above them. Longhorn sheep stand on rocky outcrops and watch them pass.

Inside the Santa Fe the heat is on and the radio is turned low to a country-and-western station coming from Butte. It is a weak signal, and it gets lost from time to time. When that happens there will be some low-hum static and then the signal comes back, still some sad lament, only a few bars down from where you'd lost it. Like nothing had really changed. It is early in the morning and the station only seems to be playing sad songs.

Carter doesn't mind the music, or the interruptions. It seems peaceful inside the car. Knowing where you stand and where you're going—that's peaceful.

The girl opens her eyes and asks, "Was it your wife who shot you?"

Carter looks at her. He is no longer surprised by the questions. It is her nature. The thoughts that are in her head, she gives them voice. Talking with your tongue. That's what it used to be called.

"Why are you asking me this now?"

"Just came to me."

"No . . . it wasn't my wife who shot me."

"But she was there?"

"Yes."

"You think that makes her just as guilty?"

"Don't think guilt has much to do with it. Things happen. When they do, other things need to happen."

"You get shot, so you need to shoot someone back. Is that how it works?"

"My grandfather used to say he didn't have enemies. He didn't allow it. . . . When you're betrayed . . . I don't see how you have much choice about what you do."

"It's a rule?"

"It's one thing leading to the next. It doesn't need a rule."

She doesn't say anything else, and in a few minutes, she is back asleep. Carter stares at her and wonders, not for the first time, why she reminds him of Tess Danby. They couldn't have looked more different, this girl blond and slight of build, his wife red haired and statuesque, this girl quiet and contemplative, his wife loud and impulsive.

It was impulse that married them, their sixth night in Las Vegas and there wasn't much else left to do. They'd honeymooned in Puerto Vallarta, after she first suggested Acapulco, wanting to go there because of cliff-diving she had seen on television as a child. She had dived off the cliffs on Danby Island and wanted to try Mexico.

But the Kaminskis did business in Acapulco, so he had taken her to Puerto Vallarta instead, where he knew many people and where they stayed in a villa on Mismaloya Beach, fifteen miles south of the city. The beach was in a small bay with an isthmus jutting far out into the Pacific. There was a small hotel and a half dozen villas. Fishing boats bobbed in the harbor every morning and there was a trail on the isthmus that brought you to the ruins of an old house built as a stage set for a Richard Burton movie. Elizabeth Taylor was not in the movie, but she was there for the filming.

In the villa where they stayed there were framed photos of Taylor and Burton on Mismaloya Beach. They wore black sunglasses in every photo. Looked unsteady on the sand. "She was still married to Eddie Fisher when those photos were taken," said the man who owned the villa, when he showed them around before leaving on the yacht anchored in the bay. "It was quite the scandal. There were many reporters here when that movie was made. It put Puerto Vallarta on the map."

"Who's Eddie Fisher?" asked Tess.

"No one remembers. He was married to Elizabeth Taylor."

There were more photos in the hotel. Burton was always smoking a cigarette. Taylor was always wearing black glasses and a headscarf. Beside the photos was a framed newspaper story from 1965 in which Taylor said she and Burton should never have left Mexico. That had been their mistake. What doomed them.

Carter doubted Mexico had anything to do with it. In the photos, they already looked doomed. Dressed in tweed suits and headscarves, smoking Benson and Hedges while looking around for a cocktail waitress on an isthmus jutting far into the Pacific. People like that get blown away. People like that don't get good last chapters.

Along the shore of the bay were royal palms, and in the hills behind the villa were yucca trees and laurel and wild bougainvillea shrubs with trailing rose and yellow blooms. They awoke late each morning and swam most afternoons. Their meals were brought to them from the hotel. She never asked why Acapulco had been a problem, or why they were honeymooning on a stretch of beach so secluded it had been chosen by the most famous couple on the planet as a good place to drink and have an affair.

In the early morning, while she slept, he would go outside and listen to wild dogs howling from the hills behind the villa. The dogs were rarely heard during the day. He liked mornings best, when the dogs began to bark, when he knew there were animals in those woods that had not been tamed. Except for the dogs, it was a quiet beach.

Only now, driving with a girl who reminded him of Tess but wasn't Tess, after he had killed his uncle and his uncle's wife at their ranch outside Las Vegas, as he was driving west with a trunkful of weapons and plans to see people who owed him something, the sun falling far down the highway and his chest wrapped with swaddling bandages from bullets fired into his back eight days ago—only now did he wonder if that had been a strange way to start a marriage.

———

IT IS EARLY twilight, the sky just beginning to darken, when Carter sees it. He pulls off the road and takes a pair of binoculars from the glove box. Gets out of the Santa Fe, walks into the woods and climbs to a ridge so he can see better.

There are two Washington State police cars parked across a county road. The cars have their roof lights spinning. He sees four cops. One is sitting in a patrol car, one is talking to the driver of a pickup truck, and two are walking down the line of cars backed up behind the patrol cars, punching license plate numbers into a cell phone. The lineup is thirty-two cars long. Stretches for more than a quarter mile. The cops aren't waving anyone through because they look all right.

He climbs down from the hill, gets into the Santa Fe, turns the vehicle around and drives to a cut in the forest he saw a quarter mile back. It is an old settlement line, long grown over, and he can drive no more than a hundred yards before he needs to stop. He gets out and starts looking for pine boughs to throw over the roof of the vehicle. He tells the girl to get out and grab her pack. They'll be walking the rest of the way.

27

WHEN I WENT for my coffee the morning after Ambrose Danby came to my room, I found Obie sitting in the kitchen. He was the only one there. He winced when he saw me walk in, then put his head down and went back to eating his cereal. He always ate cold cereal. On the coldest morning on Danby Island, Obie would be eating cold cereal.

He looked embarrassed when I sat beside him.

"Don't worry about it, Obie," I said. "That's just Ambrose's nature, doing stunts like that."

"Yeah, it is," he said, looking up from his bowl of cereal. "He knew Gordie. He could have asked those questions himself. Didn't need me."

"More fun putting two men on the spot, I suppose."

"Like I could scare anyone," he said, dipping his spoon back into the bowl. Then he looked embarrassed again and said, "It's true though. Tess has gone out to see you a few times. Everyone's noticed it."

"There's nothing going on."

"You sure 'bout that, or just trying to convince yourself 'bout that?"

"What's that mean?"

"I've seen you looking at her, Danny."

"Nothing's going to happen, Obie."

"She's a good girl, Danny. I've known her most of her life. If there's such a thing as a good Danby in this world, it's that girl."

"That's the way I see it too."

"She's just wild. It's her nature. You know those cliffs on the north shore—she used to dive off 'em. That's how wild that girl is."

"That's suicide."

"That's what Ambrose told her, but she'd seen people doing it on television, down in Mexico somewhere, and she told her dad the cliffs here didn't look any higher than the ones she'd seen on television. So, in she went."

"A dive like that should have killed her."

"You don't get it, Danny. She didn't do it *once*. She did it *all the time*. She'd do it today, I bet. The bigger the risk, the more Tess Danby wants to do it. Look who she married."

I didn't say anything to that, and in a few seconds Obie continued. "She gets herself into enough trouble, Danny. She don't need anyone helping her with any more."

"You think I'm trouble, Obie?"

"From the second I saw you."

I was so startled I had to swallow my coffee quickly, so I didn't spit it out. Obie went back to eating his cereal. Without looking up at me, he added, "Whatever you're doing, try not to hurt her. . . . Can you do that?"

"Already trying."

"Good."

We didn't say anything else, and in a few minutes, Obie had finished his cereal, put the bowl in the bin at the end of the buffet table and was heading toward the door. As he was about to walk outside, I said just loud enough for him to hear, "What did your son drink, Obie?"

"Brandy," he answered.

━━━━━

I'VE SPENT AS much time thinking about Obie Tupper as I have anyone else in the Danby case, which is saying something, a case that had both Henry Carter and Ambrose Danby, giving as much thought to an old longline fisherman.

But I've thought about him enough to believe Obie knew what was heading our way. That morning, he knew. Only one on that island who had figured it out, who already knew that a lot of the things everyone thought mattered—they didn't anymore. Up was down, down was up, and the best thing you could do was hunker down and let the storm pass.

Maybe Obie was already doing that. Maybe I'm making too much of an old man who didn't take the opportunity to betray me, who walked away from it; maybe Obie—a man who avoided confrontation— was always going to do a thing like that. But I think he knew. I've tried many times to see it a different way, but nothing else has come to me.

I was still thinking about Obie when I felt my wrist tingle that morning. I looked at my watch. That was never supposed to happen. I walked outside the hut, knelt so I couldn't be seen from the trail and hit the watch face.

"You're not supposed to be contacting me."

"Got no choice, Barrett," I heard Gardner say. "Hart needs to see you. Tonight."

"Tonight? How the hell is that supposed to work?"

"Get over to the Spyglass. He'll get a message to you there."

"I haven't been off this island since I got here. I'm being kept on a short leash. Have you guys forgotten about that?"

"You just gave Ambrose a hundred and sixty thousand dollars. Hart thinks your leash is longer than you think. Boats go to the Spyglass every Saturday night. Get on one."

"Ambrose was in my room last night asking questions about Jimmy Metcalfe. He's getting more suspicious about me, not less."

"You need to figure it out, Barrett."

"Why can't Hart just call me?"

"Ask him when you see him."

<hr>

I WALKED ACROSS the courtyard after my shift and knocked on Tess Danby's cottage door. It was a lot brasher than I wanted to be right then, but I had no choice.

I had to knock three times, although I'm sure she heard me after the first knock. I was just as sure I knew what she was doing—standing the other side of the door wondering if I'd lost my mind. When the door opened, she stared at me, but didn't say anything.

"When I finish talking, act surprised," I said. "Can you do that?"

She gasped and threw her hands in front of her face.

"When I stop talking, say, 'Really?' Say it so someone can make it out."

"*Really?*"

"I'm going to take something out of my pocket and give it to you. It's a quarter. You're going to look at it like it's a lot more valuable than a quarter."

I pulled a quarter from my pocket and gave it to her. She folded her hand over it and held her hand to her heart. She was smiling when she said, "What the hell are you doing?"

"Something's not right. Getting that combination . . . it was too easy."

"Not everything in life is hard, Danny."

"I'm going to pretend you didn't say that. . . . I want to spend one night snooping around, find out if we're missing something."

"You said we didn't have one night."

"I've changed my mind."

"You think it's a trap?"

"Could be. And if your dad is planning something like that, he'll need help. I'm going over to the Spyglass tonight, see what I can find out."

"To go drinking with the boys?" she said in disbelief. "Jean would like nothing more than to throw you off a boat, Danny. You know that, right?"

"Guess we'll finally get a chance to find out if down is down."

"What?"

"Nothing. You need to trust me on this, Tess."

She looked at me like that was the last thing she wanted to do. Looked at me like an airline passenger being told the flight to Paris has been delayed a day, but they have overnight vouchers for the Quality Inn down the highway. Would you like one?

"We go tomorrow?" she asked.

"If everything checks out . . . yes."

"You're a lying coward if we don't do this tomorrow."

"Flattery doesn't work on me."

She laughed, a genuine laugh that anyone watching would have taken as a genuine laugh. It was going better than I had expected. I knew Tess Danby would be quick on her feet. I wasn't expecting her to be blowing away the scouts at the combine.

"By the way, that quarter was a necklace of yours that I just returned," I said. "It broke and fell when you were at the hut. You're going to say thank you when I stop talking. Then you're going to give me a hug."

". . . are you . . ."

"Big thank you. Big hug."

"Well . . . *thank you*, Danny."

Tess Danby reached her arms out and pulled me toward her. I kept mine down, as though embarrassed. In a few seconds, it was hard to keep them there. When we were finished hugging, she stepped back, and it looked like she was blushing.

28

Now I just needed to get a ride to the Spyglass.

When I walked into the common room that evening, I was thanking Frank Gardner for suggesting I let a bundle of bills fall out of that gym bag before giving it to Ambrose. It was a smart call. A good, smart-cop call.

"A crook wouldn't turn over all the money," he'd said. "He'd drop a bundle."

Gardner was right again when he pointed out that this would give me some spending money if that was ever needed. Neither of us thought it would be an immediate need.

"What the fuck are you doing here?" said the giant when I walked into the room. He was playing poker. Sitting around the table with him were Skipjack, Barry the mechanic and both cousins.

"Came to make amends."

"Make what?"

"Came to give you money, Jean."

He understood that word. His eyes narrowed and he looked at me with a brief flash of interest, then the eyes widened as I took the bundle of hundred-dollar bills from my pocket, still crisp along the edges, still with the bank wrappers. Ten thousand dollars sitting in the palm of my hand.

I snapped the wrapper, took out twenty bills and threw the rest on the table.

"I'm the new guy, on probation, really, and I didn't think I could take the risk. Ambrose . . . he's a scary dude, ain't he?"

The men looked at the money on the table and laughed.

"I had to give him the bag. But the way I see it, I'd be an idiot if I gave him *everything*."

A bit more laughter.

"I figure we can split the bundle. Keep everything that happened in this room before I gave him the bag. . . . We keep that to ourselves."

"The money on the table is ours?" said the giant.

"Split it up any way you want."

All five men moved toward the money at the same time. In a few seconds, when it became obvious they were going to tip the table if they kept at it, they settled down, and the giant counted out the money. Each man got sixteen hundred dollars.

"You got more," the giant said.

I shrugged my shoulders. "Why don't you take it from me in some poker?"

"You any good?"

"Straight poker I'm pretty good. Not crazy about wild cards."

"Grab a seat."

———

THERE WASN'T ONE hand of straight poker.

It was dealer's choice, and the games were crazy with wild cards: queens, deuces and just about everything else on some hands. The giant never bluffed. The mechanic always bluffed. One of the cousins kept some high cards at the bottom of the deck whenever he dealt. The other cousin checked his bets or followed until there was a second raise and then he folded. Didn't seem to matter what cards he had showing.

Skipjack was probably the best player, and I wondered if he won every pot he could, or whether he was smart enough to win just a little every night. The more he played, the more I thought he won a little every night. Finn joined the game after a couple hours, stumbling in from the cocktails and brandy he'd had with his father during supper. He gave me a nasty look when he saw me sitting at the poker table but before he could say anything, the giant roared, "Grab a seat, Finn. The new guy's making us fuckin' rich."

About an hour later, after I had just lost eighty dollars to Finn Danby by drawing to an inside straight two draws longer than I should have been, the giant said, "Let's go to the Spyglass. I feel like shooting some pool."

Everyone stood. I stood with them. The giant looked at me and sneered.

"Who said anything about you coming?"

"I'd like to shoot some pool," I said.

"You any good?"

"Bit better at poker."

"Come on."

THE SPYGLASS WAS busy, Saturday night, and there wasn't an empty table. The kid was already at the tavern, and that made eight of us. The bartender got some men to move to the bar and pushed two tables together so we could sit down.

The giant went to the pool table and put down some quarters. There were three stacks of quarters already there, but he put his stack in front and played the next game without anyone objecting. He was a good player. I got to play him twenty minutes later, and when I scratched on the eight ball, he might as well have won the state lottery. It was only twenty bucks, but it might as well have been the Powerball.

I sat down, and when I did that the bartender came walking up to the table. "Finn, I'm out of CC," he said.

Finn rolled his head back, to look at the bartender behind his chair. "What do you mean, you're out of CC?"

"Sorry, the boat came in this afternoon, haven't had a chance to unload it."

"Well, you better go fuckin' do that, Pierre."

"I can't leave the bar. It's on the boat, Finn. Can't you go down and get it?"

"You want me to go haul your fuckin' booze?"

Danby was starting to get to his feet and the bartender said quickly, as if he'd said something wrong, "I wasn't saying *you*, Finn. Get one of your men . . . get the new guy."

Danby stood halfway raised from his chair, turned to look at me, and then he sat down.

"That's a good idea."

The bartender tossed me a set of keys. "It's the tug four slips down, the *Amanda Gay*. Cases are in the cabin."

———

THE CAPE RAGE wharf was about eighty yards long, with a boatyard next to it with slips big enough to house a steamboat, derricks and cranes big enough to lift one out of the water. The only light came from the moon and a security light at the boatyard, and I walked through elongated shadows of cranes and pulleys and chains as I walked down the wharf, looking for the *Amanda Gay*.

When I found the boat, I boarded and opened the cabin door. It was a thirty-foot lumber tug converted to a supply boat, to bring food and alcohol over to Danby Island mostly, although it did runs to some of the other San Juan Islands. When I walked into the cabin, standing next to a stack of Canadian Club, as if knowing that's what I would need, were Gardner and Hart.

Hart was wearing a trench coat and I almost laughed when I saw it—a long, gray trench coat with pleats that probably billowed like the coat of some noir detective hero if he twirled it the right way. His blond hair was easy to spot, even in the darkness of the boat cabin.

Gardner looked like a longshoreman arriving for his shift. He was wearing a black watchman's cap, black jeans and steel-toed boots. His clothing was all dark. He was hard to see. He knew what he was doing.

"The bartender is one of your agents?"

Hart cleared his throat. "He's not an agent. He does jobs for money. Been quite useful during this investigation."

"Hell of a risk he's taking."

"He's been paid more in six months than he'd make in ten years. He doesn't mind the risk."

That's right. There was always money. When nothing a person does makes any sense to you—look at their bank account.

"Any trouble getting over?" Hart asked.

"Just needed to lose a few hands of poker. . . . What's gone wrong?"

Hart cleared his throat again. When he was uncertain, or about to lie, he did that. It bought him a few extra seconds before he needed to speak—a stutter that wasn't a stutter, and he probably didn't even know about it. You could make some money playing poker against Jason Hart.

"Not sure if *anything* has gone *wrong*," he said, and he emphasized both words, to let me know they were open to interpretation, those two words. "There have been some surprises. Maybe opportunities, we're not sure yet. . . . But there are things you need to know."

"Thought you already told me everything I needed to know."

Hart shrugged his shoulders. "There were one or two things I may have left out."

Gardner snorted. When I looked at him, I saw he had a smile on his face, not his usual sneer. He was enjoying himself.

"It seems obvious to us . . . today," Hart continued, "that the Danbys were after something specific in that bank. That wasn't always obvious, Barrett . . . something always seemed a bit . . . squirrely, about that robbery. I agree with you. But I gave you the reasons why, the best intel we had at the time.

"It wasn't until we worked our way through the list of box holders that we saw it. Before you accuse us of keeping secrets, you should know that."

"What haven't you told me?"

Hart gave me a quick scowl. "We have recently finished contacting the box owners. All but one . . . the Danbys made more on those boxes than they would have made on the vault, by the way. We have the insurance claims. A damn sight more. Before you start thinking this was fuckin' obvious. It wasn't."

"Are you going to tell me?"

"Good question," laughed Gardner. "What the inspector is trying to tell you, Barrett, is that we can't interview the last box owner because the last box owner is dead. He was murdered in Tacoma the night before the robbery. And he was well known to us. Guy's name was Pete Flarety."

I thought for a second. "I've heard that name. The agent who picked me up at the airport, the day I got to Seattle, he asked me if I was there for the Danbys or Pete Flarety."

"Logical question," said Hart, glaring at Gardner and picking up the conversation. "Pete Flarety was a gangster who owned a bunch of strip clubs in Tacoma, had an interest in the Sweetwater casino too, although we were never able to prove that."

"How was he killed?"

"Shot in the head while sitting in his car outside one of his clubs. Up until now, the Tacoma cops thought it was a Haitian gang he's had some trouble with in the past."

"They don't think that anymore."

"No, they don't. Flarety is a known associate of Ambrose Danby. They go back years. The bank robbery and the murder happened within thirteen hours of each other. The Tacoma cops are starting to think it's too much of a coincidence."

"Starting to? How long have you had Flarety's name?"

Neither of them answered.

"I don't believe this."

"I still don't think it makes a spit of difference to you, Barrett," said Hart, sounding angry now. "Your job has always been stone-cold simple—find where the Danbys hid what they stole in San Francisco and get that information back to us. Stone fucking simple. The kind of work I was told you do."

I thought about what he said. It was good bluster. But that's all it was.

"This still doesn't add up. Why haven't you arrested Tess Danby? Why did you need to see me tonight?"

Hart turned away from me, as though embarrassed. It was Gardner who spoke for him.

"We needed to see you, Barrett, because earlier today we were alerted to a manhunt underway in Idaho. Washington State, Utah and Nevada now as well. Suspects are a man and a girl. They're wanted in connection with the murders yesterday of a county sheriff and a motel clerk in Meridian, Idaho. Suspect male is described as early thirties, Caucasian, six feet, black curly hair; suspect female is a teenage girl, long blond hair, five-foot-four or -five in height. Suspects' vehicle, a late-model Jeep Grand Cherokee, was found abandoned at an Amtrak station in Idaho Falls."

I knew what was coming, and maybe I didn't want to hear it.

Maybe that was the reason I asked a question I knew they couldn't answer—as if, subconsciously, I wanted to delay hearing what they had come to tell me.

"What does this have to do with Pete Flarety?"

"We're not sure, but it's all starting to seem connected somehow."

"Why?"

"There was a security camera at a gas station next to that motel in Idaho. Camera caught the Jeep coming and going. The couple gassed up there too. . . . There's good footage of the driver."

I didn't ask another question, and what followed was a pause that seemed as endless as the fall in a bad dream, one of those falls that keep spiraling and spiraling and never end.

Finally, he said it. "Henry Carter isn't dead, Barrett. And it looks like he's coming this way."

29

HENRY CARTER PUTS down the binoculars and turns to the girl.

"We'll ford the river over there," he says, and points across the parking lot of a Texaco station to a twisting river the other side of a two-lane road. It is early morning, and the mist is slow to rise off the river, as though it is being held down. The air is moist, and Carter knows when the mist burns away, there will be rain clouds in the sky. The first ones he's seen in days.

A half mile away, upriver from where they are kneeling, are the spinning red-and-blue lights of two Washington State police cars blockading the road. It is the third roadblock they have seen since they started walking last night, and Carter has no doubts now that the police know who they're chasing. Every road leading to the coast will have cops manning checkpoints, cops cruising in their patrol cars with his photo displayed on dashboard computers. He'd heard helicopters yesterday, until it got too dark for them to fly. He'll hear dogs today.

"That's a big river," the girl says.

"There are shoals just past the bend. Doesn't look like the water's much more than knee-deep down there."

"Whose knees?"

It was a fair question.

"We'll make it," he says. "Won't be another river that size after this."

The Texaco station is closed, no cars in the lot, and the mist has rolled across the highway. Rolled right up to the gas pumps and the building they're hiding behind, with a restaurant and convenience store; rolled past the building to the diesel pumps out back and the cleared edge of a towering red-fir forest. Carter walks through the mist to the back of the building. The girl follows.

He is surprised when he sees the security system. ADT alarms and a Lorex camera, a lot better than a backwoods Texaco station needs. It has been twenty-six hours since they've eaten, a long day ahead, and he wants to get inside this building. But there is no way to go through the door without setting off an alarm.

Maybe through a window? More work than he is expecting. How hungry is he? He looks at the girl. How hungry is *she*? He'll be going no faster than she's going. Unless he leaves her behind and goes on himself.

Is that what you want to do?

He is getting distracted. Asking questions that don't need to be asked right then. They are hungry and there is food inside this building. He needs to stop overthinking it.

"Stay here. I'm going to check some windows," he says.

He disappears into the mist. A minute later the girl sees headlights on the highway. Two diffused, glowing orbs that move in tandem through the mist. She watches as the headlights grow larger and more defined, a Dodge minivan now traveling behind the lights, turning into the parking lot of the Texaco, pulling around to the back.

The driver sees the girl as soon as he rounds the corner. He is a teenage boy, about the same age as the girl. Maybe a year or two older. He has red hair and freckles and a white shirt with a Texaco logo on the shirt pocket.

"We don't open till six," the boy says to the girl when he steps out of the minivan. Carter comes walking out from the mist. The boy looks at him, and Carter pulls up the zipper of his pants.

"Sorry, I couldn't wait."

"Hey, no problem," says the boy, although he has already turned away from Carter, is back looking at the girl. "You know . . . you can wait inside till I open up. I'm not supposed to do that, but there's no one else in yet. . . . Come on, I'm about to put some coffee on. We got good washrooms too. Some of them have shower stalls. Where are you parked?"

"Other side of the building," says Carter, pointing into the mist. "I thought that's where your washrooms would be."

"They are. We just aren't open yet. Come on in."

They follow the boy into the restaurant.

———

THEY SIT AT a lunch counter, staring at faded laminated menus. A cook has shown up, a middle-aged Chinese man who looks half asleep and doesn't seem to know Carter and the girl are sitting there until he starts the grill and drinks half a cup of coffee. He gives them a disgusted look and goes to the back of the kitchen. *Customers.* They aren't even open yet.

From the windows of the restaurant, Carter can see the flashing red-and-blue lights of the police barricade. "Know what's going on out there?" he says.

"Cops have a roadblock set up. They do that sometimes."

"What are they looking for?"

"Don't know. Do you want me to turn on the news?" The boy points to a television on a shelf behind the cash.

"That's all right. I was just wondering."

He is a good kid. Carter can tell that just by looking at him, short hair with a part in the side, looks at the girl a few times out the corner of his eye, then looks away, embarrassed, when she catches him doing it. And a helpful kid, knows his vague answer about the roadblock is disappointing, so he says, before he walks away with their breakfast orders, "There's a state penitentiary not far from here. Most times, when the cops are out there, it has something to do with the prison."

He goes into the kitchen, and Carter looks around. It is an old gas station, built at a four-corner intersection that must have been passed over in favor of another four-corner intersection when the interstate was built. The stools they sit on have red plastic cushions so badly cracked they look like topographical maps. A green milkshake machine the other side of the counter has a spider's nest built between the blades. The boy can probably get a better part-time job, thinks Carter. He drives; there are better restaurants along the interstate, with waitresses not much older than the girl. He wonders why he's here.

The boy keeps himself busy opening the station. He turns on the gas pumps and the lights in the convenience store. He stocks the pop coolers and the toilet-paper dispensers in the washrooms. Despite the chores, he goes into the kitchen several times to check on their order. When he puts the plates in front of them, there is steam rising from the eggs, like they had just come off the grill.

He asks if they need anything else and Carter says no. The boy doesn't walk away though, stands there looking at the girl.

"Ketchup would be nice," she says.

The boy runs into the kitchen. Comes back with several plastic ketchup bottles cradled in his arms. "Thanks for reminding me. I need to put these out on the tables."

He gives the girl his fullest bottle of ketchup, starts putting the rest on the tables. Before he's done, a car pulls up to the gas pumps in front and the boy runs outside.

"You even like ketchup?" says Carter.

"It depends," says the girl. "Sometimes I do."

They begin eating their breakfast.

"How much further you got?" she asks.

"I'll be there tonight."

She takes a few bites of her eggs and says, "*You'll* be there tonight?"

He turns to look at her. "You don't have to go any further."

"Thought you were bringing me home."

"You did what you promised. You're free to go."

They go back to eating their breakfast. When they have finished the boy comes and takes away the dishes. He is back in the kitchen when Carter says, "I'm going to ask you to do one last thing though."

"What?"

"I want you to go tell the cops that you just escaped. I kidnapped you, and you just escaped. Tell them the last time you saw me, I was heading that way." He gestures toward the woods behind the gas station. "Wait behind the building a few minutes before running down there, so I can get to the river."

The girl looks to where he has pointed, then back to the front of the station and the red-and-blue lights spinning through the windows, the river just beyond that.

"I leave and you stay; give you five minutes, is that right?"

"That's right."

"This is the first time you've lied to me."

"What are you talking about?"

"You don't want me here when you kill the boy. No witnesses. That hasn't changed, has it?"

The surprise Carter feels right then passes so quickly he is left wondering later if it had been a real emotion or just something expected of him. "He'll see which way we're going . . . when we leave."

The girl looks at him but doesn't say anything, and he continues. "It wasn't me that put a boy here. I don't get to choose these things."

"Yes . . . you do. You got free will. That thing you talk about all the time. You got it."

Carter stares at her and is surprised when no anger comes to him.

"Sometimes, you got to have faith things will turn out all right for you. You got any faith, mister?" she asks.

His last words to Huey Dalton. The girl has recited them back to him. She motions for the boy to come over. When he is standing in front of them, she says, "I'm hoping you can help me."

"Sure . . . sure, what do you need?" says the boy, anxious to please, excited to have been chosen.

"Those cops out there, they're looking for me . . . and my dad. I can't explain why. I don't have the time. But those cops will tell you all sorts of bad things about my dad, some of them true, but I've never seen him hurt a good man, or do anything he could have walked away from."

The boy looks startled, but not for long. He never looks frightened. A few seconds after she starts talking to him, the expression on the boy's face settles back to what it had been when he came over. The look of a teenage boy talking to a pretty girl, anxious to hear what she has to say.

"What do you need help with?" he asks.

"When we leave, don't contact the cops."

"I wasn't planning on contacting any cops."

". . . And when the cops come asking questions about us—they're going to come—tell them we headed into the woods behind the station. Can you do that?"

The boy looks behind him, as though seeing the woods behind the station, then back at the girl. "Sure, I can do that."

"Your cook shouldn't say anything either. Can you make him do that?"

"My dad owns the station. I can send him home soon as you leave. There's another cook comes in at ten."

"That works."

The girl smiles at the boy. The boy smiles back. A good kid. The pretty girl needs help. He doesn't have a lot of questions.

Life, briefly, as it should be. Carter is surprised to see it.

"Got any faith, mister?" asks the girl, as she gets off her stool and picks up her backpack.

"Got a bit," says Carter, and he also gets off his stool, hoists the duffel onto his shoulder. "You don't have to go any further. I didn't lie to you about that."

"Seems like I'm here for the duration. Don't it seem that way to you?"

When they walk outside, rain is starting to fall.

30

A STRONG WIND shook the bunkhouse the next morning. The panes in the window rattled. I could hear objects bumping and smashing around outside. The rain came a few minutes later.

After two weeks without it, the sky emptied in a rush, like God dumping a bucket of water onto the world. It didn't build in any sort of way, the way most storms do. There weren't the initial drops of rain, falling big and loud, sounding like bugs splatting by your feet. There wasn't stinging rain after that, or windswept rain that circled and acted like it was trying to trap you. There was enough wind for an hour or two, to have seen rain like that, but there was too much water, and it came too fast. It drowned the wind.

There would be no boats out in rain like that, and no hurry to get to my hut. I stayed in bed. I was sure everyone else in the bunkhouse was doing the same. Staying in bed. Listening to the rain. Trying to recall the last time they'd heard rain like that.

Jason Hart had told me to stand down on the robbery until Henry

Carter was caught. Said it was too dangerous, with Carter around. We needed to get him off the board before we could finish the game.

Which made no sense. Henry Carter here, Henry Carter there—it didn't affect the robbery. Not unless our boats crashed out in the channel.

I knew the real reason Hart wanted to wait—as long as Tess Danby was on this island, the FBI knew where Henry Carter was going. Tess Danby was now bait. Which I didn't feel good about. Yes, she was a criminal, she deserved to be punished for that; but what Hart was doing—you wouldn't do it to an animal. *Couldn't* do it to an animal because there are laws against baiting.

Even Gardner, who hated the Danbys, had told me in my last sit-rep that he was glad it was Tess Danby we were about to turn, who was going to get a sweetheart deal with the state. "Her biggest crime is being as wild as wild gets," he'd said, in a moment of unguarded compassion that surprised me. It would have sickened him, he went on to say, physically sickened him if the deal had gone to Finn. That didn't surprise me.

Also, something I didn't bother bringing up with Hart, as I was sure he would see it differently, was that Henry Carter wasn't my problem. I'd been brought to Seattle to help finish the FBI investigation into the bank robbery in San Francisco and the deaths of those two security guards. The best way to accomplish that goal would be to bring Tess Danby and two duffel bags of stolen goods to Cape Rage and turn her over to Jason Hart.

He could freak all he wanted, but he'd have to arrest her. She'd be safe after that.

I lay in bed listening to the storm. I had seen a storm like this once before, in Tampa, the skies opening and so much rain falling in three hours they had to close Busch Gardens, had to close I-95, had to close half of southwest Florida. But it was over in three hours. People didn't come back to the beaches along the Gulf Coast right away because the storm had come on so quick, with no warning, and people were scared it might come back just as quick. There were photographs in the *Tampa Bay Times* the next day showing Clearwater Beach with not a swimmer, beach towel or beach hut in sight, just miles of white sand and a brand-new blue sky. People had never seen it.

A cleansing rain, that's what fell on Tampa, and that's what seemed to be falling on Danby Island. In Tampa, that storm came the day before I was leaving—one case finished, another about to begin—and there were times during that storm when I felt untethered, weightless and giddy and everyone I met that day seemed to be people from my past.

When I got out of bed that morning on Danby Island, I had the same feeling. I told myself I'd only seen a couple storms like that, and it was probably a different feeling. I didn't have a lot to compare it with. But the feeling never went away, and I spent my last day on Danby Island with people who reminded me of people I used to know.

TESS DANBY CAME walking down the trail toward my hut about an hour before my shift finished. She walked the way she always did on that trail, without breaking stride, without looking around, walking with purpose until she walked right into the hut, not bothering to wait outside this time.

There was dark skin under her eyes, and it looked like she hadn't slept the night before. She didn't bother with any pleasantries.

"Are we going tonight?"

"Yes."

She brightened like a child spotting a final present under the Christmas tree. "Thank you, Danny. Thank you . . . thank you . . ."

I stopped her before she could say a fourth thank-you, knowing that when I handed her over to Hart that night, thanking me would be the last thing she'd want to do.

———

THIRTY MINUTES AFTER Tess Danby left, Frank Gardner contacted me. It was the second time something that never should happen had happened.

"Another hour and I could have been sitting in a kitchen next to a giant who wanted to know why my watch was making that funny sound."

"I'm sorry, Barrett, it needed to be done. You good to talk?"

"Talking to you now."

"Carter's been spotted. He was at a Texaco station near Lookout Mountain this morning. Bit of confusion at first about what direction he was heading, but it's a confirmed sighting, Barrett."

"How far away is that?"

"Thirty miles."

"Early this morning? I thought every cop in three states was looking for him."

"He's gone into the woods."

"He any good in the woods?"

"The Snow Corner cops have told us to round up every dog we got, and good luck."

I didn't speak for a few seconds. "This keeps getting better. Glad you boys called me into this case."

Gardner didn't speak right away either, a longer pause than mine, long enough to seem like the conversation had stalled. "Listen, Barrett, the way this has played out, I agree with you," he finally said, "it's been a bit of a rat-fuck."

"A bit?"

"Yeah . . . but it's just about over. We'll catch Carter in those woods. There's no way out for him now."

"Been no way out for him for a while now, but he's a dead man who keeps coming."

I didn't want to let Gardner off the hook. I was surprised when he spoke next in a voice that I had never heard him use before, a low, almost confessional tone of voice.

"I'm your operational commander, Barrett. I know Hart has been dropping in and out of this case, but I'm the one you listen to when you're in theater. You listen to me, not him. You understand that, right?"

"Why are you telling me this?"

"Because it's important."

"Sure, I understand. Always thought that was the case. Any other reason you're telling me this?"

Another pause. "Just want to make sure there won't be any freelance-spook problems when this deal goes down."

That voice I recognized.

"We'll have that bastard in cuffs before the night is finished," Gardner continued. "I know you're not happy about postponing the robbery, keeping Tess Danby on that island. . . . Hart didn't give you the honest reason we want to do that."

"I know."

"Figured you did. Soon as we have Carter—one way or another, soon as he's gone—that robbery has a green light. You won't be on that island much longer."

"I know."

31

CARTER AND THE girl ford the river by the Texaco station and when they are on the other side, they crouch and wait. They can't see the roadblock from there but can see the spinning lights. The lights don't move, and in a minute they continue walking.

The rain is coming hard now and they walk with their heads cast down, stepping carefully so they don't slip on the rocks. Carter takes a straight path through the woods, his duffel bag tinging from time to time, like a bear bell.

They come across a small brook that becomes larger as they walk beside it, large enough to have deep pools where they scoop water in their hands and drink. Carter is surprised to hear birds flying overhead. No bird should be flying in a storm like this. He can't see the birds, only hear the beating of wings, large wings, that sound like gusts of wind when they fly close to the tree line.

Midafternoon the rain stops, and Carter turns away from the brook, heads toward the coast. The air becomes warmer and the trees thin. They can smell salt. The sun comes out, just long enough to start slipping away toward the western horizon. They climb a small knoll, at the end of the mountain pass they have been traveling, and directly in front of them is the Pacific Ocean.

There are islands everywhere. Too many to be counted. The smaller ones, with the sun shining above them, look like gemstones: shards of jade, chunks of emerald, floating out there on a blue-ribbon stretch of water.

"You're almost there," says the girl.

"You can see it. It's that island there."

The girl looks to where he is pointing. "How you gonna get over there?"

"I'll steal a boat," and Carter swings his hand a couple inches, to point at a bay partially hidden by the line of hills running down to the ocean, "over there, in Cape Rage."

"Cape Rage? Never heard of it."

"No reason you should have. It's a company town. Unless you work for the company . . ." Carter shrugs his shoulders and picks up the duffel. He stares at the girl, before asking, "Are you sure you want to go on?"

"I'm sure."

"Why?"

"I'm here for the duration, already said that."

"That the only reason?"

The girl considers the question. "No," she admits. "The way I figure it, you protected me twice. You'll probably do it a third time if you need to . . . or maybe it'll be my turn."

"What's that mean?"

"Means we're each other's best way out of this mess," she says, and wipes her nose on the sleeve of her parka. "That's a funny thing, ain't it?"

They walk another forty minutes, until they are on flat land, approaching the ocean, surrounded by hemlock and balsam now, the sun almost gone, and they hear footsteps.

Many footsteps. At the same volume, like people are fanned out in a search line coming toward them, not walking single file down a path. There is the snap and crunch of branches being trampled. The hiss of radio static. Carter grabs the girl's hand and pulls her into the woods.

32

THERE WAS A near-full, yellow moon hanging over Danby Island that night, the sort of moon that made me think of vellum night shades and nicotine-stained enamel, candle wax on dark wood furniture. An old yellow moon for people who remember a different time.

Tess Danby was waiting for me in the pines. She was dressed in black jeans and a black sweater, had two empty duffel bags and a full daypack on the ground beside her. "Was beginning to think you were all talk," she said.

I didn't bother answering, but crouched beside her, stared through the trees at Ambrose Danby, who was staring out at the sea and drinking at one of the dining room tables. Danby would drink until he passed out, after which Enrique would leave him snoring in his chair for thirty minutes before awakening him. The waiter had learned years ago that awakening Ambrose immediately was a mistake. The old pirate needed at least thirty minutes, to let the dreams pass, or to let the dreams settle, the waiter wasn't sure.

Thirty minutes would be all we needed.

We didn't speak as we watched her father through the twisted, knotty branches of the ponderosa pine. He was perfectly lit. There were perfect sight lines. It was like staring at a cinema screen. Danby raised his rocks glass up and put it down. Laughed from time to time. Left the table once and came back. After we'd been watching him for forty-five minutes, his head rolled back, then snapped upright, then rolled back and stayed. A minute later, Enrique came to the table and removed the rocks glass, an empty wine glass, an ashtray and anything else that might break when Ambrose awoke. When the waiter disappeared again, Tess Danby hit a button on a stopwatch, picked up the duffel bags and ran toward the back of the house.

I FOLLOWED HER into the house and down a hallway, dark-colored oil paintings hanging on the walls, no windows, no light. She opened a door and light returned, the glow of the moon outside a large bay window, enough light to see a shadowy oak desk, floor-to-ceiling shelves lined with gold-stenciled and black-tasseled books. I couldn't imagine Ambrose Danby reading any of them.

She strode to a closet in the room, more of a wardrobe than a closet, a wooden structure jutting out from the wall, and opened the door. She pushed aside some clothes and found the other door. Using the flashlight app on her phone, she punched the numbers for her father's birthday onto a keypad. There was a click, and she turned the handle down, pushed open the door.

We came down the stairs, and it was something to see. Some days, I think I went ahead with the robbery just so I could see it; to make sure it wouldn't be taken away from me, the opportunity to see a pirate's treasure. I'd read *Treasure Island* when I was a boy and went to sleep for weeks afterward with dreams of pirates' gold. I wouldn't have been the only one. How many have dredged Oak Island, how many have looked for shipwrecks in the Caribbean, trying to find what was in front of me right then?

Everywhere I looked, gold glinted back at me. There were gold bars in Civil-War-era military chests. Gold coins in old postal bags. Gold jewelry pinned to black-velvet jewelry boards, so many boards they were stacked in crates like vinyl records. There were gold dishes and gold serving trays, golden goblets and golden cutlery, a gold urn and a spun-with-golden-thread christening gown. There were golden crosses of every size, and a golden nativity scene so large it was boxed, the boxes filling one corner of the room.

There was probably more money than gold. Bundles and bundles of ribboned currency—American, British, Mexican, Canadian, Japanese, Thai—stored in clear-plastic storage bins so you could make out the currency. The bins were stacked twelve high at some places in Ambrose Danby's hidey-hole.

I stared around in disbelief. As an undercover cop, you don't always see the reason you're working. The reason you became a cop and the good you once thought you'd accomplish. A senior-brass cop tells me this person needs to be betrayed, or that person needs to spend the rest of their earthly years in a cage so decent people can sleep at night. That's what I get.

Beat cops get to see the reason they're working. Homicide cops see it more often than they want. I always come later, and almost never see it.

But not this time. In front of me stood four generations of greed and avarice, a family's bloody legacy of robbing and looting. How many deadly secrets were locked inside this room? How much death and tragedy? Wealth like this always comes with a price. It's never the rich who pay it.

"We have ten minutes," I heard Tess Danby say. "We should start with the money." Not that it made a difference anymore, but as we stuffed bundles of American bills into the duffel bags, I asked her where the contents of the safe deposit boxes from San Francisco had gone.

"Looks like those bags over there are from that job, but my dad uses the same bags all the time. It hasn't been put away, whatever it is. It's a mess."

I had a look inside the bags she had pointed at while on my way to get another bin, and thought she was right. There were four duffel bags, and nothing had been stored away, a tangled mess of jewelry and money and financial papers. There were even items scattered on the ground, as though the bags had been emptied already and then shoved back together. Or they'd been thrown to the ground and the items fell out, the person who threw the bags not caring enough to pick them up. Like they were worthless to him.

We had filled one duffel and were halfway through filling the second when a tap-tapping sound came down the basement stairs. We both heard it. We had left the door in the closet open, as closing it would have locked us inside the basement, but we hadn't left it open that much. Whatever we were hearing, it would be much louder outside.

"What is that?" she asked.

The sound wasn't regular. Didn't follow a pattern. A tap-tapping coming from outside, loud enough so it couldn't be ignored. Enrique was probably shaking Ambrose awake right then.

I walked to the bottom of the stairs. It was easier to tell what the sound was when I stood there. Tess Danby hadn't moved since we first heard it, was still crouched on her ankles with bank-wrapped bundles of cash in both hands.

"Drop it," I said, and started walking up the stairs.

"What?"

"Leave everything. We need to get out of here."

"What? We're just about done!"

"This isn't a good place to be right now, Tess. We need to get outside."

"What the hell are you talking about? What's going on out there?"

"Your husband is coming."

33

PEOPLE HAD ALREADY started gathering on the cliffs by the time we got there. The sound was coming directly across the channel, a tap-tapping mechanical sound that could have been machinery, but wasn't. You could tell that from the flashes of light that came with the sound, tiny flares that came a second before the sound. A few times there were so many flares it looked like fireflies. Once, like so many fireflies that I imagined a long, kite-tailed procession of them swooping and weaving their way between the trees.

Tess Danby hadn't spoken since we left the basement. She'd gasped when I'd said, "Your husband is coming," but she hadn't asked any questions. I don't think I was ever the only one on Danby Island wondering if Henry Carter was truly dead. He never seemed like someone you could ignore, someone of no consequence, the way dead people are supposed to seem. I wasn't surprised when Hart told me he was alive. I don't think his wife was surprised when I told her.

How did I know that? She hadn't asked that question yet. If things kept moving as fast as they were right then, she might never get the chance.

The last man to arrive was Finn Danby, drunk and weaving his way to the edge of the cliffs. He looked at the lights across the channel like a child would look at the night-sky refraction of some distant fair.

"What the fuck is that?"

"What do you think it is?" his father asked scornfully.

"*A gunfight?*"

Ambrose didn't bother answering.

"Who the fuck is over there?" yelled Finn, turning to look at his father, then at the men standing along the cliff. No one answered him. He looked to where Tess and I were standing, dressed all in black, then back at the lights across the channel.

I watched the flares, heard the mechanical tapping that could have been a machine but wasn't, and knew something had gone terribly wrong. Frank Gardner was over there. The operational commander who was looking after me, giving me orders, going to evac me off this island when I was done. I stared at the flashing lights and felt as abandoned and marooned as a shipwreck survivor.

Twice, I heard a man's scream, a faint sound that just managed to travel across the channel and up the cliffs, almost lost in the wind, but it came with the unmistakable timbre of something human, something plaintive and knowing. Twice more, right at the end, there were explosions. When it happened, the background on the far shore was lit up all the way to the base of the mountains—the valley, the raised land, the pine and fir between here and the mountain—it all came careening out of the darkness with the speed and surprise of a sucker punch.

Then it was gone, and an awkward silence followed. The men stood on the cliffs and shuffled their feet, craned their heads like the crowd at a fireworks show wondering if that had been it.

It was in that silence we heard a bell. A single bell that right then seemed as lonely and sad as a funeral chime ringing out over some shadowed valley, some mournful place. A fire had started after the last explosion, and as we listened to the bell, we watched flames begin to lick the trunks of the trees, smoke begin to roll out over the water. The bell chimed until Ambrose took a phone from his pocket and then the chiming stopped.

He stepped away from us, but there was no need. He never spoke. The phone was back in his pocket in twenty seconds. The men circled around him and although no one asked a question, he gave an answer to the question everyone had.

"That was Henry. He told me I can stop looking for what he stole. He's bringing it back."

No one said anything. We looked out at the smoke, at the high branches of the fir, which were silhouetted now by the fire below, so they looked like human arms reaching out from the flames. In a few minutes, everyone started walking toward the house.

34

SMOKE TWIRLS AMONG the trees, mixing with the mist rising from the water. It is hard for Carter to find the girl, although she is where he left her, sitting on a pine stump a hundred yards from shore.

He kneels beside her, careful to prop up the rifle strapped around his neck. Behind him, a fire has started at the base of a large redwood and the air is filled with the acrid scent of gunpowder.

"If you stay here, you'll be all right. No one will be coming back into these woods tonight."

The girl rocks back and forth on the tree stump. Her fur collar is turned up, so it frames her face. When Carter looks at her, there seems to be no background, no foreground.

"You sayin' goodbye?"

Carter doesn't answer.

She says, "You still love her, you know."

"I know."

"It's going to be harder . . . someone you love."

". . . You know something about it, do you?"

The girl keeps rocking back and forth on the pine. "Just heard stories," she says. "It damns a soul so it can't be fixed no more. Worst damnation God ever invented. There's only one way to save yourself after something like that."

"What?"

"Stop another soul from making the same mistake."

They don't speak for a minute. Eventually Carter says, "Bit late for me to be worrying about souls, don't you think, girl?"

"Never too late for a soul. That's why God invented them."

"What are you trying to tell me?"

"That I'm praying you don't get a chance to do what you're going over to that island to do."

"Praying? That's a funny thing to say."

"Why?"

"I'm not sure . . . just seems funny."

Although he has told the girl he is in a hurry, Carter stays crouched, staring into her face. She holds his gaze and he says, "There's a good chance I won't be able to keep my promise . . . about bringing you home."

"Good chance of anything in this world. When you're ready, I'll be waiting for you."

Carter smiles at her. It is a gentle smile, something peaceful about it, something joyful and young, nothing forced or undecided.

"I suspect you will."

He turns away and the girl watches him walk into the mist, heading toward a police boat bobbing in the bay.

35

How THE FUCK can he still be alive? He got a full shotgun blast dead square. You weren't more than five feet away from him when you shot him. He was fuckin' *cut in half.*"

Finn was pacing and waving his arms in the courtyard, yelling at his father as though Ambrose had done something wrong.

"Thought you checked him," his father said quietly.

"*He was fuckin' cut in half.* I just told you that."

"Wasn't a dead man that just phoned me."

Two fatigue-green cargo boxes had been brought over from the garage and placed in the middle of the courtyard. Every light on the main floor had been turned on, along with every light on the veranda. The rifles in the open bins glinted and flashed in the glare of so much light.

There were thirteen men standing in the courtyard: along with me, there was the giant, Skipjack and the kid, Obie and the two cousins, Peter and Barry, Enrique and Hank, Ambrose and Finn. There was one woman.

The two cousins took the weapons from the chests. The rifles were a mix of automatics and semis, AR-15s and Uzi Pros, the Uzis going to people higher up the pecking order; Ambrose and Finn, the giant, Skipjack and the kid got Uzis. Everyone else got an AR-15. Obie took his rifle with both hands outstretched, like he was being handed a baby that needed to be changed. Peter shook his head no, then had to grab a rifle when a cousin shoved it into his chest, the barrel of the gun hitting the boat captain's chin and drawing blood.

The giant and Skipjack took their guns and immediately checked the clips. Snapped the magazines in and out. Adjusted the nylon shoulder straps. Their checklists were identical, their speed about equal, and they moved in unison, as though performing a synchronized act.

Ambrose took an Uzi and brought it to his daughter. She looked at the gun and shook her head. "I won't shoot him again."

"He'll shoot you."

"If he gets the chance . . . yeah, that's probably what'll happen."

"You want to die? Henry wouldn't do that. Play the cards you've been dealt, girl."

"That's what I'm doing."

Ambrose stood there a few more seconds before lowering his arm and walking away. "Go wait in the house," he said. As he walked past his son he said, "Take your sister inside. Make sure she stays there."

Finn Danby looked confused for a second. Then, and it was hard not to notice, he looked relieved. His body went slack; the pinch-white knuckles gripping the stock of the Uzi went back to their normal color. He almost smiled. Stay inside the house and guard your sister. That was a good assignment.

"Don't trust her, eh?" he said, his voice now surly. "Don't blame ya."

Ambrose looked at his son like he was looking at an idiot.

———

SKIPJACK, THE KID, one cousin and Enrique were given the wharf. That's where Carter would likely come ashore. The obvious spot, not only because there was a wharf there, but because there weren't a lot of options. You would need to rappel up the south or east side of Danby Island to reach the top. There was no other way. And it would be an eighty-yard nighttime rappel up those cliffs. Not many things in life are truly impossible but getting up the south or east side of Danby Island at night would be two of them.

The west side was possible. Where I had been stationed for ten days. The path Tess Danby walked down to see me at the hut continued to the old cannery, then to the wooden beams and timbers that rose from the ocean where another wharf had once been.

Carter could land anywhere on the west side of the island and make it to the bay, then through the heathered field running to the back of the house. The giant, the second cousin, Peter and Barry were sent to the west side.

"Go to the hut and spread out in a line," Ambrose told them. "He'll be heading to the field, if he comes up that way."

"We should hear a boat, right?" said the giant.

"You should."

"Why not jump him as soon as he comes ashore?"

Ambrose thought about that. "If you heard the boat coming . . . if you knew where it was coming ashore . . . yeah, you should do that. Cut Henry down right on the shoreline when he's wading through the break." He smiled, as though imagining what something like that would look like. "Yeah, you should do that . . . but keep your position in front of that field if you don't hear anything. Don't bunch up. And no fuckin' smoking."

He gave the giant a hard look and then moved on to Obie and Hank. The oldest men in the room. One busted-up sailor and one busted-up cook. The last ones to be picked. Looking a little embarrassed by that, but like every player ever picked last, quite willing to go home and forget about the game if that was the group consensus.

"Go to the south cliffs and watch the shipping channel," he told them. "See anything approaching, call it in. Don't fuckin' think 'bout it—call it in."

Hank nodded. Obie stood, not nodding, not looking at Ambrose, staring at the AR-15 in his hand. He looked at the rifle as though trying to determine what it was, exactly, and how it got there.

"I ain't good with guns, Ambrose," he finally said.

"Good night to learn, Obie."

————

AS THE MEN were leaving, I managed to position myself close enough to the gun crates that I could duck behind one if needed. Maybe close enough to turn the crate over as I dove, the weapons tumbling out. Maybe the riveted, metal crate would give me the protection I needed for a few seconds. Maybe the right gun with the right matching clip would roll out right in front of me.

A lot of maybes in the best plan I had if Ambrose turned nasty. I wasn't sure what he'd do right then, but I knew he'd been keeping an eye on me. Even as he was handing out the assignments, determining which man got an AR-15, which man got an Uzi, he was keeping an eye on me. His world spinning out of control, doom tracking him down in the darkness—he had time for me.

When the men had been dispersed and it seemed that something needed to be said soon or bad things would follow, I asked, "Any assignment for me?"

"Where were you earlier?" he said.

"Standing right in front of you."

"Before the shooting. You didn't come from the bunkhouse."

"Came from the kitchen."

"Kitchen's closed."

"Cook leaves a coffeepot going. You know that."

"Drinking coffee? That's what you were doing?"

"Yeah, what did you think I was doing?"

"Don't know . . . don't think you were drinking coffee."

I thought about arguing with him, but it seemed silly to have an argument like that right then. Convince Ambrose Danby I was drinking coffee. Like that mattered. With FBI agents lying dead or dying on the far shore, armed men taking up positions around Danby Island, a mass killer heading toward us—an argument about coffee?

Ambrose must have felt the same way. He closed the lids of the gun crates, put several clips into the pockets of his vest, motioned with his Uzi for me to start walking toward the house and didn't say another word until we were walking through the doors of the house, when he asked, "Was Tess drinking coffee with you?"

36

Tess Danby was sitting at a table by the windows of the dining room. Her brother was sitting the other side of the table, a Glock 9 mm in his hand, pointed at her chest. Ambrose saw them and let out a loud snort.

"What the fuck are you doing, Finn?"

"Keeping an eye on her, like you said."

"She got a gun?"

"No . . . she doesn't."

"Think you need to keep a gun drawn on an unarmed woman?"

Finn blushed. Tess gave him a pitying look that probably stung as much as her father's words. "Not trustin' anyone tonight, Dad . . . like you said." A few seconds after that, Finn Danby slipped the gun into the waistband of his jeans.

"What's he doing here?" he said, looking at me.

"Don't think it's a good idea sending this boy out tonight."

"Why not? Thought he was good at shit like this."

"Just a feeling I have."

"He doesn't have a gun?"

"No, he doesn't. Let's wait and see if he needs one."

A confused look flashed across Finn's face. Tess gave him another pitying look, then looked out the windows of the dining room at the near-full, yellow moon hanging over the ocean.

"He's going to get on this island," she said. "You know that."

"I don't know that," her father said.

"You're fooling yourself."

"Twelve men to one, Tess. Your husband is good. He ain't that good."

"Don't think Henry will be doing the math that way."

"No other way to do it."

"Variables change."

This time it was Ambrose who had a confused look on his face. His eyes narrowed, and his breathing turned shallow. He was just about to say something when we heard the gunshots.

They came from the west side of the island. Where my hut had been, where the giant, a cousin, Peter and Barry had been sent, the boat captain marching into the night with an awkwardly held AR-15 and a plastic pocket protector clipped to his shirt.

We heard three bursts of automatic gunfire. Three-second bursts repeated in three seconds. The person firing knew how to fire a gun. Then there was a loud, white-noise squawk and Ambrose pulled a yellow radio transmitter from his pocket. I heard the giant scream, "We got him."

"What's happening?"

"We spotted Henry's boat. He tried coming in below the cannery. I just lit him up."

"He's dead?"

"Fuck, Ambrose, the boat is on fire. I hit the fuel tank."

In the background I could hear more automatic gunfire, no longer controlled, no longer coming in short bursts, men firing without a sense of danger, or purpose, the giant laughing and screaming—"Henry is fuckin' target practice, Ambrose. Yeah, he's dead."

"You see his body?"

"Just see one big fuckin' bonfire. Boat's drifting in now. Give me a minute."

No one in the room talked. No one moved. Henry Carter being dead—a second time—didn't remove any of the tension. Ambrose held the radio transmitter so tightly I thought the case would crack. Finn's eyes darted around the room like mercury pellets, a chapped tongue licking his lips from time to time. Tess kept staring at that yellow moon, not looking at her father, not looking at the radio, like she hadn't heard what was happening at the west-side bay, or it didn't matter much to her.

The gunfire subsided and the silence in the room was near total for a minute. Ambrose was smart enough not to ask for a sit-rep. The giant would contact him when field conditions allowed.

And then the gunfire came back. The short, controlled bursts we'd heard earlier.

"What the fuck . . ." we heard the giant yell, and that was the last time we heard him. Last time we heard anything from that radio. For the next minute and a half we heard short bursts of gunfire coming across the heathered field, interspersed with occasional screams. It was hard to tell who was screaming, although one time, quite clearly, I heard Peter say, "This isn't fa . . ." and after that, I heard him scream.

When the shooting was finished Ambrose said, "The bastard swam in beside the boat."

Tess Danby finally turned from the window. "How's the math now, Dad?"

AMBROSE TRIED FOR a minute or two to reach Skipjack at the wharf. He stopped when he heard the first motor. It was brass-knuckles brash for each man to steal a boat and run away, although when I thought it through later, it made sense. It must have occurred to them that they weren't coming back to Danby Island, and they might as well start the next chapter of their life with a boat.

The boats took off one after the other: a motor starting, idling for a few seconds, then revving high and fading away in about ten seconds. One after another. Like men were helping each other tie off and get underway.

Ambrose tried reaching Obie and Hank but never got through. He got angrier and angrier, shouting obscenities and threats through the radio, telling them what would happen to them when he saw them next, describing the quartering of a man in detail, until finally, in a rage, he threw the radio on the floor and started stomping it. He stomped until the glass had been ground to dust and yellow shards of metal were strewn across the floor.

When he stopped, he was a spent man. Sweat was pouring off his head, running down his face, into his beard, turning the hair into something that resembled the strands of a mildewed mop. He sat in a chair to catch his breath. When he had recovered, he gave me the look of a man who wanted nothing more in this world than to kill what he was looking at. As though all his days and dreams had come to it.

It was only his exhaustion that saved my life. I've thought about it enough to know that's a fair and accurate statement, to know that if he'd had the strength to do it as soon as he wanted to, I would have died in that room.

I was unarmed. Thirty feet from the nearest exit. Ambrose Danby had an Uzi Pro with a full clip. I've run the scenario a bunch of times, given myself heroic abilities to jump and roll, to run and duck, but each scenario ends with me dead.

But the time Ambrose needed to recover was the same time his son needed to panic. And that's what saved me.

"We can't just fuckin' sit here," yelled Finn, just as Ambrose was rising from his chair.

"Not now, Finn."

"What the fuck do you mean not now? Now is all we fuckin' got, Dad. That psycho is coming right for us."

"We all know that."

"We can't just fuckin' sit here. Henry will pick us off one by one."

Finn's head snapped sideways and he stared at the windows; stared like he was seeing them for the first time. The bank of eight-foot windows running down the west and south sides of the dining room, a line of shadowy islands the other side of the window, a reef that was showing at low tide, a yellow moon that looked close enough to come sailing into the room and touch him.

"*The fuckin' windows*," he whispered.

"Henry ain't a sniper, Finn. Sit down."

"We don't know what the fuck he is, Dad. No one does."

With that, he ran from the room. Ambrose tried to grab him, but he was too late. His son went right by him, through the door, and you could hear him running across the veranda after that, then hear him on the gravel road leading to the wharf. A few seconds later we all saw a light flash behind the garage. We saw it reflected on one of the windows of the dining room.

It was hard for me to believe someone would make a mistake like that, but people had probably been saying that about Finn Danby for years, and old habits—they never go away. They walk hand in hand with you right to the end.

We heard gunfire a minute after we saw the light. It wouldn't have been more than that. Coming from right where you would have expected it to come: the gravel road leading to the wharf, about a hundred yards from where Finn Danby had turned on his flashlight app after he must have run off the gravel road and lost his bearings.

It was a short burst of gunfire. Only one.

I couldn't be sure if Tess Danby was crying when I looked at her after hearing the gunfire, but it looked like she might have been. Finn Danby hadn't been much of a brother, but growing up together on this island, there must have been a time when they were close. A time when they were brother and sister, and all seemed right with the world.

Ambrose sat back down, looking like he was in shock. Or looking like he had been beaten into no longer caring if he moved or didn't move, if he saw or didn't see, breathed or abandoned all human promise and future. Shock, perhaps, before it gets diagnosed and given a word.

It didn't last long. Within a minute, he started looking around the room, at the windows, the white linen tablecloths, his daughter, me, the service bar, back to me. I was staring right at him when he remembered that a few minutes ago he wanted to kill me.

He made it out of his chair this time. Bolted out in a rage, yelling something I couldn't understand, maybe it wasn't even language, just a blind-rage scream as he rushed toward me, moving faster than a man his size had any right to move.

I was ready for him this time. He'd made a mistake, leaving his Uzi behind on the table, his rage about to be his undoing. He charged with his arms spread wide, getting ready to grab me and not let go until he was holding pieces.

I fell to the floor, spun on my back and kicked him in the right shin. He stumbled and nearly fell but corrected himself. "That's how you want to fight, Danny!" he roared, but I didn't bother answering, just crabbed over and kicked him again. He roared one more time and dove to the floor.

If he'd landed on me, it might have been over right then, but I rolled away just in time. Most men don't think of diving to the floor when someone goes Brazilian jiu-jitsu on them. They stay standing, and that's how they get beaten. Ambrose was smart and wasn't going to be like other men.

But he'd made another mistake. As soon as he was on the floor, grabbing his Uzi was a better play. I sprang up and ran toward it. Danby saw his mistake and yelled, "I should have tossed you off the cliffs days ago! You're a rat-fink cop, ain't ya!"

He sprang back to his feet and we were running side by side when we heard a window smash and a metal cannister, about the size of a small soup can, landed beside us.

It was a curious thing to happen, although neither of us had much time to think about it. Ambrose may have slowed a little, to look at what had landed by his feet, but he had too much momentum and too much purpose to do much more than slow. Certainly, he never had time to stop or go in a different direction.

I saw the metal cannister roll behind him but can't remember if I started putting the pieces together. I had wondered earlier that night about the explosions across the channel, and what might have caused them. I might have wondered about it again, just before I heard a loud bang, and the world went black.

37

 A MBROSE DANBY BORE the brunt of the explosion. When I awoke, what was left of him lay scattered around me: a purple brocade vest, scraps of burned canvas and black hair, pools of blood. I'd seen men who had died in car bombs and knew there would be pieces of Ambrose Danby all the way to the front door.

I didn't know how long I'd been unconscious, but it seemed a long time, for when I awoke, I was in a different world. Not a different place, not a different town or country, but a different world, one without reference points, where nothing was normal and nothing was the way it should have been. A stiff wind was blowing over me and the floor was covered in glass. White linen tablecloths billowed above my head. There was a fire burning in the kitchen. I could *see* the kitchen now because a wall had been blown away. The burnished steel of the appliances showed the flames, made it seem like I was looking at a fake fire, perfect yellow-blue flames licking their way up and down the steel.

I was lying on my stomach and still scanning the room when I felt the first jolt of pain. It was in my chest, like someone was squeezing something inside there. I winced and got another jolt, then another, then a burning in my left leg, so painful it felt like I was suddenly being branded. I looked over my shoulder and saw blood pooling around my waist. The spindles of a chair were lying across my legs.

I felt another sharp pain, but it wasn't as bad as the first ones. I was expecting it. I was getting used to it. When it passed, I took a deep breath, and it didn't hurt. There were no burbling sounds with the exhale. No blood in my mouth. Perhaps I wasn't going to die any minute.

I was about to try and stand when I noticed what else was in the room, what I'd missed in my first scan, because of the smoke and the billowing tablecloths, what I saw now in the far corner of the room. Tess Danby was still alive. She was standing where I'd seen her last, by the bank of windows on the south side of the room. A man I'd never seen before was standing ten feet in front of her, holding a Glock handgun pointed at her head.

In the past two weeks, as I'd heard stories about Henry Carter, he had taken on the aura of someone mythical, someone from an old folk song, or an old newspaper clipping from the '30s, front-page stories about Baby Face Nelson and Pretty Boy Floyd, a boxed story in the upper right corner about Henry Carter.

Now, there he was. Flesh and blood. Wearing a dark-gray suit and white shirt, heavy-soled black shoes, dripping wet, but other than that, no signs of battle, no signs of distress. He could have been waiting for a maître d' to bring him to his table, waiting for the doors to the boardroom to open. He was that calm. There was water pooled around his feet, and when I saw that I knew he had been standing there awhile. Same spot. Not moving.

The side of the dining room where they stood was in better shape than the rest of the room. Some of the tables still had their place settings. There was glass in some of the windowpanes. There was smoke twirling around them, because of the fire in the kitchen, and the wind was whipping the tablecloths around, so they billowed out like flags, but the rest of the room looked normal. Right down to the near-full, yellow moon peering through the window, just like it had been before the explosion, only closer now, as though it had grown curious about what was happening inside this room. In the far distance, behind the moon, I could make out the white cliffs of Cape Rage, shimmering in the darkness.

There was a ringing in my ear that went away slowly, and as it faded I began to hear what they were saying. Like turning up a volume switch, Henry Carter's voice the first one I heard.

". . . makes any difference, Tess."

"You don't think so?"

"Some things you don't walk back from. You know that."

"Even the things you never started?"

"Even those."

Tess, like the room where she stood, looked unchanged from before the explosion. Her face was unmarked, her red hair still tied back, no dirt or soot on the black jeans and sweater she had worn to break into her father's vault.

"You're thinking about family, aren't you?" she said. "You're thinking about the Kaminskis, and what you had to do back then."

"Been thinking about a lot of things, Tess."

"And San Francisco, what you needed to do there . . . thinking you were protecting me . . . that's what you're thinking about."

Carter didn't answer. The moon seemed to have inched a little closer, hung just outside the window now, like some peering face trying to see inside the room; the bloated, glowing, leering face of a child that has snuck out for the night.

"It doesn't have to be this way, Henry. Not this time . . . if that's what you want. . . . It can be different."

"You think they're the same, Tess? What I did in Snow Corners and what you did out on that logging road?"

"What did I do, Henry? I didn't know my dad's play. In your heart of hearts, you know that. You *must* know that . . . right?"

Carter didn't answer.

"Henry . . . I had nothing to do with what happened on that logging road. I didn't know what my dad was going to do. One second, I'm talking to you, the next . . . the next . . . you know."

"Yeah, I know."

Carter's outstretched arm hadn't moved, hadn't so much as twitched or wavered in the time I'd seen them talking. His eyes hadn't moved off his wife either. I'd seen the stance and the look before. The first movement I saw from Henry Carter was going to be a small, almost-unnoticed gesture; a finger moving back, a finger moving forward.

Tess Danby wasn't as stone-stoic as her husband, but she wasn't doing bad. She was smart enough not to be moving around or making any sudden gestures. It was taking some effort to stand as still as she was. I could see that from the way she rolled her shoulders from time to time, to straighten her spine. She wasn't going to break down and plead. Wasn't going to be weak and helpless. She knew her husband. Probably couldn't have acted like that anyway. I had seen her cry once, but I had never seen her play the role of victim.

"What would you have done, Henry?" she asked him, almost angry now. "Can you tell me? I'd really like you to tell me, because I've been thinking about it, thinking about you—spent as much time thinking about you as you've spent thinking about me—and I don't know, Henry, what would you have done? Should I have been killed right after you? Is that what I should have done on that road? Die for you?"

"Why not? . . . It's what I'm willing to do for you."

The answer might as well have been a bullet. Tess Danby's head snapped back. Her eyes went wide. A second after that she raised her hands to her mouth, to stifle a scream, to keep out the bad spirits swirling around the room. . . . It was hard to tell exactly what she was doing.

Although I knew what I was looking at. The two sides of love—what makes you do good; what makes you do bad—it was right in front of me, broken down to its most basic elements: two people, one gun and only a few words left to say.

"Henry . . . please don't do this . . . I love you . . . you love me . . . why are we doing this? . . . Let it be different . . . for once . . . please."

It looked like Carter was considering it. I've wondered long and hard about that, whether I imagined it, but I'm sure his gun barrel dipped right then, looked like he was lowering his arm. I looked around to see if any of the weapons that had been in the room before the explosion had landed near me. I saw Ambrose's Uzi near a pile of purple fabric: the barrel badly bent, the cartridge clip empty. I saw a handgun, far enough away I'd be dead before I could crawl to it.

I was still looking around when I heard the shot.

I wish now I had never taken my eyes off them. Wish I knew if Henry Carter kept lowering his gun, and if Tess Danby died knowing her one love had always been her one love; that it had never altered or bent.

But I didn't see her die. Just heard the shot.

When I turned back, she was already gone. Carter was there, pointing his handgun where it had been pointing the last time I saw him. But Tess Danby was gone. It took me a few seconds to find her, lying on the ground near the window, blood just beginning to pool around her head. I was still looking at her when I heard a man's voice say, "You were always going to shoot her, Henry. Bitch betrayed you. I just saved us some time. Put the gun down, so we can talk."

I recognized the voice. I was still trying to place it when out of the burning kitchen stepped Jason Hart.

HART HAD A handgun pointed at Carter's chest, but Carter stared at him for no more than a second before he rotated his body, repositioning his still-outstretched arm so his gun was now pointed at the FBI agent's head. The move surprised Hart, who took a step back.

"Slow down, Henry," he said. "She betrayed you once and she would have done it again if you were stupid enough to let her. Think it through and you'll see I'm right."

Neither man spoke for a while. I took another look at the handgun lying on the floor. Decided one more time it would be suicide to move toward it. I hadn't been noticed yet and keeping it that way might be my best play.

"We're the last men standing," I heard Hart say. "Why don't we sit down and talk? We've earned the right."

"Were you on shore with Gardner? I didn't see you," said Carter.

"I came after. No one knows I'm here, Henry. That means I'm in a position to help you. Why don't you put the gun down."

"Where's the girl?"

"What girl?"

"The girl I left there."

Hart didn't speak for a minute. He cleared his throat a few times before saying, "The girl you were traveling with? . . . You care about that girl?"

"I asked you where she is."

". . . Where you left her, Henry. Why don't you put that gun down, give me what you took, and you can go see that girl."

"You killed her, didn't you?"

Hart didn't say anything right away. When he spoke, it wasn't an answer to Carter's question. "Do you have what you stole?"

"'Course I have it."

"You caused a lot of problems, Henry. Do you have it on you?"

"What do you think we're doing here—practice runs?"

Hart smiled. "You're a crazy fuck, Henry. Should have made a deal with you instead of Ambrose. Give it to me and disappear. Go grab that girl and run."

"Sounds like a bad deal. You'll just come looking for me."

"Fuck—last thing I want to do. I want you to disappear, Henry. I'm going to say you fell off those cliffs. That can be the end of you."

". . . You left her where she was? You didn't kill her?"

"She's alive, Henry. . . . Why would I lie?"

Carter seemed to think about that. For about five seconds. Wouldn't have been more than that. When he was finished, he shot Jason Hart in the head.

I HAD CLEAR sightlines on Hart's body when it fell to the floor. The head was bent as though the neck snapped from the velocity of the bullet. The legs were splayed out like a cursive letter. It was an unnatural, awkward position, although aside from the position and the countersunk hole in the middle of his forehead, Hart's face looked fine. Eyes open. Mouth in a smarmy smile. The blond, feathered hair just beginning to turn into a bloody sponge.

Carter slipped his gun back into the shoulder holster and wiped his hands on one of the linen tablecloths. He walked to where Tess Danby had fallen. When he was there, he knelt and lifted one of her hands. It looked like he was checking for a pulse, but he held the hand a lot longer than he would have needed.

I had begun to think of Tess Danby as someone who needed my protection, someone I *could* protect, but there was no deal in the world that was going to save her now. Carter stood, took a linen tablecloth from a nearby table and placed it over her body. It seemed like I was spying on some intimate act I had no right to see, and I closed my eyes.

I kept them closed, and for the next several minutes listened to Carter move around the room. By the sound of his footsteps—getting louder, getting quieter—I could tell that he was checking the remains of Ambrose Danby, the fire in the kitchen, went back to Tess Danby a few times.

When the footsteps finally approached me, I thought about continuing the play-dead routine, but knew it would never work. Thought about lunging toward the gun that was just out of my reach but knew that wouldn't work either.

So, I opened my eyes and watched Carter walk toward me. There didn't seem anything else to do, and besides that, I'd told myself a long time ago that I would leave this world with my eyes open. I would take it all in—all that was offered, all that would be—to the last second. No one was going to take that from me.

He approached until he was standing right beside me, one more step and I would have been straddled, one leg on either side. Then Carter looked at me and cocked his head. Turned it one way, then the opposite way. If he'd thrown his head back and sniffed the air, he would have been reenacting a scene from the San Francisco CCTV tape.

He stared at me for what seemed a good minute, while I stared back. I wasn't going to speak until he did. Even stone-cold killers usually have a line or two before they kill a stranger. Seems impolite not to make an introduction before saying goodbye.

I would wait for him to speak, and I would respond to what he said. So long as I was responding, I was alive.

Eventually, he said, "You must be a cop."

I didn't know how to respond to that.

38

I SAT WITH Henry Carter at one of the tables that had escaped the explosion. The place setting was perfect: no cutlery missing, two wine glasses just waiting for Enrique to arrive. Although Enrique would not be arriving tonight.

To the left of me lay the body of Jason Hart. To my right, the remains of Ambrose Danby. In a far corner lay Tess Danby. Blood had soaked through the first tablecloth and Carter had placed another one over her. He had put out the fire in the kitchen too. The only light came from the glowing embers in the kitchen and the moon outside the window, although there was no window anymore and it seemed as though the moon had rolled right into the room.

Carter had helped me to my feet, then to the chair where I sat. He checked to make sure I didn't have a weapon, then asked if I wanted a drink. The scotch tasted good. Dulled the pain in my chest. I stared at him across the table, his own rocks glass of scotch next to the handgun he'd put there. He was handsome; Tess Danby had been

272 | RON CORBETT

right about that. Just beginning to transition out of being a young man into a middle-aged man. Had some girth around the middle, some gray in the black curls. His mannerisms seemed to be changing too. He had a cocky, youthful smile on his face from time to time, but it never stayed long, and each time it disappeared it seemed as though he had just remembered something.

Learning restraint. Learning not to overreach. I was familiar with the lessons.

"How'd you know I was a cop?" I asked him.

"Cops all over the place. And I don't know you."

I nodded. That was possible. Pretty damn smart, but possible.

"Why did you shoot Hart?"

"Lying prick. I was getting tired of him."

I almost laughed. "What did he want from you?"

"His life . . . when you look at what he did, everything he put into play . . . it had to be that."

I took another sip of my scotch. "Sounds like you don't know."

"I don't."

"That doesn't make any sense."

"Bit late in the game to start looking for sense, don't you think, cop?" He put a hand in his coat pocket and pulled out a thumb drive.

"Here it is. What all this was about."

"What's on it?"

"No idea. Haven't been around many computers lately. But it's what Ambrose was after in that bank."

"How did you get it?"

He moved the thumb drive from hand to hand. I watched it go back and forth. "I heard them talking about it the day we left. Ambrose wrote out the box number for Finn. The one they were after. Had to write it down, so Finn would remember. Three numbers. Do you believe that?"

"I believe that."

"I popped all the boxes and switched out the box they were after. Pocketed what was inside. It was only this thumb drive."

Back and forth. Back and forth.

"If you have no idea what's on it, why did you take it?"

"Whatever this is, it's valuable. Ambrose hit that bank just to get it."

"That's why you took it?"

"Something that valuable, I thought it would be best if I had it."

He put the thumb drive back into the pocket of his jacket.

"Was it Hart that pulled you into this?" he asked.

"It was."

"You've been played, cop."

"I'm beginning to realize that. Who's the girl he killed?"

"He didn't kill her. He never saw her."

"I don't understand. You just said. . . . Who is she?"

And he told me. He started the story with being shot in the back and waking on a patch of fern moss in a redwood forest north of San Francisco.

———

WE DIDN'T SPEAK for a long time after Carter had finished. He had just confessed to kidnapping, armed robbery, multiple homicides. It was the sort of story you told people you weren't worried about or expecting to see again anytime soon. The dread in the room right then was so palpable it might as well have been a color.

"What was her name?"

"I never asked."

"She never tried to run on you?"

"No."

"Why do you think she did that?"

"I've wondered. She never seemed all that scared. Never seemed all that uncertain either. . . . Maybe she had nowhere better to be."

"Running with you until the guns and the dogs show up? You believe that?"

Carter smiled but didn't answer. "You can't walk away from this," I continued. "You must know that. It's way too far down the road for that. Don't know how it's going to help your situation any, killing another cop."

Carter started looking around the room, as though he hadn't heard me. I saw his gaze touch upon Ambrose Danby, Jason Hart, the smoldering embers in the kitchen, the vulture's moon sitting at the table next to us. But he kept coming back to the body of Tess Danby. He was looking at her when he said:

"Have you ever met people, and somehow you knew, first time you met them, you knew that whatever was happening on the outside, inside, they were flashing like tinsel. Just burning up with life. Ever meet people like that?"

"I'm not sure . . . maybe."

"No, you'd remember. Those people are rare. It's like they were born with the stars inside of 'em, not outside the way it is for the rest of us." He didn't take his eyes off Tess Danby when he spoke. "I've only met two of those people. One was my wife. One was that girl. Like angels run to ground, that's what they were, but the world doesn't know what to do with people like that, does it? We shun them, fear them, long time ago we called them witches. . . . What can you say about a world that punishes the people who love it too much?"

He finally turned away from the body of his wife. Looked at me, like he was expecting an answer, like he hadn't asked a rhetorical question.

"Not much."

Carter snorts. "Yeah, not much. You got that right."

"I got to know your wife a little," I said. "I was hoping to get her off this island. I was working on it. What she was telling you . . . at the end . . . it was true. She loved you."

"I know that."

"She didn't betray you."

"Not by choice. But betrayal . . . it's not always free will, is it, cop?"

I tried not to look startled, but I'm sure I failed. It sounded like Henry Carter had spent time asking the same questions I'd been asking since I left Detroit. Coming up with some of the same answers.

"Well . . . we'll have visitors soon," he said. "It's time we finished this."

With that, Carter picked up the handgun from the table and moved it back and forth in his hands. He twirled it, let it rest for a second in the open palm of one hand, then the other, then he flipped the gun and placed it carefully on the table. He was opening his mouth, about to speak, when he suddenly began to laugh.

"I told you about this, didn't I?"

"You did."

He reached into one of his coat pockets and pulled out another handgun. He looked at it a few seconds, before saying, "Yeah, this seems right—we'll end this the old way, with guns in our hands."

He put the gun he'd taken from his pocket in front of him and bumped the gun already on the table toward me. When it didn't reach me, he stood and bumped it a little further, until it came to rest a couple inches from my rocks glass.

He sat down and we stared at each other. We stared until I started to count the wrinkles under his eyes—seven wrinkles in total, an uneven number, the left eye having one more wrinkle. I wondered if that was unusual. He was inhaling his breath every eight seconds. Never seven. Never nine.

"You want me to put it in your hand?" he asked.

"If you could."

Carter laughed again. He seemed to be having fun. "Where you from, cop?"

"Back east."

"That's what I get? Think your answer's going to matter in a minute?"

"Detroit."

"Ahh, had some good times there. Used to be a good town, wide-open town. My granddaddy had Jimmy Hoffa at his house for lunch once. He had photos. That where you live?"

"Where I grew up."

"Where you live now?"

"Nowhere special. I move around."

"I bet you do."

We went back to waiting. In another minute, Carter said, "I wish I had a hip holster right now so we could stand and do it the old way. You wish we had hip holsters?"

"No. I wish you were already dead."

He slapped the table a few times, a big, broad smile on his face. "I'm glad it's you, cop. . . . Come on, let's see if you get your wish."

His hand reached toward his gun, and I reached for mine. I didn't try to lift mine but let my right-hand forefinger curl around the trigger and pull back. Carter's Glock had barely risen from the table when my first bullet hit him in the chest.

I grabbed the gun and kept firing, throwing myself out of my chair at the same time. I landed on my back, both hands on the gun now, firing bullets up and through the table. It looked like every bullet was hitting Henry Carter.

He didn't fall right away. The bullets spun and danced him across the floor, jerky limb after jerky limb, until he crashed into a bank of unbroken windows. His body slid to the floor only after the last bullet had struck him; a slow slide, his head tilting to his chest as he fell. When the slide was finished, Henry Carter's crumpled body lay before the blood-splattered glass like a man kneeling in prayer before a gallery-sized Pollock.

Right after that, I passed out for the second time that night.

39

I'M FALLING DOWN a black hole that gets narrower as I fall, until I'm choking and gasping for air when I shoot out the other side . . . and land in a field of sweetgrass, the world around me more colorful than normal, than what was comfortable, a world high on peyote, shot up with tracing iodine. The grass swaying over my head becomes the tentacles of an algae-covered sea monster; the sky becomes a royal blue, with sheet lightning in the distance, flashes in the sky that could be artillery fire but must be something else. There is no sound.

I lie on my back and the sweetgrass blows over my face, neon strand by neon strand, until the grass disappears, and suddenly I am back on the cliffs of Danby Island, looking out on the Georgia Strait, minke whales crying their lonely, edge-of-the-world song, fog rolling onto Cape Rage, the lighthouse flashing to my left, then to my right, then far out at sea. There are no reference points left in the world, only a tempest that engulfs me as I stand on the cliffs of Danby Island, waiting to be swept away.

When I awake, I am lying in a hospital bed. A man I have never seen is standing in a doorway, staring at me.

———

THE MAN'S SUIT is rumpled enough to look like he's slept in it. A toothpick is in his mouth. He keeps staring at me, chewing on the toothpick until he steps backward, out of the doorway, and waves to someone in the hallway.

A nurse enters the room. Then a doctor, and then another doctor. They crowd the bed. The doctor who came in last asks how I'm feeling, and I say, "All right . . . where am I?"

"University of Washington Medical Center," he answers. "You came in by air ambulance two days ago. You'd lost a lot of blood. You may end up with the record at this hospital for most pints put into a person. I'll let you know."

He asks again how I'm feeling, and I say fine, maybe a little hungry. He looks at me like that is a strange answer. Then he shakes his head and leaves. The man who had been standing in the doorway walks out with him. The nurse adjusts the IV needle in my arm and leaves without speaking. The man in the rumpled suit comes back.

He stands in the doorway again, leans on the frame, still chewing his toothpick. He is tall and lanky, with gray eyes that never stop moving.

"They tell me you're going to live," he says.

"What I hear too."

"Shrapnel wounds. Don't see that every day."

"Not recommending it."

"Better than a bullet to the head. Two of the people dead in that room with you, that's what happened to them. Bullets to the head. Another guy had all sorts of bullets in him. Another guy . . . well, that guy was just a mess."

He stays in the doorway. Hands in his pockets. The toothpick moves from one side of his mouth to the other.

"How you feeling?"

"All right. Haven't tried to do much."

"Head's clear?"

"Head's clear."

"My name is Ed Turner. I'm a senior special agent with the San Francisco FBI office. I flew up here yesterday to see you."

I nod. He hasn't asked a question.

"I'll be honest with you, the doctor thinks I should come back tomorrow, leave you alone for the day. Problem is, I'm in a hurry. I guess I should apologize to you for that. Would you like me to apologize?" The toothpick slides up the corner of his mouth like a flag being raised.

"Why are you here?" I ask.

"I need to get a statement."

"Why? I'll be filing a report."

"And who's going to be getting it? . . . They're all dead."

He finally comes into the room. He looks around, as though he doesn't already know where everything is, then he takes a chair from the corner and drags it to the side of the bed. He sits down, takes the toothpick out of his mouth and puts it in a pocket of his jacket. He puts his hands on his knees and leans forward.

"I know you've been through a lot, pal, but you've got the entire fucking FBI waiting to hear what happened on that island. Forget the report. I need a statement from you now."

"WANT ANYTHING? GLASS of water? Something to eat? You said you were hungry, right? Want me to wave down a nurse? Don't know what sort of food they have here, but they tell me hospital food is getting better. Want me to talk to someone?"

Turner has his chair pushed back and is talking to me as he pulls a cell phone, a pen and a stenographer's pad from the pockets of his suit jacket. He flips pages in the steno pad until he comes to a clear one. The constantly moving gray eyes look sad when I see them up close, watery, and opaquer than I was expecting. But they never stop moving, eyes that are also filled with curiosity, like the sad, earnest eyes of a graduate student who still wants to learn but has begun to doubt his studies. A sad, curious man who asks one more time, "Want anything?"

"I'm good. Where would you like me to start?"

"How 'bout the day you met Gardner and Hart."

I'm not sure how long it takes to tell the story. My watch is gone. No clock in the room. He doesn't ask any questions until I'm finished, and I'm surprised by his first one.

"How did Gardner and Hart seem to get along?"

"They hated each other . . . that was plain to see."

"Never had any doubts about that? Never thought they were playing you?"

"Always thought they were playing me. But they hated each other."

"Why do you think that was?"

"Don't know if it was anything specific. Hart would be the sort of man Gardner didn't like. Being his boss wouldn't have helped any."

He nods a few times, then flips through his steno pad until he stops at a page near the start of the pad, crosses something out, then flips back to where he was.

"Looks like this was Hart's play. Gardner had nothing to do with it."

"You thought he did?"

"We've known for a few months there was something wrong with the Danby investigation. It was starting to stack up like something crooked. Gardner was the operational officer." He shrugs his shoulders.

"That phone call Gardner made to me, the one a few hours before it all happened . . . it sounded like he was suspicious about something, like he was trying to warn me about something."

"He might have been. He was trying to track down Hart that night, but never found him. He might have figured it out. He might have started thinking about it a while ago . . . that would explain the hatred. A good cop knowing he was working with scum."

"Did Gardner make it?"

"No."

Anger flashes in those gray eyes, and I wait a few seconds before asking, "How many didn't make it?"

"Four agents dead on the shore, including Gardner. Five in the hospital here, just down the hall."

"There should have been two men on the island."

"Edwin Tupper and Harold Perkins. They're in custody."

"What about the girl Carter was traveling with?"

"Never found her."

"He was traveling with a girl."

"We know that. We have her on security camera, from that motel in Idaho. We haven't found her."

"She has to be there."

Turner shrugs his shoulders one more time. "What can I tell you? She's not there. We've still got dogs out looking, but she should have been found by now . . . one way or the other."

"In the water?"

"Possible. We got boats out too. She also might have taken off the moment Carter left her, gone down the shoreline to Blaine and caught a bus out of Dodge. That's what I would have done."

"You've checked for her in Blaine?"

"Not yet . . . not sure if we will. We don't want her for anything. That security tape shows her sitting in the Jeep when the sheriff and motel clerk were killed. If she's healthy enough to get to Blaine and get on her way . . . why should I go looking for her?"

"She seemed important. And to make sure she's all right."

"If she's hightailed it out of here, she's of clear mind and making good decisions in my book."

He stares out the window. It looks like it has rained again. The needles on the pine are wet and slick, and the sky is the electric blue you get sometimes after a good, hard rain.

"Ever figure out what Carter stole?" he asks.

"A thumb drive. I don't know what's on it."

"We found it in his pocket. I've downloaded it to my phone."

Turner touches a button on his phone, then touches another button, and hands me his phone. I'm watching a video. Seven minutes and thirty-seven seconds. Recorded in a strip club it looks like, a woman in the background spinning on a pole, neon Coors and Miller Lite signs twinkling in the shadows, a round table in the foreground, a private room of some sort, two men sitting at the table, one fat and sweaty, one young and fit, his blond hair feathered and running past his collar.

Shot with a stationary camera. Money on the table. Stacks of hundred-dollar bills still with the bank wrappers, more than a dozen bundles on the table, and the fat man says, "You don't want to count it?"

"Why would you short me, Pete?"

"Yeah, you're right. Smart guy you are."

The young man doesn't bother answering. He picks up an Adidas gym bag, puts it on the table and starts putting the bundles inside. It is an old-style gym bag, one with the stiff plastic coating that always cracked if you used it regularly. The girl on the pole is finishing her set. The DJ is asking the crowd to clap for Tiffany. The fat man says, "I'm taking a leap of faith on you, buddy."

"It'll happen."

"I don't need to tell you what will happen if it don't?"

"You don't."

"Good, we can keep it friendly. You want Tiffany to come in for a dance?"

"I'm in a hurry."

"That's why I said Tiffany. She just finished her set."

The younger man laughs. The fat man raises his arm and waves a hand. The girl who had been on the pole comes into the room and the fat man leaves. The video ends with the girl sitting on Jason Hart's lap.

I give Turner back his phone. "The fat man is Pete Flarety?"

"Yeah."

"What year is the video?"

"Two thousand and seven. October fourteenth. Three days later, sex-trafficking charges against Flarety were dismissed when a witness recanted her testimony."

"Have you tracked down the witness?"

"Re-interviewed her. She said Hart paid her five thousand dollars to change her testimony."

"Looks like there's a hundred fifty thousand on that table."

"He was a cheap prick."

"And Flarety got the whole deal on video, to blackmail him."

"We don't think it was straight blackmail. Looks more like they were helping each other. Flarety set up some of his competitors for Hart. Those arrests made his career. Hart was in line for assistant director. Would have happened in two or three years."

Turner is silent for a few seconds. The thought of having a bent agent that high up the chain of command silences him.

"Hart thought it was time to get rid of Flarety," I say, filling in the silence. "But as long as Flarety had that video sitting in a safe deposit box in San Francisco, Hart was screwed."

"He was—as long as the video stayed in the bank," agrees Turner.

The pieces fall together so quickly it is like getting pelted, a sudden cloudburst of revelations and truths. "Hart hired Ambrose to rob the bank and get the video."

"He didn't hire him. Hart was already squeezing Ambrose, had been for years. The Seattle office could have arrested the Danbys a long time ago, but Ambrose was a confidential informant. Hart didn't give him a choice about doing the robbery."

"Ambrose brought Henry Carter along to help."

"Yep. Carter was good with boxes."

"Why did Ambrose kill him?"

"Carter was too smart. Ambrose didn't want anyone to know he was an FBI informant, and Carter was starting to figure it out. He was *going* to figure it out. I think that was always Ambrose's plan, kill him right after the robbery."

"Use him and lose him."

"Yep."

"In front of the guy's wife. That's cold."

"Yeah . . . it was."

He keeps staring out the window. Eventually, he says, "I don't know if I've ever seen a bigger rat-fuck. Hard to know who fucked up more—Jason Hart when he got Ambrose to rob a bank for him, or Ambrose Danby when he thought it was a good idea to bring along Henry Carter. . . . Do you ever wonder about it?"

"Wonder about what?"

"When the bad things start. The first mistake. I've read your file. Some of your cases . . . it's been like combat for you. . . . Do you ever wonder?"

"I do."

"What have you come up with?"

"Still working on it."

"Yeah . . . I suppose you would be."

Turner stares out the window a little longer, then closes the steno pad and picks up his phone. He gives his back a stretch before standing, then he squeezes my arm and says, "Take care of yourself, pal. You did good work here."

He starts toward the door, is halfway there when he turns and says, "Oh, one last thing. You'd probably like to know this. If I were lying in that bed, my life still flashing in front of my eyes . . . does that happen to you?"

"It does."

"Yeah, of course . . . well, if I were lying there, I'd like to know something like this—you were never going to die, Barrett."

"Why not?"

"Carter's gun was empty."

He is looking right at me when he says it. To see my reaction. A curious man. When I look surprised, he says, "You really didn't know, did you?"

"No . . . he tried to fire on me. Said he wished we had hip holsters, so we could draw on each other, like in an old Western movie."

"His gun was empty."

Outside the hospital window the sky is turning darker, is a cobalt blue now, a thick lustrous color, the world wet with rain, the first star of the night sitting high. I remember Carter talking about people being born with the stars inside of them, and a world not knowing what to do about that.

"Doesn't seem like the sort of mistake a man like Henry Carter would make. Any thoughts about that?" Turner asks.

In that fingerpaint swath of an evening sky the colors seem to come alive, thicken and transform into a lipstick streak of setting sun, a blue pool of electric sky, and against that background that high star looks embossed, looks like it's sticking out from the heavens, shining from a place you only see in a twilight sky after a good, hard rain.

"Nothing comes to mind," I say.

EPILOGUE

I HAVEN'T STOPPED thinking about it. Not really. The gun. The girl. What happened at Cape Rage. I've given it a lot of thought.

When I first started thinking about it, I had these crazy ideas. Especially about that girl. How she managed to disappear without a trace, and how could she have done a thing like that? I don't know what I was thinking back then. Must have been running a fever.

I went so far as to try and track down the security tape, the one showing her in a Jeep parked outside a motel in Idaho, two men getting killed inside. Just so I could see her, and know she was real. But no one thought to keep the tape after the case exploded and no one was left standing to bring to trial.

A few months after I left Seattle, Ed Turner got in touch with me though, to say some hikers had found an abandoned cabin in a redwood forest north of San Francisco. The cabin was on old timber-rights land that was now a state park, most of it closed to the public for reforestation. From some of the items found in the cabin, the FBI believed it had belonged to Wally Moss, a bank robber who had been on their most wanted list in the early 2000s.

The reason Turner contacted me was that Moss had a daughter. He sent me a picture of her. From another security camera, the photo taken years earlier. The girl would have been ten, and she looked the way the missing girl had been described. Small girl. Long blond hair.

Seeing that photo settled some things in my mind. She looked like a girl who might not want to be found, who was moving from one place to the next and didn't have time to stop. I have begun to tell myself that must have been what happened. I only wonder about her from time to time now.

I've thought a lot about Henry Carter and that empty gun too and have come to believe Turner was right. It wasn't the sort of mistake Henry Carter would make. When I talked to Carter that one time, he seemed tired, disappointed with the world, talking about people being born with stars inside of them, like they were magi or something, talking all sorts of crazy nonsense.

He was in a bad place. Same with everyone else on that island. There are places like that in this world, and from having seen a few of them, the only advice I can give to you if you stumble upon such a place is to get away as quick as you can. A bad place won't ever change. Won't ever be anything different. Like Cape Rage, you can try to call a bad place something else, even pretend it's something else for a while, but the trick never works long term. If you get born into a bad place . . . I'm still not sure how to feel about people with that sort of luck. People like Tess Danby. People like Henry Carter. I hope to figure it out one day.

Also been thinking about the question Ed Turner asked me in the hospital—When do the bad things start? It's his question that has got me thinking about beginnings and endings and whether we ever see what's really happening there. If we ever get that right. Some days I think we do. Other days I think I never want to take a guess at stuff like that again. It's too easy to embarrass yourself.